JAKE AND THE HOBO

MY SUMMER OF LOVE

By NAMAYA

VERMONT ART POETRY PRESS

Copyright © 2024 Namaya *All rights reserved*

Published by Vermont Art Poetry Press
Guilford, Vt.
info@vermontpoet.com
www.vermontartpoetry.com

ISBN   978-0-9990844-4-1   *Paperback*

Dedicated to

Sharon Spencer –
Writer, teacher, traveler, friend

ACKNOWLEDGMENT

Thank you to the people who helped in the creation of this book. Hannah Morin did a superb job editing. Nookie Rivera was terrific with formatting and designing the book. Zoe Kopp who was there at each stage of the novel and an invaluable reader. Wendy Baez Brown for your insights and guidance.

Contents

Introduction

Twenty years ago, I took a journey that changed my life. The day I met Erasmus P. Hobbs, I was a skinny, frightened, soaking-wet girl of sixteen standing on the side of the highway without a clue as to where I was going or what to do. Then he rolled up in his metallic yellow Airstream RV, called *Emma Goldman*, and introduced himself. "Hi! My name is Erasmus P. Hobbs. How can I help you?" For three months, we wandered across America…helped at homeless shelters, met fellow hobos, saints, and revolutionaries, cleaned up parks, planted gardens, and met the woman who became my *Fairy Godmother*, the herbalist and healer Sojourner. I learned how to read, write, and how to tune up Erasmus's Airstream home. In that *Summer of Love*, I learned so many things every day. I will tell you more about my extraordinary summer, but before I get too far ahead of myself…most importantly, I learned something I never thought possible. The hardest lesson was to love myself unconditionally.

It's been twenty years since I last saw the man who changed my life and probably the lives of everybody else who met him. My name is Jake, and this is the story of my *Summer of Love* with the extraordinary Erasmus P. Hobbs—my hobo saint who came dancing into my life on a rainbow of possibilities.

CHAPTER ONE

Kismet

He pounded the thin plywood door to my bedroom, a tiny room the size of a closet. Harry, my mother's drunken boyfriend, shouted, "Come on, Jake! Let me in! You're the only person I can talk to. Your mother is worthless, but you're fine!"

I knew what he wanted, and it wasn't talking. The door almost busted loose as I threw on my thin army jacket. Despite the cold night, I had no choice, I had to leave. I already kept my clothes in a backpack, as we never knew when we would be evicted. Moonlight looked like shadowy ghosts breaking through the pine trees on the hillside as the wind blew a shriek of bitter cold across the land. My sneakers hit the ground as I heard the door crack inside the trailer and Harry roared, "Jake, where are you? I want to talk to you! I need you!"

I had the address of my Aunt May, who lived in Ohio, hundreds of miles away. Though I had never met her, I thought, *maybe she could take me in for a while.* I headed to the interstate to find the truck stop in Jonesville. The narrow moonlit path led through the forest along the muddy logging road that snaked across the hillside. I followed the path for miles. A cold drizzle of rain began, but better wet and cold than raped. I kept rubbing my frozen hands together, and my sneakers were soaked. I must've walked at least three hours when at last, the first feeble light of day appeared over the mountain. I ate the only food I had, an apple and a bag of potato chips, but it only made me hungrier.

I came to the roadside of a long stretch of empty highway. There was no sign of where the truck stop was. I put out my thumb to hitchhike, and then waited and waited until I saw a small yellow sparkly RV slow down and pull over to the side of the road. A man about six feet tall stepped out. He had long silver-white hair tied back into a ponytail and a neatly trimmed silver-white beard. He wore a faded green baseball hat that said, "Veteran for Peace," a worn dark blue work jacket, faded jeans with a work knife on his belt, and black work boots. His face was tanned and rugged with bright blue-green eyes.

He said, "Hi! My name is Erasmus P. Hobbs. You look like you need some help."

"Not really. I just need to get to the truck stop," I said through chattering teeth.

"The one in Jonesville?"

"Sure. Can you get me there, Mister?"

"I can, but it's about fifteen miles the other way!" He pointed down the highway in the opposite direction I had been heading.

"Damn! I thought it was closer."

"Can I come over and talk to you?" Then a fluffy black and white cocker spaniel with a playful yap came from behind him, waddled over to me, and licked my jeans.

Reluctantly, I put my hand out. "Does he bite?"

"Of course not! Socrates will lick ya' to death before he bites you!" I bent down to pet him, and Socrates leaped up into my arms and licked my face.

He extended his hand. "As I said, I'm Erasmus P. Hobbs, and this lovely fellow licking you is Socrates. We'd like to help you. Can I give you some dry clothes and something to eat?"

"I don't need help. A dry shirt if you have it, but I can walk to the truck stop if it's not in the direction you're heading."

"Really? Fifteen miles in soaking wet clothes and without having eaten anything?"

"I walk fifteen miles every day! I'll take a dry shirt, but no funny business. Besides, what kind of name is Ramus?"

"Erasmus," he said. "I don't want anything from you. I only want to help. How about I give you some dry clothes, make you something to eat, and then you can walk the fifteen miles if you like, or I can give you a lift?"

"Thank you, Mr. Erasmus. I don't want to cause you any trouble. Give me a dry shirt and an apple if you got it, and I'll go on my way."

"What's your name?"

"Jake."

"Okay, Jake. Let me help you."

"No funny business," I repeated.

He smiled. "Right, no funny business! Nice to meet you, Jake. Can I make you breakfast? After you eat, I can drive you to the truck stop or your parents' house."

I didn't have parents who wanted me. I never met my father, and my mother had long been sucked into her world of pills and whiskey. I hadn't heard anyone in a very long time ask, "Can I make you breakfast?" Most times, I waited for something to eat at school, like most of my friends.

Even if it was awful, at least it was hot.

I cautiously stepped into the yellow RV. It smelled like sandalwood and candles. The inside had polished wood and a wall of books about eight feet long and five feet high. There were small lights, wood cabinets, a kitchen with a slate gray counter, and two guitars hanging on the wall. I had never seen anything this fancy or fine.

"Take off your wet sneakers, Jake, and I'll find you some dry clothes."

He searched in the cabinet. "Here are some clothes and a pair of sneakers that should fit. You can change in the bathroom, take a shower, and put your wet clothes in the cloth bag."

Why is he being nice to me? What does he want? I know where the door is and can get out if anything weird happens.

"Here's a dry towel. The shower is only hot for a few minutes, so enjoy it. And I'll make you breakfast."

I locked the bathroom door, pulled it twice to make sure it was locked, and let the hot shower pour across me. I was exhausted. I dried off and dressed in the clothes he'd given me, a big flannel plaid shirt, sweatpants, and clean white socks, and the sneakers fit. I had a funny thought; maybe I was Cinderella at the ball?

When I came out of the bathroom, he put a big bowl of steaming hot oatmeal with fruit in front of me for breakfast. "There's hot chocolate too. Okay?"

"Sure. What are these lumpy things in the oatmeal, Mr. 'Rasmus?"

"Erasmus. They're roasted nuts and sesame seeds, good protein for you."

I devoured one bowl of oatmeal and then another and slurped down the hot chocolate with whipped cream.

I was full and sleepy and fell asleep on the couch. When I woke, I was alone and wrapped in a soft green blanket. What happened and where was I? I realized I was in the stranger's RV and Socrates was sleeping next to me.

I heard a guitar outside the RV and I stumbled out. Erasmus and another man were playing guitars.

"Where am I? What happened?"

Erasmus said, "You're at the truck stop, and it's twelve o'clock. You ate like a hungry puppy and fell asleep. I drove us here while you slept and met this talented guitarist, and we've been playing guitar and waiting for you to wake up."

The other guy was in his twenties with long brown hair and blue eyes, a gold earring, a faded straw cowboy hat, patched-up Levi's, and worn boots with steel tips. He said, "My name is Matt and I'm a guitar-picking truck driver. How do you do, Miss?"

Man, this is a good-looking guy, I thought. "Nice to meet you, Matt! You sure play a mighty fine guitar."

"Erasmus, thanks for letting me play with you, but I've got an eight-hour drive ahead with the Magic Flyer, my trusty 18-wheeler."

"My pleasure, Matt. I'm sure we'll meet before too long." Then Socrates jumped up on Matt's lap and gave him a lick on his bearded cheek. "Ha! Ha! Socrates is a love muffin!"

We watched Matt pull away in his rig, and he gave a toot on his horn. Erasmus said, "Let me fix you my world-famous black beans, rice, and tofu scramble with garlic."

"Toe what?"

"Tofu, and soybeans. Have you had it before? The way I make it, it will make you cry with joy."

"Cry with joy?" Then I looked at this smiling man with lovely green eyes. "I'll try it, though I've never had toes before."

"Tofu!" He laughed. "You're playing me. We'll get along fine. I know a place on the river about two miles from here with a lovely sunset view and a picnic table. I'll cook, and we can talk. Unless you want me to drive you home?"

I bit my lower lip as I tried not to let the tears out. I felt alone and scared. "Mister, I'm sorry. It's just when you said 'home' I realized—I ain't never really had a home." I took a deep breath and began to cry. I sobbed against his green flannel shirt, and he gave me a red bandana.

"It's okay to cry," he said softly.

I cried for all the slaps, beatings, and times I was hungry. At school, even the other kids who were as poor as I was called me *white trash* because my clothes were raggedy and didn't fit. I cried for all the times I was afraid of my mother's boyfriend. I cried for being alone, frightened, and watching my mother disappear into her world of drugs and whiskey. A flood of pain burst through the dam, and I couldn't stop crying. Erasmus sat and listened. When I screamed, he gently held my hand.

An older couple came by, and the man said, "Miss, are you okay? Do you need help?"

I shook my head. "No. I'm okay. Really. Thank you. I'm having a bad day."

"Mister, do you need anything?"

Erasmus said, "Can I trouble you for a small black coffee and water for my friend?"

Fifteen minutes later, the couple returned with a tray of bean burritos, soup, coffee, milk, water, and brownies. "We thought you both could use a little more than coffee. It's on the house!"

The woman touched my shoulder and said, "Honey, we all need a good cry and a friend to help. Enjoy your lunch!"

I must have looked ridiculous, my eyes swollen and my hair a mess. "Thank you."

He said to the couple, "Thank you for your kindness. My friend Jake is having a little rough patch."

This was the circle of kindness Erasmus created. He reached out, and other people spontaneously helped. He once said, "It's the circle of love. We can all be part of it if we choose."

We were famished and devoured lunch.

Erasmus said, "The diner cooks terrific food! Man, this is delicious."

"Damn, I didn't realize how many tears I had inside of me."

"Not to worry, Jake. We all have tears we need to let go of."

The sun burst through the grey clouds and there was an orange-violet streak of light. We drove to the picnic area by the state park on the border of West Virginia and walked up to the mountain caves with Socrates in the lead and a hawk soaring above. The air smelled fresh with pines and hemlocks. I said, "Though I don't live too far from here, I rarely left Black Mountain."

That night, I fell into a heavy sleep. I dreamed I was running hard, but the wind was blowing against me, and I kept getting pushed back. The more I tried, the stronger the cold wind blew me back. Erasmus appeared on a white horse wearing a cowboy hat. Socrates was yapping. "Jump on board, Jake. We'll get through the storm!"

In the morning, I awoke to the call of a blue jay and smelled pancakes.

"Oh, Mister Erasmus, good morning," I said sleepily.

"Just Erasmus. Good morning, sunshine! Here is a cup of tea, and when you're ready we'll have breakfast."

He went back outside where he was flipping pancakes on the griddle, whistling like a bird, and the pancakes landed on a plate. We were surrounded by tall oak, ash, and beech trees. A robin was tweeting, a red cardinal raced through the morning, and the sunlight shimmered against the river. There were three rough-looking men with Erasmus.

"Jackson! Smith! And Jamal! Wash up, set the table, and here are plates, forks, and cups for coffee. Oh, and use this tablecloth."

The picnic table soon filled with a morning feast…pancakes, fruit, coffee, hot chocolate, and tea.

Erasmus said, "Before we eat, can we say a word of grace?" We joined hands, and Jamal raised his head, and through his broken teeth emerged the song "Amazing Grace." We held hands and sang the first verse.

We all said, "Amen!" The big stack of pancakes soon disappeared.

The strangest bicycle, with solar panels painted in rainbow colors, suddenly appeared. The tall man riding had long, knotted silvery hair and a beard that touched his chest. "I'm sorry to bother you. Can I join you? I have granola and nuts."

Erasmus looked surprised and said, "Now, this is a party! If it ain't Phil the Tinker! Welcome! We always have a place for you." Erasmus stood up, and they hugged. "Phil, how in the hell did you find us? We're in the middle of nowhere and like stardust you fall from the sky."

Phil said, "Pure serendipity! I was jaunting along heading to a Grateful Dead concert when I saw *Emma Goldman* flying by yesterday. I couldn't believe it. Erasmus P. Hobbs! I knew you always liked this picnic area, so I took my best guess, and voila! Here we are! Kismet!"

Erasmus said, "Yes, kismet, divine fate. Friends, I'd like to introduce you to Phil the Tinker, who can fix anything. Phil, this lovely young lady next to me is Jake, and these handsome gentlemen Jackson, Jamal, and Smith are Knights of the Noble Order of Vagabonds. Welcome!"

Phil the Tinker was a handsome man with a weathered face, a long flowing silvery beard, and strange gray hair about two feet long. Later I found out that the 'strange hair' was dreadlocks. He folded his hands and said, "Gratitude for you, fine people."

We devoured our pancakes while the butterflies were dancing across the blue cone flowers, and the hummingbirds darted among the bright red bee balm.

"Jamal, are you okay?" Erasmus asked.

"Yeah, I got this little headache."

"Let me see if I can help." Then he stood behind Jamal and began a gentle massage, a bit of a crunch, and rubbing his scalp. "How is that?"

"Wow!" He shook his head. "All the pain I've been having in my head and neck is gone. What did you do?"

"Only a little TLC!"

I asked, "What is TLC?"

"Miss Jake," said Jackson. "TLC is what Mister Erasmus does best. His mojo magic changes the world with tender loving care."

Everyone laughed!

I nodded, and though I had just met Erasmus, I knew exactly what Jackson was talking about. Erasmus personified TLC. I laugh now, thinking about how I didn't even know the word *personified* until I met him.

When we finished our breakfast, the guys helped clean up and wash the dishes. Jackson reached inside his coat pocket for a flask. Erasmus quietly said, "I'd rather you didn't do that. Jake is here."

Jackson was flustered and smiled. "Of course. No problem."

This gentleness made Erasmus a giant, and he didn't make anybody feel bad. He dealt with each person with loving kindness. That was one of the key lessons he gave me, "Start with loving kindness, and the rest will follow." At first, I thought it was stupid. Almost all the people I had known were cruel, mad with pain and booze, and ready to steal from you. I had lived all my life at the bottom of a steep ravine where a coal mine had closed down years ago. The sun rarely shined there. Everything seemed like a huge mountain to climb, and I was always at the bottom.

After breakfast Erasmus said, "Who would like to help Jake and me clean up the picnic area?"

We looked around the park. Trash was in big heaps, the swing set was broken, and it was generally a mess.

Jackson said, "Miss Jake and I can pick up the trash."

Phil said, "I can fix the swing and benches!"

Jamal tied back his long hair and rolled up his sleeves. "I'm here to help!"

A broom, rakes, saws, hammers, and big plastic bags came out of the back of the RV. It was like the scene in Mary Poppins where she took all kinds of things from her purse. Erasmus was whistling and helping to clean up, and everything was going fine when a cop car showed up with flashing blue lights.

"What do you think you're doing?" the cop asked.

I was worried that the cop would pick me up as a stray kid. Erasmus smiled and said, "Hold on, Officer, if I could talk to you for a few moments."

He walked over to the cop. I couldn't hear what Erasmus said, but the cop switched off his blue lights and picked up the radio after a few minutes. "Yes, I want a pickup truck from the sanitation department over here. Some fine citizens have cleaned up the entire picnic area down by the river. No, it can't wait 'til tomorrow!"

Soon, a town pickup truck came, and two workers pitched in to help load up the broken boards, bags of garbage, and the stack of tires. Phil the Tinker fixed the see-saw, made new seats, and replaced the chains.

The cop then made a second call. "Yes, Dominos. This is Sergeant Jack from the police department. Three large…what was that, Erasmus? Vegetarian?

"My friend Erasmus wants the pies as vegetarian. I know it's weird, but sometimes weird is good. Ain't it?"

Erasmus walked over to the shoulder of the playground with Jamal and dug in the soil. They turned it over in their hands.

"What do you think, Jamal? What plants might be best here?"

"The soil looks poor, but probably hellebores – you know, Lenten rose, and some periwinkle would be good along the edges. Black-eyed daisies will look terrific around the swing. Do you have anything like that?"

"If not, I have something pretty close. I keep a pretty good assortment of seeds in my RV. Jake, do me a favor. Get me a shovel and one of the rakes, and we have some seeds in *Emma*. The first cabinet on the left."

"Of course!"

Everything in the thirty-five-foot palace was precise. As Erasmus once told me, "She's my masterpiece my Galetta. According to legend, the sculptor Pygmalion made a statue of the beautiful Galetta, fell in love with her, and she came to life. Except, in this case, the statue is the RV *Emma Goldman*. It took a team of friends and me about a year to make her the beauty she is—mostly made from recycled wood and parts powered with vegetable oil and diesel, and solar panels to make the hot water and electricity."

Phil said, "Not to be immodest, but I did most of the interior wiring with Sojourner, and it was one of the most fun building projects I've ever done."

"It was a glorious summer in Vermont and you're right, it was incredible fun!" said Erasmus. "Thanks, Jake, for the seeds. Now, let's get to work and make a flower bed."

Wherever he was, he would plant flowers. With Jamal, we planted the edge of the playground with a bed of seeds. He turned to the guys from the Public Works. "Would it be possible to look after these? By the fall, there'll be colorful flowers everywhere."

"Sure thing! My kids will be happy to come and play. We never really thought about cleaning this up. You know how it is. You live in a place, ignore it, and get used to the trash."

In the late afternoon, the sheriff, the men from the road crew, and their kids came by with watermelon. This was the magic that Erasmus brought.

He said to me, "This is the best kind of fun I have. It's kind of like my art. I meet all these wonderful people on the road, we play together, and sometimes in our play, we make things like this garden."

"How do you get paid?" I asked.

"Next year when I come by, there'll be flowers and the children will have a playground. Won't that be payment enough?"

I began to understand his way of doing things slowly, and now I call it the *Economics of Erasmus*. Many things were done for free, sometimes items were bartered for, a lot of things were repaired, and as he said, "The most important thing is to recycle and reuse." Nothing was wasted.

"In some ways, it's how we lived in Black Mountain, where no one really had money. We traded and bartered. My mother's boyfriend broke into buildings and stole the copper pipes."

Erasmus said, "I know what you mean. It's called poverty. I grew up in the northeast kingdom of Vermont, and most people were dirt-poor farmers. Everyone cared for each other, even though we didn't have much money. But like where you grew up, poverty and desperation lead people to do crazy and dangerous stuff."

"Like my mother and her addiction to pain pills and whiskey?"

We cooked a big pot of chili over the campfire for Jamal, Jackson, Smith, the sheriff and his family, and the folks from the Public Works Department. Phil the Tinker was making jewelry using the heat from the campfire. Erasmus took out his guitars and drums, and we sang by the fireside. The sheriff was a terrific singer and sang songs like "Peggy Sue" and country-western songs like "Crazy." I never knew that people could have this much fun. Jamal played along on his harmonica, and Jackson played the recorder. I was always shy about singing and tried to sing quietly, but Erasmus said, "Jake, sing 'Wade in the Water.'"

The playground was now clean and tidy and filled with music. The fire had burned down low, and the stars shined brightly above us.

The men from the Public Works Department said to Jackson, Jamal, and Smith, "We have some state money to hire workers this summer. Would you like to stay and work with us for the next few months? There's a bunkhouse on a farm nearby for you to stay. We'd love to have you."

Jamal said, "Really? Man, that is so nice of you and the town." He looked at his friends. "What do you think?"

They all nodded in approval and said, "Thank you." Years later, I found out the three of them liked it so much that they stayed in that little town, settled down, and had families.

The guy from Public Works said, "How about you, Phil?"

Phil said, "Thank you very much, but as much as I've loved this magnificent reception, I am a wandering tinker and there are many places along the way that need my help."

A few rare people know their destiny, and Phil was one of them. "Ever since I was a young teenager, I've made the road my home, and what I love to do best, like Erasmus, is to fix things. In every town and village I travel through, people bring out their pots and pans and anything else that is broken, and most times, I can fix them."

"That's why we love you, Phil!" Erasmus said. "You're one of the stellar angels of the Noble Order of Vagabonds."

The next day it was time for us to go. After we cleaned up from last night, we had a breakfast of leftover chili and fresh corn tortillas and tidied up. Then the *Three Amigos*, as they now called themselves, were picked up by the Public Works Department.

Erasmus gave them each small booklet.

"What's this?" asked Smith.

"Every few months, I print a small book of poems that I wrote. This collection is called *Love More*."

"Thank you, Erasmus and Jake." The three of them surrounded us with a big bear hug.

We watched them drive away. Phil turned to us to say goodbye. "Erasmus, it was fabulous to see you again. As always, we had a blast in making loving revolutions!"

"When did you two meet before?" I asked.

"Phil and I met years ago when we were creating our exquisite *Emma*. There are many of us, like Phil, Sojourner, and more. This is a tribe, if you will, without any church or ideology, but what binds us together is our desire to help people. Some of us live in one place, like Marty and Liz, who run an outreach center in New Orleans. Others wander the globe. Without being exalted or grandiose, our mission in life is to help people. Sometimes we are seen as weirdos, freaks, and even worse. Some of us are a little crazy, but Father Marty once said, 'The real craziness is to live and not help other people. It's not because God or anyone told me to do it. It's the right thing to do, and it feels good!'"

"Kind of like angels?"

Erasmus said, "As you'll find out, there isn't a thing that's angelic about me. I've got plenty of faults and flaws."

"Me too!" Phil said with a laugh. "I'm hoping that if I continue fixing things long enough, I can also fix myself."

Then Phil climbed onboard his four-wheel electric bicycle. It had a canopy and roll-down sides. When the flap came down, it said, *Phil the Tinker NDAA.*

"What is an NDAA?" I asked.

"No degree at all," said Phil.

"Oh, by the way," said Erasmus. "Here's a gift from Jake and me. Fresh walnut bread and a casserole with fruit."

"You guys are too kind! Here's a present for Jake." He gave me a heart-shaped copper pin and in the center, it said *dream*. "I made it last night as I was watching you. It has two hearts."

"Phil, this is great! But two hearts?"

"For a love that is greater than love." He smiled and looked at both of us. "You are blessed in your love for each other."

We all embraced, and then Phil threw back his long grey dreadlocks and a stream of rainbow banners flew from the top of his cart. "Thank you. I love you both!" He put on his bowler hat, sat astride Phil's Flying Machine, and he was off.

Then Erasmus, Socrates, and I were alone at last. We sat by the river, watching the sunlight play on the water.

He asked me, "Jake, what would you like to do? Do you want to go home? Shall we try to find your aunt in Cleveland? Or is there someplace else you want to go?"

"Where are you going? What's your next stop?"

"I have to go to New Orleans, to Arizona, and to Northern California. I have to see some friends and a few doctors along the way one last time."

"What do you mean? One last time?"

He seemed surprised. "I meant—never mind. I need to see some friends before the end of the summer. But as for you, my new friend. How can I best help you?"

I had no idea where I wanted to go. I couldn't go back to my mother and her boyfriend. That part of my life was over. We were about four hundred miles from Cleveland. "Can I come with you?"

"Absolutely. We can go to your aunt's house together. You know, in the few days we've known each other, I feel like I've known you all my life. Is that strange?"

"Not strange at all," I said. "What was that word you used, destiny? I feel the same exact way. I've been waiting all my life to meet you." Socrates jumped on my lap and gave me one of his big licks across my face. "I guess Socrates doesn't want to be left out of this."

"Socrates thinks this is a good idea as well. Let's find your aunt. Can you call your mother to tell her you're okay?"

I nodded. "She doesn't have a phone, but I can leave a message with a friend who'll tell my mother I'm safe. Is that okay with you?"

He said, "Absolutely. Let's go to Ohio and see if you can stay with your aunt. I only have one ground rule – our relationship is like a grandpa to a granddaughter. Understood?"

"Grandpa to granddaughter?" I knew what he meant and though it was hard for me to trust anyone, I trusted Erasmus and felt safe with him. I looked into his eyes and said, "So, Erasmus. No funny business?"

He chuckled and threw a pillow at me. "Exactly, lots of fun, but no funny business. I think this is the start of a very good friendship."

We shook hands and I said, "Yes, a very good friendship."

CHAPTER TWO

On the Way to Ohio

My world completely changed after I met Erasmus. A short while ago, I was a frightened sixteen-year-old girl who knew little about the world beyond Black Mountain, West Virginia. Before I met Erasmus, my future was bleak and the choices limited—drop out of school, get pregnant, go on welfare, sell drugs or sell sex for drugs, have kids, and then, like my mother, watch my life vanish. I didn't think that I could ever be happy.

Today, we drove north to Cleveland to find my aunt. Socrates, the fluffy black-and-white cocker spaniel, napped on my lap. The trees were starting to blossom, bright yellow forsythia dotted the edge of the forests, the sun peeked through the clouds, and the wind was cool and fresh. I opened the window to let the spring air in, while classical guitar music played on the CD.

"Isn't it a thing of beauty? This is my friend Miguel from Spain who taught me how to play guitar. It's called *Memories of Alhambra*."

"I've heard of Spain, but what is the Alhambra?"

He told me a story about this enchanted Alhambra in Granada and the Court of the Lions. Long after I had last seen Erasmus, I made it a point to see as many of the places he'd taught me about as possible, and when I finally saw the Alhambra years later, it was truly as magnificent as he'd said.

"The Moors came to Spain in the 8th Century and created a country of tolerance, culture, and art. While Europe was in the Dark Ages, all the Moorish cities like Cordoba, Granada, and Seville throughout the Iberian Peninsula flourished and welcomed all people—Muslim, Christian, and Jew."

When I closed my eyes, I could follow him as he walked along the winding cobblestone streets of Granada that lead to the Alhambra and the Court of the Lions. "The Court of the Lions represented Muslims' vision of the earthly paradise."

I'd never met anybody who had traveled much beyond West Virginia, and his stories sounded as fantastic to me as if somebody had taken off in a rocket ship and landed on another planet. Erasmus spoke about all the places around the world that he visited as easily as most people talked about their hometown.

When I heard his stories of Granada, I thought of my home in Black Mountain filled with broken trailer homes and junk cars rusting away. Being poor is like getting caught in black water—the coal sludge rivers that are worse than mud. The coal dust is in your skin, mouth, hair, and so much a part of you. I never realized how awful Black Mountain was until I left.

When we crossed the state line over the Ohio River into Ashland, I thought I was in a dream.

"Erasmus, I love your stories. Why aren't you a professor at a college?"

"I taught for a while at a small Quaker college, but I prefer being a professor of Hobo College."

"Huh? Hobo College?"

"Hobo College is the college of life and all the lessons one learns on the road and riding the rails, or in my case, riding in *Emma Goldman*. Hobos were men and women who rode the trains looking for work, but they often tried to avoid a regular job, and sometimes during the Depression, there was no work. They had their own secret language code and ethics. Look behind you on the cabinet. There's a diagram of all their codes. A code for *nice lady*, *good food*, *work available*, and so forth. These are the signs they would mark in chalk on curbs and houses. Many of them couldn't read, and the signs and symbols were a way for all of them to communicate with each other. Also, look to the left, there is the hobo code of ethics."

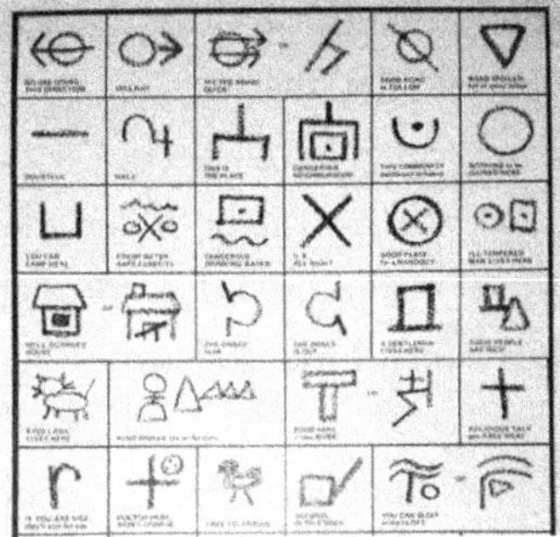

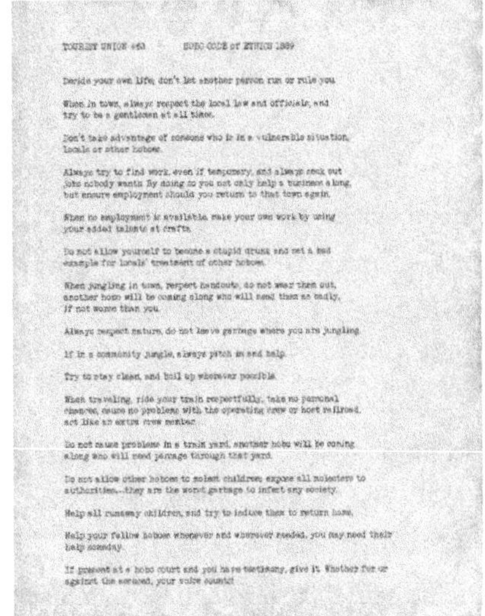

The first line sounded like him. *Decide your own life, don't let another person run or rule you.* "This sounds like common sense. Be nice to people, take care of the land, don't cause trouble, and share what you have with others."

Erasmus said, "This is why I like it—simple, reasonable rules of behavior for all people."

As I read the page, I stopped at the line, *Help all runaway children and try to induce them to return home.* But I knew I couldn't go back.

Erasmus said, "Since the beginning of time, there's been a tradition of wanderers, people who have chosen to live on their terms, not hurting or harming anyone, helping others, and cleaning up after themselves. The noblest code of the hobos is to live with integrity, humility, and kindness."

"That sounds cool! I want to be one. Can I sign on?"

"I think you have already. Let's stop here at Lake Vesuvius. It has the sweetest little campground."

We sat at the wooden dining table, made tea, and he took out a three-ring binder. "This is my bible. I keep a log of when the maintenance on *Emma* needs to be done."

I opened it, and it had elegant calligraphy on the front that said, *Emma Goldman*: *If I can't dance, I don't want to be part of your revolution.* Every page was written in the neat handwriting of Erasmus. It was almost as if he had typed it. The date, the service procedure, and a reminder of when to do it again were in columns. He recorded every service with the time he changed the fuel filter and the oil, rotated the tires, cleaned the drain lines, and the hundreds of other things that made *Emma Goldman* run like the swift gazelle she was.

"I'd like to help you, but I don't know anything about fixing."

"Not to worry, you'll know soon enough. You'll be a terrific mechanic's assistant. Necessity is the mother of invention. I didn't know much about RVs and how to maintain them until I met Sojourner."

"Who's Sojourner?"

He smiled and sighed. "She is one of the most intelligent and graceful people I've had the pleasure to know. She saved my life."

"She sounds like an incredible person. When do I meet her?"

"You met her in a way— she helped to design and build my lovely *Emma Goldman*. More importantly, because of her love, patience, and strength, she saved my life."

"How did she save your life?"

He breathed deeply and fell back onto the grass. "She loved me unconditionally!"

"Like boyfriend-girlfriend love?"

"Deeper than that, maternal love that heals all the pain. When I was alone, angry, and very sick, she found me and nursed me back to health. She believed in me when I stopped believing in myself."

"But you seem…I don't know the word. You seem the exact opposite."

"Redeemed is the right word. I had lost my way in life I was doing drugs and alcohol, eating the worst food, and allowing the demons to take over my life."

The words hit me.

Here was this man who, to me, was the most extraordinary and healthiest person I had ever met, and now he was telling me how he had been like me. This didn't make any sense.

"How did you turn it around? How did you become you, Erasmus?"

"It wasn't *me*. It was Sojourner's fearless power of love. Even when I was mean and stupid, she loved me. When I was lazy and selfish, she kicked my butt. She let me fall when I was learning to stand on my feet. Despite all reasons to the contrary, she remained and helped me through it all. When I was better and learning to be on my own again, she gave me a big bone-crunching hug and kicked me out. 'Now, find your damn way!' Ghosts from my past had haunted me—things that I could've done and should've done." He took a deep breath and sipped his tea.

"I don't mean to burden you, Jake. I should've been a better father to my son. I could've been a better husband. I could've been more helpful to my friends. I can't change yesterday, but I can change who I am today." I saw the sadness in his green eyes.

I reached across the table and held his hand. "Though I've only known you a little while…I don't know how to say this. You're a very good person."

"Thank you, Jake."

A son? A wife? Family? Sojourner? I was constantly discovering who he was, a complex person who, through his struggles, and failures, was a gentle man of wisdom, and compassion who endeavored to be a friend to all.

He never liked to bother people with his troubles, and even towards the end of my time with him, when he was sick, he didn't like to be helped. Even when he was struggling, he'd say, "No bother, it's only a trifle."

"But, you seem happy now."

"I am happy, but that was never my goal. I made many mistakes with drugs and alcohol to deal with the pain and loss of the war. The thing that helped me the most was that I enjoyed helping people. I didn't need or want to make much money, though I thought I did. I guess the saying is true, every saint has a past, and every sinner has a future. I'm somewhere in the middle of that journey."

"What does that mean? Every sinner has a past, and every saint a future?"

"You almost got it, Jake, but it's the reverse. With a rare exception, each of us can rise above our failures. No matter how far we've sunk, we can always rise. Trust me. There isn't a thing about me that is a saint, but I'm marching back up that hill to a life where I can be proud of myself again." His eyes darkened, filling with tears as he looked away.

"I don't believe we can rise above our mistakes," I said. His conversation brought up thoughts of my mother, her chaos, pain, and all the alcohol and drugs. I breathed so deeply that I almost fell over. Hearing his story, a flood of anger poured out.

"Other kids, even ones just as poor as me, called me white trash. I was so ashamed of being poor and dirty. My mother was often high or drunk, and couldn't remember to buy food and soap, and there was rarely hot water. Sometimes my ragged clothes smelled because I couldn't wash them. I had to sneak into school early to wash myself. How crazy is that?"

"I'm sorry this happened to you."

"Damn it! I hate being this ugly white trash!"

"No, these are the lies other people say because it's what they believe about themselves. Never believe the lies!"

"Look at me! Pimples, fat face, my hair is a mess, I'm ugly!"

"Jake, look at me. You're beautiful."

I was shaking. I never knew that I had all this anger and pain inside. He wrapped his arms around my shoulders and we walked out into the sun. I was exhausted. I didn't realize how many tears I had.

"Jake, thanks for telling me this. I'm sorry you've been through this. Let's for a hike up to Lake Vesuvius."

"Yeah, I need to scream or take a long walk."

He smiled. "Yup, that's what I do when I need to chase away your blues. By the way, you're going to need these." He handed me a box wrapped in brown paper. "Open it up."

I slowly unwrapped the box. "I can't believe it! New boots!"

"Try them."

"This is the first pair of new boots I've ever had. It must have cost a fortune."

He said, "Not too expensive, but they'll last at least ten years. I bought them for me, not for you. If you're going to keep up with me, you need boots you can run in. It would be a pity if someone your age couldn't keep up with an old guy like me." Then he gave me a wink and a smile.

I threw a pillow at him. "There ain't a damn thing old about you!" I reached over and kissed him on his cheek. "Thank you. I'm sorry to whine. I don't know where that all came from."

"Not to worry. Here are some socks that go with this. But trim your toenails, or it'll be painful when you hike." He handed me scissors and showed me how to cut my toenails.

This was weird. Here I was, a sixteen-year-old girl, and somebody had to show me how to cut my toenails correctly.

All the emotional junk vanished as we walked up toward Lake Vesuvius. We walked along the Iron Ridge trail, and I could run with my new boots. I felt like I could almost fly. I was more at peace than I ever thought possible. We walked in silence, breathing the clean mountain air and feeling the peacefulness of the old forest of oaks, birch, and pines. The trails were cushioned with a fragrant quilt of pine needles. He saw an exquisite blue flower in the woods and said, "Great Blue Lobelia. If you use it correctly, this plant makes an excellent tea for respiratory stuff, and it's terrific for wounds, but it will make you sick to your stomach if you drink too much of it. Do you see that pimple that was bothering you?" He took some leaves and a little water, crushed them in his fingers, and put them on my cheek.

"This will help my skin?"

"Yes. I have plenty of herbs and potions from Sojourner inside *Emma*, and we can pick some more along the way."

We stopped by the rock ledge and sipped some water. "How come you know all this stuff?"

"Like, this is Tinker's Cave, where Shep Tinker, the horse thief, would hide and trade horses? Or the plant juice that we made? Or that this ledge was made during the last Ice Age, and the iron ore gives it that strange color?"

"All of that stuff! Damn, how do you keep all this stuff in your head?"

"I'm a learning junkie. I don't learn or know stuff to impress people, but I want to know how things work. When I was a boy in Vermont on our farm, we had to figure out how to make do and fix machines that didn't work. We didn't have money to hire a mechanic. My dad said, 'The fool asks no one and thinks he knows it all, but the wise person admits what they don't know and asks all the time.'"

"Your dad sounds like he was a smart man."

"Yup, a Vermont dairy farmer with a world of wisdom that he learned from working the land."

Lake Vesuvius shimmered like sparks of diamonds in the evening light. The setting sun warmed my bones, and the wind skated across the water.

He stood on the rock ledge, ripped off his clothes down to his shorts, and swan-dived fifteen feet off the rocky ridge. Then he emerged and called back to me, "Jake, come on in! The water is chilly but delightful!"

"I hate to tell you this, but I don't know how to swim. I'm afraid of water."

He said, "It's okay. Socrates will be your lifeguard, and you can swim and splash by the edge. Are you okay with that?"

"This is crazy! It's freezing." I splashed around a little, and then he swam in a smooth, straight line 200 feet across the lake and back.

He stood in the fading light and his body was strong, thin, and more like a man in his twenties, not someone as old as him. I was a little embarrassed thinking of him in that way. *Damn*, I thought, *he looks good*.

When we returned to our campsite, we spent about a half-hour cutting up fresh carrots, rinsing chickpeas and green peppers, and sautéing onions and tomatoes. Though we had some wild greens and berries growing back home in Black Mountain, our vegetables came out of frozen food bags with little taste. I said, "The only spices we ever used were salt and pepper."

He soon had a steady fire going with a few twigs and some logs. Like most things during that summer, I didn't realize that ordinary things like making dinner could be fun. He would make enough stew for several days and offer it to anybody who showed up.

I heard someone call out, "Hey, neighbors! I'm Shoshana! I smelled your dinner and wondered if I could join you. I don't have anything fancy, but I have a big salad and brownies."

Shoshana was a slim woman with long silver hair neatly tied back into a long ponytail and wearing a purple dress.

He said, "Sure, there's always plenty of room. I'm Erasmus P. Hobbs, and this is my friend Jake Meadows. Pleased to make your acquaintance."

She helped to make supper and said, "I belong to a tribe called the Purple People. Some of us live on the road, and others live in communities in cities and towns around the globe."

"But why the color purple? Why not orange or pink?" I asked.

"Maybe because we like purple?" she said with a smile. "The founder of our tribe, Adam, said purple signifies royalty. We believe everybody is royalty. If we treat everybody like a king and queen, with all due respect, the world will be much happier and more peaceful."

We sat by the fire, eating a fresh salad of wild greens, dandelions, nuts, and fruit. She said, "I picked most of this around the park yesterday. Jake, parks are like free grocery stores."

"Amen!" said Erasmus. "Can we say grace? Please, Shoshana, lead us."

"Give thanks for this abundance of friends. Give thanks for this blessing of food. Give thanks for life. Give thanks for this Earth."

"Let's eat!" I said. "I'm hungry."

Socrates barked his approval, and soon, he lapped his vegetable stew.

Shoshana told the story of her life as a wanderer. She said, "When I was younger, I went to San Francisco during the *Summer of Love* and lived in a VW bus."

"Sorry to interrupt, but what is a *Summer of Love?*"

"Ah," said Shoshana. "In the *Summer of Love*, we hippies believed that the world was going to change, and we were going to lead that change. We thought that this Age of Aquarius would bring enlightenment and love to the entire planet. Perhaps that's why I crashed and burned out.

I realized there was so much more work to do. Too many people were greedy," she said with a heavy sigh. "But then I met the Purple People. They had this commune on the Lower East Side of New York City. They had taken over an abandoned warehouse. It became a home for dozens of people, a daycare center, and a free food kitchen. The only obligations were to help fix up the home and no hard drugs. If you were a druggie and didn't want to work, you had to go someplace else. At the Purple People's commune, I had found my tribe at last. It's strange, that moment in life when you feel like you found your tribe."

"Amen, sister!" Erasmus said. "I know what you're talking about. I know who they are and have even met Adam Purple, but my journeys took me elsewhere."

"Are there a lot of weirdos like you around?" I blurted out. "Wait, I didn't mean that. Not weird like weird, but like you and Erasmus. Different. I'm sorry."

They both burst out laughing. Shoshana said, "We are weird, because weird originally meant magical and extraordinary."

I was embarrassed as I realized what I had said. "I'm sorry!" They were rolling on the ground with laughter. They made up a song and sang, "Who's a weirdo? Are you a weirdo? I'm a weirdo. We're all weirdos."

"Don't worry, Jake! Aren't we all weirdos in our own way?" said Erasmus.

We were all laughing so hard that it almost hurt. I didn't realize I had this much laughter inside of me.

Later, Erasmus said, "I was a little put out that she didn't tell us there was pot in the brownies. Generally, I stay away from pot and such."

"I thought you were a hippy or something like that."

"To all appearances, I am a hippy with long hair, living in an RV, and traveling around the country. I've smoked more than my share of pot, but I realized I don't need it and rarely imbibe it. However, periodically it's okay."

I had never smoked or eaten pot before. For most folks in Black Mountain, their drugs of choice were moonshine and any pills they could find. I liked the buzz from the chocolate brownies. I don't know what made me laugh more—Shoshana, the silly jokes, playing the guitar, Socrates dancing on his back legs, the brownies, or me dancing. After my anger earlier, I felt much better with the swim, dinner, and this funny lady.

When the stars came out, Shoshana and Erasmus sang "Freight Train." "Come on, Jake! Join in."

"You guys sing and let me listen."

"That's silly! Of course, you can sing!"

With a bit of prodding, I sang along with them.

"Go, girl!" said Shoshana. "You sound like my granddaughter."

"Your granddaughter?" I asked. "Does that mean you're old?"

Shoshana giggled. "Erasmus, where did you get her? She's priceless. My granddaughter is twenty years old, but there isn't a thing about me that's old. In some ways, she reminds me of you, and she's also a terrific singer."

That night, I learned songs by Woody Guthrie, Pete Seeger, and other folk singers. A few people came by from neighboring RVs and everyone joined in the singing of "This Land is Your Land."

"That's a fabulous song. Can we sing it again?"

We sang it through, and then Erasmus sang it in Spanish.

I never imagined I could be this happy. But I was exhausted and yawned, "Goodnight, all. Thank you! It's time for bed!"

Shoshana and Erasmus reached over and gave me a big hug. "Goodnight, Jake. We'll see you in the morning."

I sleepily made my way to the back of the RV and kicked off my boots. Socrates came in and snuggled next to me. I thought, if life should end tonight, I could not imagine a happier way to go. I felt genuinely loved. It was strange at sixteen to say that I finally felt loved and cared for, and, just as importantly, I felt safe.

I said, "I love you," to no one in particular. Socrates snuggled close, and I fell into the most peaceful sleep.

I awoke to the smell of pancakes on the griddle and sleepily stumbled out to a glorious morning by the lake. Erasmus and Shoshana were laughing and giggling while they made breakfast. I thought little of it then but realized where he had been last night. He had slept with Shoshana, and I was afraid he wouldn't want me around anymore, but

I said nothing. That morning he had a little extra twinkle in his eyes. Shoshana was giggling like a schoolgirl with him.

Blue jay and robin songs filled the air, a red cardinal sailed by, the puffy clouds drifted across the sky, and I was at peace as I sat down for a cup of coffee. Erasmus said, "The first cup of coffee each day is my best meditation."

After my coffee, Erasmus said, "Jake, I want to introduce you to Robert and José, who will join us this morning. Would you please set the table? Robert and José, please help Jake and Shoshana. Breakfast is almost here."

We watched the geese flying across the lake. Shoshana said grace, and we all joined in, "Give thanks for this abundance of life. Give thanks for this food. Thanks for the circle of family."

José said, "I've been living in this park for a few years, and this is the first time anybody has invited me to such a delicious breakfast. I am blessed. So, can I tell you a bit about the trees surrounding us?" He then told a fantastic story about the tulip trees, the various types of maples, the beech trees, the black walnut, the pines, and the reasons different trees grow here. "For example, willow trees always like to be next to the water, and the leaves can be used in tea to soothe a fever, and the bark is a natural aspirin and a salve that can ease muscle aches. These black walnuts also grow by the riverbank and have been used by Native Americans as an antibiotic and essential food in the long cold winters."

Everyone was quiet and listened to this captivating story.

"I hope I didn't talk too much," said José. "I rarely talk to many people, and I appreciate your gracious company."

"I liked learning from you, but why didn't you tell them about the twee tree?" I asked.

"Twee tree? I don't think I know that one."

Everyone looked at me.

"Yes, the twee pines growing next to each other there." I pointed to the pines.

José looked at me and the three pine trees next to the lake and roared with a laugh that shook the table. "Of course, that is the best one of all! The twee trees."

After breakfast, we washed the dishes and picked up all the trash in the bushes.

Shoshana, José, Robert, and I planted flowers on the pathway's edge. Shoshana said, "We'll put some periwinkle on the edge, then some tulips, and we can mix it up on the pathway down to the lake."

"That will look fabulous! But remember some of the purple flowers as well," I said with a smile as I helped her with the planting.

"Yes, purple is the passion!"

Erasmus changed the fuel filter and oil, and Robert came over. "I'll help you. I'm a fair hand with cars and trucks."

Over the next few hours, the two worked together while Shoshana, José, and I planted the flowers.

That evening, word spread about music and food by our campfire. As the fire blazed, more people showed up with potluck, others came by with guitars and drums, and soon a crowd of about fifteen people gathered near *Emma Goldman*. We made a cauldron pot of vegetable stew. Then after dark, a jeep with lights flashing came by, and out came several park rangers. Several people stepped away and disappeared into the shadows, and one of the park rangers came closer to the fire. He said, "Do you know that there is a curfew on music."

Erasmus stepped forward and reached out to shake the hand of the ranger. "We were having some supper. Would you join us for yummy stew and fresh-baked bread?"

"That's mighty generous! We'll join you! But before we do, we need to get a few things from the patrol car." He strolled back to his jeep, and to our surprise, they came back blowing a harmonica and a saxophone. They had a local blues band and joined us for supper. Erasmus told them about Robert, José, and other people's work cleaning the park.

"We wish everyone could be so thoughtful to this park. Many times, people are drinking and causing damage."

There were twenty large plastic bags of bottles and trash neatly stacked. "We left the recycling bags and bottles, and they're ready to be picked up, or should we drop them off?" asked Erasmus.

"We can have the park crew pick them up tomorrow."

Around eleven, when the campfire was burning low, some fifteen people gathered around the park rangers, Tyrone and Jasper, who led us in singing "Hound Dog," "Johnny B. Goode," and other songs that I had never heard of but grew to cherish.

I fell asleep that night cozy inside *Emma Goldman* with Socrates beside me.

The following day, we headed up to Cleveland. I awoke to the sound of Erasmus playing guitar, and I couldn't believe I had slept until nine. The sun was already glorious, and the day looked promising. Erasmus made me a bowl of granola and yogurt.

Shoshana was packing up and joined us for breakfast. "Erasmus, I'm sorry to see you and Jake go, I've had such a fabulous time. That is the poignancy of life on the road, sometimes you meet such extraordinary people, and then you have to leave."

"I know that too well, Shoshana. I've met many people on the road and sometimes if I'm lucky we meet again. It has been a joy to meet you, but we need to find Jake's aunt in Cleveland."

Shoshana waved as she stepped inside her purple RV and raised her fist. "Purple power is the power of love!"

We drove north to Cleveland, and Erasmus said, "We have to stop at Kent State College to pay my respects to a friend who was killed there."

"I'm sorry. Was it a car accident?"

"No, it was something that shocked me and the nation. Long before you were born, there was the horrible shooting of college students by National Guard soldiers. I want to honor the students at Kent State who protested the war."

When we arrived at the Kent State campus, there were large crowds of college kids lying on the lawn, some studying and others playing Frisbee. We parked *Emma Goldman* and Socrates and I followed along. He took his prayer beads and zazen bench. "I won't say anything to you for a while. I need to sit and meditate on the commons where the killings took place."

"Do you need me to sit with you?"

"Yes, sit with me. This was the turning point in American protest against this tragic, unnecessary war where millions of Vietnamese were killed by the French and the Americans. This shooting woke people up to the consequences of war, and the massive protests helped to stop it."

Erasmus put down his blanket, zazen bench, and a small brass bell on a grass clearing. At noon, he rang his bell, folded his hands, and meditated amid all the students. Students who had been playing came over and quietly sat on the green grass by him. One girl sobbed quietly, and another girl sat next to her and held her. Today was the day the Ohio National Guard had killed students: Allison Krause, Jeffrey Miller, Sandra Scheuer, and William Knox Schroeder, and nine others were wounded.

Though few students knew much about the events, everyone had some idea of what had happened that day. After a half-hour, Erasmus looked up and rang the small bell that resonated throughout the commons. Over one hundred people were sitting on the grass—some with their eyes closed and everyone silent.

He turned around, folded his hands, and bowed to them. "Thank you all for sitting in this moment of witness to these events on May 4th, 1970. If anyone would like to talk more about it, I'll be here, and as best as I can, I will tell you about some of those events."

"Draft dodger!" said one student as he stormed in front of him. "You can sit here because all these brave soldiers died to protect your damn freedom."

Erasmus looked up at this hulking guy who seemed like he was ready for a fight. "Sit down, and let's talk about this."

"I don't want to talk. People like my uncle went to Vietnam and fought so we have freedom and democracy!"

A girl said, "Chuck, sit down and talk to this man. He's not going to hurt you."

"It ain't gonna change my mind. Hippies like him are the reason we lost in Vietnam."

"Chuck, my name is Erasmus. Tell me about your uncle. I'm a Vietnam veteran too and it was a complicated time."

Chuck looked at him. "I'm sorry, I didn't know you were a vet. I'm an ass. I'm angry that my uncle is in a wheelchair and sick with cancer."

Erasmus reached over to touch Chuck's shoulder. "It's not fair that he went to Vietnam, and got sick from this Agent Orange shit." Chuck started to cry. "All he wanted to do was fight for his country."

"Chuck, I'm also sick because of Agent Orange disease. Twenty-five percent of southern Vietnam, Laos, and Cambodia are contaminated with this poison that we poured all over their countries. When I was a young medic in the Army, I saw the sky thick with clouds of Agent Orange. We were told it was safe, but we knew it was a lie. When I returned to Vietnam last year, I met hundreds of children born after the war with terrible birth defects because of this."

"Why would we do this?" asked Chuck.

"As General Butler said a long time ago, 'the only purpose of war is to make the rich richer and the poor poorer.'"

"I want to join the Army after I graduate and serve my country."

"Chuck, that may be one way, but there are many other ways to serve. You need to decide. There's Peace Corps and AmeriCorps, or teaching in poor communities, which are all as important. There are many other ways to be patriotic without serving in the military."

"Again, Mr. Erasmus, I'm sorry I got mad. Thank you for your service."

"I always tell people, if you want to thank me for my service, work for peace."

Chuck reached out to shake Erasmus's hand. "I got to go, Mr. Erasmus. Thank you so much for talking to me."

Erasmus took off his *Veterans for Peace* hat and gave it to Chuck. "This is for your uncle. Tell him that a fellow vet is thinking of him and wishes him well."

Chuck put on the *Veterans for Peace* hat. "Thank you, Mr. Erasmus. Thank you for your service...for peace."

Erasmus patiently sat and spoke with the people about having compassion not only for the victims but for the National Guard as well. He was tired, but his eyes were bright and his energy never flagged.

A man with long gray hair came over. "Erasmus, thank you. I was a professor here on this day in 1970." He pointed to the offices above the commons. "I watched the protest unfold with the National Guard as they threw tear gas and opened fire on these students." He bit his lip. "I think about those students killed and wounded every day. Unfortunately, I don't have your wisdom or compassion. I can't forgive those soldiers for what they did."

"To be truthful, I'm not sure I can forgive the National Guard either, but I can understand the terrible situation they were put in. Like soldiers in Vietnam, they followed orders, and like many of us, they were frightened and did incredibly stupid things. Forgiveness is not black or white, it's made of infinite shades of grey. I've tried to forgive myself for going to Vietnam. My brother Henry refused the draft and was willing to go to jail."

"Did he go to jail or leave for Canada?"

"Strangely, he got a deferment because he's dyslexic and can't read. However, he was a very smart guy. If someone read it, he could memorize a tractor repair manual."

The professor said, "I admire your brother's courage."

We were there on the commons for more than three hours. Though Erasmus was tired, he and Jay spoke to the students and faculty who came by. People brought us lunch. I knew almost nothing about the Vietnam War. I didn't know what this Agent Orange thing was that Erasmus was sick from. Sometimes he was as tired and needed to be by himself, but I thought it was because he was *old* – even though he could walk and swim further than I could.

"Thank you all for coming to the commons, listening, and talking with us. Thanks to people like Chuck who had the courage to say what was on his mind."

In the months we were together, I learned how compassion was at the root of everything he did. Before we got into *Emma Goldman*, he turned and bowed deeply with folded hands toward the commons.

Leaving Kent State, we were quiet for a long time. Sometimes, there isn't anything to say. I was exhausted, though all I'd done was sit, listen, and watch.

We camped in Cuyahoga Valley. Erasmus was very tired. I'd always seen him as vibrant, but it was an emotionally draining day. Erasmus said, "I'm going to let you sleep in the arms of *Emma Goldman* tonight while I sleep out in my hammock under the trees. I need to be alone for a bit."

"Are we okay, Erasmus?"

"Us? We're terrific. I'm just exhausted from everything today. Thank you for being so supportive."

"I don't think I did anything. I was mostly quiet and listened."

"Sometimes, being quiet and listening is the most important thing one can do."

The next day we woke up early and cleaned up our campsite area. Erasmus looked perky. "Jake, how was Kent State for you yesterday?"

"Not sure. I'm still processing this. All the conversations with the students and Chuck, who wanted to punch you and wound up crying, and Professor Jay, who saw the shootings, and you. I didn't realize you had this Agent Orange thing. How sick are you?"

"Let's talk."

He made us some spiced tea, and we sat by the river. "It's complicated, but not too complicated. I have this cancer from Agent Orange. I'm one of the lucky ones. Some say more than four hundred thousand Vietnamese died from Agent Orange. Millions of Vietnamese are sick from this along with millions of soldiers from the US and other countries, like me. I also have prostate cancer and hepatitis C. When I met you, I was on my way to see a doctor and Sojourner."

"Can you cure this Agent Orange?"

"It's not that easy. Unfortunately, with Agent Orange syndrome, sometimes people have mild reactions and sometimes it's fatal. Agent Orange could have caused my prostate cancer, but hepatitis C is from somewhere else. The good news is that I feel incredibly healthy, although sometimes I'm tired and need to go slow. Also, I'm sure that being older slows me down a little."

"You walk faster than me and swim like a fish. How can you not be healthy?"

"Let's take it day by day. The important thing is—are you okay still traveling with Socrates and me?"

"Are you kidding? I've had the most – I don't even know the words. In the past weeks, my world has changed. I feel like Cinderella, and I don't want the ball to ever end."

"Let's see if we can find your Aunt May in Cleveland."

I was looking forward to meeting my Aunt May. We were heading to her address at 1400 Chapman Avenue. Everything I saw on the street was scary. The most haunting of all were the people who seemed lost and alone. There was a gunshot in the middle of a sign that said, *Welcome to East Cleveland.*

"Erasmus, this might not be such a good idea."

"Let me check the city map. Even I'm cautious about going into a war zone."

The bright yellow *Emma Goldman* made a spectacle driving along Euclid Avenue with the boarded-up buildings, empty storefronts, and people smoking and drinking on the street corners. I went from my insanity in Black Mountain to this broken city. We drove by the check cash stores and the gated liquor stores and turned up the road to Chapman Street. It was an empty lot. 1400 Chapman was a pile of bricks. Did we get it wrong?

The telephone directory had no information about her. I didn't know my Aunt May had moved. We got a postcard now and then, which was a treat since the only mail we usually got was from collection agencies. My mother once said about May, "She walked down to the truck stop with fifty dollars, a suitcase, and took the first ride heading west. I wish I had her courage."

After driving through the city with burned-out buildings, I wondered, is this America? I was told in school that the USA was the wealthiest country in the world, but it didn't seem to be true. We, in Black Mountain, were part of this brokenness. The sun came up late in the Black Mountain ravine and went down early. In the winter, people burned coal in steel barrels, and the air was always thick with smoke. We always saw the world through this glaze of gray, even when it was sunny. My grandpa died of emphysema and black lung and had a shriveled tattoo on his right shoulder that said, "Coal is king." The last time I saw him, he was on oxygen, gasping for breath, and dying. This coal dust was in my skin, in my lungs, it was in the water, and the worst part is that I had thought it was all normal.

After driving around this war zone of East Cleveland, we both knew that we would never find my Aunt May even if she were around.

"I was hoping we could find my Aunt May, but it was only a fantasy." I felt a bit lost without this dream. Even though it may have been an illusion, it was a comforting one – like Santa Claus.

"Let's make the best of this and enjoy Cleveland. I want to visit my friend Alice, whom you will love. She is one of the most fun people I know. I need some art supplies, and you need some new clothes. Then we can talk about the next steps for you."

"New clothes? Like Walmart?" I was excited at the thought. "Remember I don't have any money. New clothes and I don't go together."

"Don't worry about the money. I have a friend who has an art store and gallery in downtown Cleveland, and he said he wants to buy some of my drawings." He took out a pastel drawing of me. I was standing next to *Emma Goldman*, holding Socrates. "I have an extra copy for you."

"He wants to buy them?" I looked at the drawing and was shocked to see myself, almost like I was grown-up, not a kid.

"Don't seem so surprised. Since you were the model, you earned money to buy clothes. If that's okay with you."

Now, without being able to connect to my aunt, the last attachments to my old life fell away. My mother once said, "The day you were born, I was finally happy, but your dad wanted a boy, and so I chose the name, Jake, hoping he would help. Six weeks after you were born, he left a note and five dollars. '*Gone west. Rite soon.*' That was the last I heard from him."

Over the last few weeks with Erasmus, I was like a butterfly coming out of the cocoon. I was still wriggling in the web and the tangle of all the lies and craziness of Black Mountain. I still had this tough shell. The toughness kept me from being devoured by the pain.

Erasmus said, "We rarely arrive at a place intact and whole. All of us, me, you, the saints, the icons, we are all fragments coming into wholeness."

We parked *Emma Goldman* in a public parking lot near city hall. I was always astonished at how he could park the big old Airstream as easily as someone would park a car. Even more unbelievable was that after another month I would learn to drive *Emma Goldman*, even though I was terrified.

"My friend Alice is here. She also traveled all over the world and finally settled down in Cleveland." We walked into the funkiest and coolest store, with rainbows and art all over the place. It seemed huge. Erasmus called out, "Alice! Give me some love!"

Alice was a six-foot-two woman with streaks of pink, blue, and green hair in a glorious billow. "Erasmus P. Hobbs! Saints alive!"

Socrates barked and did a roll on his back. "Oh, yes, Socrates, my smooch boy." She gave him a bear hug and scooped up Socrates. Then she stepped back to look at me. "My, my, aren't you a vision of loveliness?" She reached out and gave me a hug that made my back crunch. "Jake, I've been waiting for you. Erasmus told me all about you, but he failed to mention how pretty you are."

I blushed. "You're pretty good-looking yourself."

She made us tea and biscuits, told us about her shelter for women, and then asked how we met.

I said, "I was in a bad way standing on the side of the road, soaking wet, and trying to hitch a ride. Then Erasmus showed up. He made me hot chocolate and oatmeal, and I fell asleep for hours."

Alice said, "That sounds about right for him and Socrates. You never know what will happen in life."

Erasmus, "Yup, it was pretty magical meeting Jake. Kismet in a major way." We chatted and chatted, and the two of them laughed and gabbed like old friends.

"Erasmus, it's been fun chatting and catching up, but now it's girl time. Jake and I got some serious fun to do. We need to pick out some new clothes for her, and we'll see you in about an hour!"

"Sure enough. Do you know what she needs? Jeans, some nice things, and some—"

Alice put her hands on her hips. "Ras, hush up! I know what she needs."

Alice said to me, "Ras and I go back a long way. We met when he was returning from Vietnam, and I was an Army nurse in Hawaii. These days, I have my store and the homeless shelter I run." Then she paused, smiled, and closed her eyes as if she was in some magical moment long ago.

Alice whirled around the store with me for the next hour and gathered everything I needed—underwear, socks, sandals, dresses, and bras. I had never really thought about bras. My shirts were often loose enough and truthfully, I didn't have much on top.

"Look at this! Pink bra and bikini. That's hot! Wait 'til Erasmus sees this." Then I blushed more than I ever thought possible. "Maybe it's not such a good idea?"

Alice smiled. "Sometimes it's good to keep things under wraps?" We giggled like it was nobody's business. "When you go dancing, you'll need something flouncy."

"Flouncy?"

"Yes, a girl needs something sexy and fine when she goes dancing. All the twirls and whirls will set your love's heart aflutter."

"Damn, that is a fancy way of thinking about it," I said with a laugh.

Then, as tidy as could be, new underwear, socks, bras, jeans, shirts, and a straw hat neatly fit into a duffle bag. Alice said, "One more thing, you need a dash of pink lipstick!" In a flash, I had a bit of lipstick and a dusting of makeup on.

Erasmus came back with a huge grin and pretended he didn't recognize me. "Alice, where's Jake?"

"Look, it's me!" I twirled around with my purple and pink silk dress, sandals with a bit of heel, and straw hat. My hair was tied back with three red, gold, and blue ribbons. I saw myself in the mirror and stopped and stared.

"What's wrong, Jake? You look fabulous!" said Erasmus admiringly.

I looked at them and started to cry. "I'm sorry."

They came over and hugged me, and Socrates, in Erasmus's arms, gave me sloppy dog kisses. "I'm not sad. I'm sorry to be a silly girl. I just never thought I could be happy or pretty."

We all laughed, and I showed off my new clothes, but not my pink underwear.

"Thank you, Alice! Don't worry. I got money," I said. I took out the biggest chunk of money I'd ever had—a brand new fifty-dollar bill! "I'm a model, and I got paid!"

Alice smiled at me and looked at Erasmus. "Thank you, Jake, but Erasmus and I spoke earlier and it's a little Christmas gift from the both of us."

"Six months early?"

"Yes! Every day is Christmas!" said Alice.

"Well, since you gave me a gift, I want to give a fifty-dollar gift to your women's shelter."

Erasmus told me later, "I was incredibly proud of you, Jake, you gave all your money away to help someone else. The love we can give is boundless and can change the world. This is the *Law of Relationship* and paying forward."

"What does that mean, paying forward?"

"Like what you did, you selflessly gave all the money you had, without expectation of being paid or rewarded."

Alice said, "I know this great little Middle Eastern place for dinner! Let's celebrate and then go over to the Fine Arts Museum."

We walked around the corner to Rumi's Palace which had foods I'd never heard of, like falafels, baba ghanoush, tabbouleh, and more. The man who greeted us was tall with long black hair, a dark beard, and dazzling brown eyes. His name was Rumi, and Erasmus was chatting with him in some foreign language.

"What are you speaking?" I was confused.

"A little Arabic I learned while traveling through the Middle East."

"You like?" asked Rumi. "Can I make you more? My grandma taught me great food. What do you think?"

"Rumi, this is delicious. All this food, and I don't know how to pronounce any of it."

"English is the same for me! It's strange—how is it that I *ate eight* pieces of candy? I have some delicious baklava for dessert and mint tea." He brought us a silver teapot and four glasses of tea. "This is a famous mint tea from Morocco." He raised the hot tea three feet above each glass and poured it without spilling a drop.

Rumi sat down with us and told us of his hometown of Baalbek in Lebanon. "I miss my mountains. Baalbek Jamila! The moonlight dances in the ancient Roman temples, and the snow brilliantly glows. On a full moon night, my wife, Aisha, and I would walk through the ruins. Though it was cold, we would huddle under a blanket and watch the moon." His eyes glowed at the memory. "Some people didn't like that we were Sufis, so we came here to America, but I will go back home to my mountains. But now, eat some more," he said with a laugh and brought another tray of sweets.

Rumi got up to greet people, always with a big smile. "Welcome, Marhaba! Welcome."

I asked Alice, "What is a Sufi?"

Alice said, "Sufism is a mystical religion for peace that believes people should treat each other with charity and kindness."

"If I had a religion that would be for me."

A man who looked confused and dressed in ragged clothes came in. Rumi smiled at him. "Jacob, welcome, take the table in the corner and I'll bring you nice soup today and beef kebab!"

"Thank you. Sorry, Rumi, I ain't got no money today. I might have some tomorrow," Jacob said shyly. "But I can clean up behind your building."

"Perfect. Not to worry! Now, have something good to eat!"

I went from only knowing the emptiness of Black Mountain to meeting extraordinarily kind people like Erasmus and his friends, Rumi who feeds the poor and serves them the same as his paying customers, and all these people that Erasmus called the *Noble Order of Saints and Hobos.*

Jacob finished his dinner and was dozing off in the corner. I loved the pictures of the mountains of Lebanon and promised myself I would see them one day.

Rumi came over with a big smile as we got up. "You like everything?"

"We loved it. I hope you don't mind. I made this drawing of you. What do you think?" said Erasmus.

It was a pencil drawing of Rumi with a big smile that looked exactly like him.

"This picture will go in the middle of the wall until I can get a frame." Rumi pinned it on the wall and said, "Alice and Erasmus, thank you both for coming. Alice, I'll see you at the end of the week, but Erasmus, when will I see you?"

He smiled and said, "I'm not sure. Jake and I are heading to New Orleans, but I hope our paths cross soon." Then he and Rumi warmly embraced like they were more brothers than new friends.

"And you, my dear Jake. It's a pleasure to meet you. Here is a little package of extra baklava and a book *The Prophet* by my favorite poet, Kahlil Gibran! I hope you like it."

The inscription in the book said, *Let there be spaces in your togetherness and let the winds of the heavens dance between you. The Prophet* soon became one of my favorite books.

"Thank you, Rumi!" I remembered what Erasmus had taught me. I said, "Shukran, ya Habibi!" Which means, "Thank you, my dear."

Rumi and Erasmus's laughter shook the room.

"That is wonderful. When you come back, we will study Arabic together, but the best Arabic is Lebanese," said Rumi.

"What an incredible guy!" I said as we left.

"Absolutely!" said Erasmus.

Alice said, "He comes over every Thursday and teaches my ladies how to cook Lebanese food, and we all have a feast. As my Jewish friends say, 'He is a mensch!' A real inspiring man!"

That evening, we went to the Cleveland Museum of Fine Arts. I felt grown up and stylish. Weeks ago, I was a girl shivering cold and alone, standing on the side of the road, and now I was wearing a silk dress from Alice with a matching handbag and stylish sandals. Erasmus wore a blue sports jacket with bright daisies in the front left pocket and his dark green fedora, and Alice looked like a princess wearing her lilac flowing dress. Socrates was guarding *Emma Goldman*.

There is one picture that I have carried with me all these years—Alice, Erasmus, and me in front of the *Thinker*.

"I've never been to a museum. What will it be about?"

Alice said, "It will be about discovery. Let's start with the Egyptian section."

Erasmus said, "My favorite is the post-impressionist painters like Van Gogh and others like Picasso, especially from his Blue Period." With this extraordinary journey with Erasmus, I felt like Cinderella, but the ball never stopped.

Alice led us through the museum and took us to her favorite paintings. "Look at this painting!" It was Salvador Dali's *Dream*. I was transfixed. It was a head that seemed to float in space, blue and serene. The Picasso painting *La Vie* of a young man and woman together had an entire world of a story. I didn't realize pictures could say so much. What grabbed my attention most was a photograph, *The Sharecropper's Wife*. It was the face of poverty. It looked like my mother or me.

"Come, Jake! Erasmus is waiting for us."

"Sure, but I want to come back. The only picture we had in the house was a poster of Elvis Presley."

Alice said, "Jake, I'm sorry your aunt wasn't here in Cleveland, but I'm happy to have met you. I wish I could join you on your trip to the West Coast, but I'll catch up with you before too long. Here is a little present for you." She handed me a black velvet sack. "Open it."

I opened the bag, and a deep purple amethyst necklace on a silk cord tumbled out.

"Alice, this is a gorgeous necklace. I've never had anything like it." At Christmas, all I wanted was anything new, but it was usually something bought at the second-hand store. "Thank you!" I leaped over and gave her a ginormous hug. I put the necklace on and looked in the mirror. I almost didn't recognize the girl I saw with hair neatly combed in ribbons, wearing a pretty silk purple dress. The amethyst crystal was the most beautiful thing I had ever worn.

"Jake, you're precious, and I'll see you before too long. Any time you need to come back here and stay, I always have a place for you." She hugged me close and kissed me goodnight.

"Alice, thank you for everything."

That night, when I laid back on my bed, I didn't undress. I wore the dress and the necklace, though I did kick off my new sandals and placed my purse by my pillow. I was afraid this dream would end, and I would wake up with a dress of rags back in Black Mountain. I was exhausted from all the emotions and events of the day: my aunt not living in Cleveland, meeting amazing Alice, going to my first museum, having dinner at Rumi's, my gorgeous new clothes, and something that I didn't think was possible—I felt profoundly loved and cared for.

"Buenas noches, cielo. Sueños con angelitos." That was how he said goodnight to me for the three months we were together. "Goodnight, my dear, sleep with the little angels." Then he kissed me on my forehead and drew the quilt up.

Socrates snuggled next to me and I fell into an exhausted, happy sleep.

CHAPTER THREE

Dignity Village

We drove to Dignity Village in Celo Valley, close to Burnsville, North Carolina. "One of my oldest friends, Captain Jim, now called Roshi Kanji, lives there with his community. I haven't been there in a while, but it's the most incredible place. You'll love him and meet Sojourner."

Over from Burnsville, then down mountain roads, we followed the signs to Celo Valley.

The road narrowed to a gravel driveway. "Hold on. It might be rough, but *Emma* will get us there." Above the village gate was a sign with a rainbow that said, *Welcome to Dignity. The first day of your life.*

It was evening, and we heard a booming gong. "Dinner! We came at the perfect time," said Erasmus. There were several large wooden buildings, a dozen Quonset huts, and tents in uniform rows. We parked by the side of the big building in front of a sign that said, *No parking!*

In a few minutes, we heard a voice. "Who the hell is parking in the no parking space?" roared a huge black man, over six-foot-five, with a shaved head, a small gold earring, a long mustache, and an athletic t-shirt with the sleeves ripped off.

"Of course, it's Erasmus P. Hobbs! The devil himself!"

"Jim!" He strolled over to the man, who lifted Erasmus off his feet like a baby and kissed him on both cheeks.

"Ras, man! I missed you!"

After the dust and hollering subsided, the man looked at me and said, "How do you do? My name is Jim or as they call me here, Roshi Kanji. Pleased to meet you." Then he gave a slight bow with folded hands.

I bowed back to him the way he had. "Hi, I'm Jake...the Apprentice Hobo."

Erasmus said, "Hardly an apprentice! Jake is my new friend, and we've been having a lot of fun!"

The bell sounded again—a resounding gong. "Come, dinner is ready! I'm truly happy you're here, Jake. Thanks for bringing Erasmus back!"

We walked with Roshi Kanji with his right arm around Erasmus's shoulder and his large left hand resting very gently on mine. We walked into the dining hall, and the dinner bell rang again. Everyone immediately stood at attention. All folded their hands and bowed in the traditional Buddhist way.

Everyone then wrapped their arms around the person next to them and formed a chain of people around the room.

"Friends, let us bow our heads in gratitude for this abundance of food, fellowship, and this community of love. We open our minds, bodies, and spirits to the love that joins us." In unison, everyone recited a Buddhist prayer, *Gokan no ge.*

Gokan no ge pertains to Buddhism's "Five Reflections" or "Five Remembrances." A large banner was on the dining room wall:

First, let us reflect on our work and the effort of those who brought us this food.

Second, let us be aware of the quality of our deeds as we receive this meal.

Third, what is most essential is the practice of mindfulness, which helps us to transcend greed, anger, and delusion.

Fourth, we appreciate this food which sustains the good health of our body and mind.

Fifth, we accept this offering to continue our practice for all beings.

We ate in silence. When people were done, they quietly pushed back their chairs and took their trays to the service window. This was the rhythm of Dignity Village. It followed the Zen traditions under the guidance of an ordained Buddhist Monk in the Soto/Rinzai tradition. This Roshi was Erasmus's lifelong friend, Captain Jim, now known as Roshi Kanji. The name Kanji means complete compassion.

Everybody finished dinner by six. Those who were on the kitchen and cleanup crew reported for duty. Other men went to various groups—some for evening prayer services and meditations ranging from Buddhist to Christian to Muslim, along with Alcoholics Anonymous and Narcotics Anonymous. The men in the Dignity community set their own schedules for the day, the activities, the service projects, and their recovery programs. Erasmus explained, "This has taken Roshi and his council of Elders years to figure out and refine. The men are interviewed, and those they think can fit into a year of sobriety, celibacy, service, prayer, and working their butts off are considered for the program."

"Celibacy?" I asked. "Do you mean – no sex? That's kind of weird for grown people. Ain't it?"

"This is a spiritual community for recovery from the pain of life, PTSD, and addictions like sex, drugs, and alcoholism. Over the past fifteen years, Roshi Kanji created this village with the help of many. Celibacy is part of their discipline and recovery. There is nothing wrong with sex, but the men have chosen this path, and it seems to work."

"Did you help?"

He smiled. "Yes, for two years in the beginning the only thing here was an old broken-down hunting cabin. Jim, a handful of veterans, Sojourner, Father Marty, myself, and whoever showed up built the first houses. Sojourner was the best tractor and excavator driver. We cleared the land, built the first dormitories, and began our recovery."

"Recovering from what?"

"Everything. We're all recovering from traumas, addictions, pain, and loss in life, and this is all grist for the mill."

I was a dry sponge soaking in every bit of wisdom, even if I didn't understand it.

There were no locks on the doors or in the rooms. I asked Roshi Kanji, who said, "We're all in the process of regaining our self-respect and dignity. We depend on one hundred percent trust. Many of the men, myself included, have been homeless, lost their families, and gone to prison. Others had been successful but lost their way in life. We all have the one goal of recovering our self-respect and dignity. There are no locks anywhere. We're trying to rebuild our trust in ourselves and each other."

"It must cost a fortune."

"The cost of staying here is enormously expensive. We ask people to invest their sweat, hearts, minds, and guts in putting their lives on the line. As for dollars and cents, people pay no money to be here."

"How do you pay for the food, the land, and all that stuff?"

"Benefactors, and largely through the men who have already been here and dedicated themselves to sobriety and dignity."

"How many men make it through the year?"

"They have a one-month trial, and they're allowed three mistakes. If they make it through one month and follow the program, about ninety percent finish up the year. Out of that, about twenty percent stay here for a second year and become part of the Elders. Then some like me are always here unless we're setting up other Dignity programs. Once men complete the program, they come back every year for two weeks or longer," said Roshi. "This has been the greatest gift of my life. With all the crazy, shameful stuff I did in the past—the army, drugs, alcohol, sex addiction, betrayals, lies, and all the waste and madness of life, I am grateful to help others. This program is for me as well. Last year, I was asked to head a large Buddhist monastery in California. I declined. I prefer the work of Dignity. I'm afraid I would get too big for my britches.'" He folded his hands.

Erasmus said, "Jake, come, let's help clean up in the kitchen!"

We joined about ten men in the kitchen. Roshi was next to me and lifting the heavy dish racks. "Everyone cooks, cleans, and washes, but I'm in charge of cleaning toilets," said Roshi.

"Roshi Kanji, I thought you were a big shot. Cleaning toilets?" I asked.

Roshi Kanji laughed. "A big shot! Me? A big shot, huh! I love ya' Jake! No wonder you travel with Erasmus. The truth is that the bigger the shot you think you are, the more critical it is to do the most menial of tasks. We clean all the toilets every morning before sunrise with a crew of four people. Sometimes other people take over, but it's a meditation for me. I sometimes wish people like the President of the United States, or other so-called big shots, would scrub toilets before the start of the day."

"Cleaning the toilet is a meditation? That's strange. I thought meditation had to be sitting quietly like in a church?"

"Good meditation is all our daily stuff, from washing the dishes, cleaning the toilets, raking leaves, and the most ordinary tasks. All these are meditations. One teacher reminded me to imagine you're washing the baby Buddha. He said, 'As you clean the dishes, breathe and wash slowly. Each plate, cup, and knife are cleaned with this same kind of attention and care.' This mindfulness is the journey of healing. That is the main work of our community, mindfulness of our hearts, spirit, and fellow beings in this journey of love."

"Wouldn't it be easier if you had a dishwasher?"

"This is the beauty of dishwashing, it slows us all down. We're all in too much of a rush in life. See, this isn't so hard, is it, Jake? Washing each spoon, fork, or plate like you are washing the baby Buddha?"

"Not so hard. You talk like Erasmus! You two could be twins."

"We're twins! Twins of different mothers. I love him as dearly as my flesh and blood. He saved my life."

"Saved your life?"

"That is a longer story than we have time for."

We finished washing the dishes and swept the dining hall. The last bit of sunset lingered on the Great Smoky Mountains as I sat with Erasmus and Roshi.

Erasmus said, "Jake, tomorrow you'll go up to Sojourner's community on the mountain. During this year of recovery, we found that it was better to have a men's only program."

"You'll love Sojourner," said Roshi. "She is our closest friend and mentor."

Erasmus said, "Come, we'll park *Emma* underneath the trees. I'll tell you more about Sojourner and her community of women and healers."

That night we settled in, and Erasmus finished his evening meditation and played guitar. I couldn't meditate. My mind was racing all over the place and it was hard for me to focus on one thing. Erasmus was always patient, teaching me to simply breathe to slow my mind down, but right now my mind was jumping around like so many wild monkeys.

The evening bell rang at 10 p.m. and it was time for lights out, even for us parked back in the oak grove, away from the cabins. We needed to respect the rules and quiet of the community.

Erasmus told me the story of how Captain Jim became Roshi Kanji. "I met him in Saigon, Vietnam, where he was a Green Beret on his third tour of duty. Most people were drafted, did their year of service, and never thought about Vietnam again, or at least they tried to forget it. Jim told me, 'I felt most at home on the front lines. I thought I knew what was right and wrong. My job was to kill the enemy. One day I woke from that world of shadows and lies when I was about to kill a Viet Cong soldier, who was a teenage girl. For one instant, we looked at each other, not as enemies, but as two humans. She had the drop on me and could have killed me, but she stepped back and disappeared into the forest. Suddenly, I was consumed by the hurt and shame of what I had done in Vietnam. This teenage girl had the courage of compassion, even amid battle. She had more courage than I could have imagined.'"

Erasmus said, "I saw the villages, rice fields, and jungles sprayed with Agent Orange and burnt by Napalm, and it dawned on me the horror of what we were doing in Vietnam, Laos, and Cambodia. Even years after the war, Vietnamese grandchildren are born with congenital deformities. Over twenty percent of the country is still contaminated with it. I've tried to atone for participating in this travesty. My brother Henry refused to be drafted and was willing to go to jail. Henry said, 'I don't have a single quarrel with the Vietnamese or anyone. The only arguments I have are with my cows on our farm.'"

I said, "He sounds as stubborn as you are."

"Me, stubborn? Maybe. I wish you could have met him. He was a dairy farmer who never traveled much beyond Vermont, and he once said to me, 'I know where I was born, and I know where I'll die, right here on the farm.' He was right. At forty, this man, as strong as a bull, went to bed one night and never woke up, same as my dad. I miss my brother, Henry. Even though we were very different, we shared a love of the land and our farm. I had the wanderlust gene that he never had."

He continued his story of Jim. "I only knew Jim briefly. It was difficult to miss a six-foot-five black soldier built like a tank. I was a medic for the last three months of the war and stationed in Da Nang, where I was exposed to Agent Orange. Though I am sick from it, it pales compared to the constant poisoning of the country and the Vietnamese. I know many veterans who are profoundly wounded mentally and physically. The war is the ghost that haunts my generation. Nearly sixty thousand US soldiers and over two million Vietnamese were killed in the war, and four hundred thousand Vietnamese died because of Agent Orange poisoning. The poison remains in the water and land decades after the war. I was in Vietnam last year and worked with some of the rehabilitation places for victims of Agent Orange and unexploded bombs. I am still horrified and ashamed of what we Americans did in the name of democracy." He breathed deeply. "What a shameful waste. A day doesn't go by that I don't think about it."

I knew a little about Vietnam, and I knew a few veterans, but they never spoke about it.

"Erasmus, please tell me more."

"I was with Jim briefly while traveling in India but lost touch with him, and years later I was in Venice Beach, California. A big fat man was sitting on a bench drinking a jug of wine. He looked up at me and said, 'Erasmus P. Hobbs. Remember India, and before when I had been shot and you patched me together? Thanks, man!'

"'Jim, you remember me?'

"'I never forget a face. I remember the faces of all the people I killed in Vietnam. That's why it's hard to sleep at night. The only thing that helps is pot and booze.'

"We were both drinking and doing drugs. We were in terrible shape, fat and depressed. We both had hit bottom, but we discovered a path out of our pain. Sojourner saved us. She ran a shelter for runaway kids and the homeless. Despite our shameful behavior, she helped us find our way."

A shout arose from the dining hall. "It's Louis! He's freaking out!"

"Jake, stay here," said Erasmus.

Erasmus raced to the dining hall. I followed behind and peeked into the dining room from the window. Louis, a skinny old man, screamed, "I got a knife! No one comes close. Back off!" Chairs were thrown around the room, glass broken, and tables overturned.

Twenty men of different ages and backgrounds formed a large protective circle and sat on the floor twenty feet from Louis and closed their eyes.

Roshi had been a black belt karate instructor in the Green Berets and was twice the size of Louis. He said later, "I opened my soul as wide as I could with all the compassion I could muster. I opened my heart to all the mistakes and heartache. I opened my heart and breathed. Louis suffers from terrible PTSD from the war."

Within a few minutes, Louis stopped as if suddenly awake and fell on the floor sobbing. Roshi and Erasmus walked over to Louis, sat on the floor, and held him as if he were a baby. "Louis, we love you. It's okay. We love you."

The men sat on the floor and surrounded Roshi, Erasmus, and Louis.

Then everyone got up and embraced Louis. He was shaking and sobbing. He spent that night with the Elders and a psychologist. After Louis slept, they walked to the retreat cabin, and Roshi Kanji stayed with him. The following day, Sojourner visited him and gave him some herbs and homeopathy, and a counselor stayed with him.

I had seen my mother in her addictions, alcoholism, and the madness that devoured her, but I had never seen someone like Louis in such a state of panic.

"Erasmus, what happens to a person like that?"

"I have been with a lot of people who have been in crisis, even myself. He still has PTSD from the war and hasn't been able to shake it. He is much better than he was."

"Have you ever been like Louis?"

"Not in the same way, but when I was at my worst with drugs and alcohol, I was a million miles away. No one could reach me, and the worst part is that I couldn't even reach myself."

"It's strange. You're the exact opposite now. You look healthy and happy. I couldn't keep up with you when we were climbing the mountain. Even with my new boots."

"Half right. I am happier than I ever thought possible," said Erasmus quietly as we sat by the campfire with Socrates on his lap. "You've brightened my spirit so much over these past weeks, and I'm grateful. I am sick with this Agent Orange disease and other stuff, but I am feeling strong, and if I can get help from Sojourner and the other doctors, I can beat this."

"I know you will." I wrapped my small hands around his strong ones. "We can beat this, Erasmus," I said with all the optimism I could muster.

"Damn right!"

He reached over for his guitar and played a blues. Then a harmonica was playing nearby and came closer. It was Roshi Kanji. Stars were bright, and Erasmus said, "Look, there is Orion, the hunter, and Ursa Major, the great bear."

Erasmus sang, "Goodnight Irene."

"Come on, Jake, I taught you this. You can do it."

I forgot the shy Jake, leaned my head back, and sang, "Me and Bobby McGee."

Erasmus said, "Go for it, Jake!"

Roshi Kanji said, "With all the excitement today, this is medicine for my soul! If we could sing a bit more that would be fabulous."

Roshi Kanji had a warm baritone voice and loved gospel songs. We sang the songs I knew from the gospel church on Black Mountain like "Wade in the Water." Starlight appeared, and when the Bonsho bell rang, we were on our last chorus of "Amazing Grace."

It *was* amazing grace! It was the first time I truly felt the power of music as love.

"Goodnight, Jake and 'Rasmus." Roshi's large arms embraced us both. "I love you. Thank you." Then, quietly, he walked through the tall grass.

Erasmus tucked me in and said, "Thank you, Jake. Sueños con angelitos."

"Erasmus, no matter what happens, I'm there for you."

"Thank you. And…"

"What?"

"You are my extraordinary friend."

"Yeah, Erasmus. I love you too, but no funny business."

Erasmus said, "Life is funny business, ain't it?"

Socrates curled under the covers with me.

The next day the sun rose in a glorious orange and golden light over Dignity. The Bonsho bell rang first for meditation and then the second bell rang for breakfast. After breakfast and cleanup, there was the dharma talk—an hour-long talk given by Roshi.

Roshi began with his hands folded in the Buddhist gassho and bowed to the group. Gassho, as Erasmus taught me, is a deep reverence for all living creatures. Then he sat down on a cushion, and the room of fifty people bowed to him.

"Yesterday, our brother Louis had a crisis. I am grateful for the compassion and love from those who were part of that circle. Today's talk on compassion is a subject I've spent much of my present life trying to understand. As an army captain in the Green Berets during Vietnam and afterward, I was a lost alcoholic and drug-addicted man. In my recovery process, I was saved by the compassion and love of many people. Every moment of the day at Dignity is built on the brick-and-mortar of compassion in our ongoing journey. One brick at a time. Learning compassion and love for ourselves and then extending it to touch everyone. Too much of the world relies on the opposite—anger and passion. I had spent too many years in anger and ego. Now, I am like you on the road to recovery. During our recovery process here at Dignity, we change and focus on the power of loving compassion. Loving compassion is not a single act. It's not for one moment, but for every breath we take and every action. The greatest compassion is to be one hundred percent present with the person in pain. Even when your pain is screaming."

You could hear the heaviness in the room as he spoke. "How do we keep that thirst for compassion alive when we've lost hope? How do we love?"

Tears came down my cheeks. Erasmus placed his arm around my shoulders and said, "It's okay to cry, Jake."

Roshi started to chant. I didn't understand a word, but later I discovered it was the Heart Sutra, the prayer that opens the heart and soul. He rang the bell, and tears rolled down his face.

We walked outside in the morning sun for the kinhin line, the slow walking meditation. Nearly fifty people put their hands on each other's shoulders, stepping forward in a snake-like walk. We were one person walking through the grass. It was like we were breathing together.

I was exhausted and skipped lunch to nap. I fell into a heavy sleep and dreamed I was in a sailboat at sunset—Erasmus, Socrates, and I, with the wind filling the sails. I stood on the upper deck, and the wind blew through my hair. I looked behind, and Erasmus was smiling and playing the guitar.

Then his voice woke me from sleep. "Come on, Jake! You're going to sleep the day away."

"How long did I sleep for?"

"At least an hour. I figured you were tired after the talk by Roshi and the chanting. Come, I brought you some lunch, and then we're going to Sojourner's."

We sat outside of *Emma Goldman* under the awning in the late afternoon as the glorious Blue Ridge Mountains stretched out in the distance and the sun broke through the hazy clouds. "You'll stay with Sojourner for a few days, so pack up, and then we'll head south. I'll stay here with Roshi Jim, and if you need anything, I'll come, but knowing Sojourner, you won't even think of me."

"Where are we going after here?"

Erasmus took out a map and drew a line toward New Orleans. "The goal is to end up in New Orleans in another week. My good friends Marty and Liz run a community center down there. You'll love them. What do you think? A few days with Sojourner, and then we head south?"

These past weeks with Erasmus were beyond words. They were not only life-changing but soul-stirring. I'd been writing these experiences down, savoring each moment, afraid I would wake up from this extraordinary dream and find myself back in Black Mountain. I wrote a letter to my mother, though I am not sure she cared. I was worried about her, but not her stupid boyfriend. Simply I said, *Mom, I'm fine. I've met some fine people who have been taking care of me. I am very healthy and happy. I hope this note finds you safe and well. Love, Jake.*

Erasmus said, "I know you're angry, and you have the right to be. I know your mom has problems, and writing the letter is a good step for you."

We walked up the steep path towards Sojourner, and Dignity Village was spread below with its Quonset huts and temple with solar panels.

I heard drumbeats on our way up the trail. I came to the open meadow, and there was a wooden cabin with a woman on the porch drumming. Her face was a light coppery bronze, her cheekbones prominent, and her hair flowed down to her waist in silver-grey dreadlocks with ribbons of gold and purple. She wore a lilac silk robe and was drumming on a large conga drum. We sat down in the meadow to listen. The sky was a crisp blue, filled with the lightest of clouds. She stopped drumming and, when she saw us, said, "Welcome, my children!"

She stepped from the porch and opened her arms wide. "My delightful Erasmus! This must be the lovely Jake I have heard so much about." She was over six feet tall, with gold hoop earrings and a copper necklace on her chest. I felt a profound peacefulness as she held us close.

Her arms surrounded us both. I was on her left side, and Erasmus was on her right. Then she started to hum. It was a song without words.

Before I met Erasmus, I wouldn't have believed them if anyone had told me I would be standing in the Blue Ridge Mountains holding a seventy-year-old man and a six-foot-tall woman humming a song without words. As Erasmus had reminded me about the book *Through the Looking Glass*, it feels like we're all going down the rabbit hole in this journey we take together. In this new world with Erasmus and on this extraordinary journey, I felt like I was constantly sliding down the rabbit hole and never knew where I would wind up. Many years afterward, when I felt lost or frightened, I would close my eyes and imagine him and Sojourner holding me.

There was lemonade, oatmeal cookies, and a fruit bowl when we sat on the porch. "Sojourner, dear sister, I've missed you," said Erasmus. "I even play music for you when I'm traveling."

"I hear you, Erasmus! The blues, flamenco, and songs. I especially loved hearing Jake singing 'Goodnight Irene' yesterday."

"You could hear us? We were more than two miles away."

Her voice was rich and deep, and she spoke in carefully measured words. "In the valley, music and sound travel. I always hear the Basho bells from Dignity Village. We'll have some more time to sing and drum. Erasmus, it's been far too long since I've seen your lovely face." She held his hand and brought it next to her heart. "Far too long, my dear brother. How did you find your lovely daughter?"

"Excuse me, ma'am. I actually found him!"

"Is that so?" said Erasmus. "Perhaps we found each other."

Sojourner gave a big laugh. "You both are precious. It seems like you've known each other all your lives. How about lunch? I have rice and beans, salad, and more lemonade."

We stepped inside her small cabin. The cabin was the same size as our *Emma Goldman*, and its woodwork, furniture, and bookcases looked similar. The front door was oval, with a large stained glass window. There were weavings and carpets on the floor of red, blue, and yellow geometric patterns, a couch covered with colored blankets, and a white antique iron bed in the back corner.

Erasmus said, "When Sojourner and I first met years ago, and after we built some of the houses at Dignity, we built this house together. Of course, with a number of our friends like Roshi. That's why some of the furniture may look the same as in our home *Emma Goldman*." It was the small ways through which he let me know I wasn't simply a hitchhiker along for a ride, but that *Emma Goldman* was *our* home together. Before I met him, everything was uncertain and I had always felt like a stranger in my life. I know that is peculiar, but I never felt at home in Black Mountain. I came to discover that home was where my heart was, and my heart was with Erasmus and these kind people I had met.

It was a joy to see Erasmus and Sojourner laughing and having so much fun. I have to admit I was a little jealous. I wish I'd had all that time with him before. There is a whole world of stories, friends, relationships, and family he had for many years before we met. I wish I could've been part of each one of those stories.

We sat down to lunch, and there was rice, beans, and salad. Sojourner said, "Please let us join hands and say grace together." Quietly, she said, "Mother, Father, God, all the spirits that guide us, we give thanks for this food, for this blessed abundance, in this circle of family."

After we had eaten lunch and washed the dishes, I said, "I hate to be a party pooper, but can I take a nap?"

"Of course, Jake! Sojourner and I are going to take a walk."

"I won't even miss you. Maybe only a little," I said with a wink.

As I laid back on Sojourner's wrought iron bed, her calico cat leaped up to sleep with me. "Esmeralda wants a nap with you as well," Sojourner said while she covered me in a quilt. "Sleep well, my dear. We'll be back before you wake up."

The bed overlooked the rolling meadow filled with flowers and the soaring Blue Ridge Mountains in the distance. I was at peace. As I grew older, I realized how rare that was. Though I was only at the beginning of my journey with him, and it would only last for three months, it was a journey I would be on all my life. The journey of our lives is our journey home to ourselves.

When I woke up, Erasmus and Sojourner were chatting on the porch and brought me a cup of tea. "How was your beauty sleep?

I said, "Well, do I look more beautiful?"

"Absolutely! I need to go down to Dignity for a few days. One of the guys down there is a terrific truck mechanic who will help me with *Emma*. Of course, I need to spend time with Roshi Jim too. I'll see you in a few days. Is that okay?"

"Erasmus, will you be okay without me?"

"I'll somehow muddle through the next few days. I am sure you'll have fun playing music and harvesting herbs with Sojourner, and you'll hardly know I've gone."

"Love ya, Ras! I'll see you in a few days. Don't worry about me. I have a feeling I'm in good hands with Sojourner."

As he left, he whistled one of my favorite songs, "The Whistling Gypsy," the story of a gypsy and a lady who fell in love.

Sojourner was a powerful and extraordinarily loving presence. "Jake, I'm happy you came to stay with my tribe of sisters and me for a few days."

"Sisters? Are there more of you?"

"Didn't Ras tell you? We're a group of healers and herbalists. We take care of the men at Dignity and all the people in the valley with our herbs and potions."

"Are you witches?"

"Of course we are! But we're the good witches, not like the bad ones in the movies and fairy tales."

"You mean you won't turn me into a frog and boil me alive?" I said with a smile.

"'Rasmus was right about you. You have a wicked sense of humor, and we're going to be terrific friends. Come, let's go out back, and brew some of our witch's potions in the barn."

The barn behind Sojourner's wasn't any ordinary old barn, and when I walked in, I was shocked. It was a laboratory for making herbs, and about a dozen people were there.

"Hi, everyone! Say hello to Jake the hobo. She came into town with Erasmus and has been traveling with him, and she thinks we're all witches. How about that?"

The women stopped what they were doing, came closer to me, and made witch-like cackling and howling noises. I started to howl and cackle like the witches I saw in *The Wizard of Oz*.

A very old woman named Sister Drum said, "Welcome to our coven of witches! We've been waiting for you! Tomorrow will be the full moon, and many others from around these hills will join us. I'll show you how we make herbs, potions, and medicines."

I knew some of the medicines Erasmus made, the teas and tinctures. The building was as big as a barn. It was clean and neat despite the mountains of weeds and herbs, laboratory glass, mixing bowls, machines to grind the herbs, and the hundreds of things you needed to do to make herbs.

"Please, help us."

Sojourner said, "Go with Sister Drum, and she'll show you around."

I had a hundred questions per minute, and Sister Drum said, "The easiest thing to do is to show you how to make a simple."

A simple is precisely that, a simple blend of herbs like peppermint or fenugreek. Erasmus taught me that. I was surprised that I knew some things already, like peppermint and chamomile tea for tummy aches. In Black Mountain, no one was a herbalist, but weeds and such were all over the mountains. No one knew how to mix herbs, put them in alcohol, or the other chemistry involved. "I only know how to grab some mint or chamomile and boil it in water when someone has a tummy ache. Or to take jewelweed and rub it on the skin when someone steps into a patch of poison ivy."

"You know more than a lot of others about this."

"It ain't anything fancy. It's common sense. Even in Black Mountain where the sludge and river run black, some of the prettiest flowers grow on the hillside."

"I know," said Sister Drum. "I'm from outside Morgantown. Like yours, my family were coal miners, and all the wildflowers grew on the hillside, the coneflowers, monk's hood, and other plants that I had no idea are healing herbs."

I was mesmerized by all the glass bottles, boiling pots, herbs hanging from the rafters, the storerooms, and glass chemistry set-ups. "We sell a lot of the herbs in bulk, and then for our clinics and herbal schools, we sell them directly. Sojourner and I make all the formulas and are the main teachers. We also have our clinics in Asheville and Burnsville. This was the only kind of medicine since the days of the Cherokees and we want to share the knowledge and healing."

While I helped Sister Drum grind down the herbs, I asked, "I keep hearing about Sojourner from Erasmus and Roshi. She seems amazing - what is she like?

Sister Drum said, "Observe her, and you'll learn everything you need to know about her. She's Cherokee who grew up with her grandmother, and became a physician, but Sojourner said, 'Even with all my doctor knowledge, I was always a herbalist and a healer.'"

I spent the rest of the afternoon helping make tinctures, taking the bulk herbs to the drying sheds, and learning from all the women. It wasn't work, it was fun, and I loved learning how these plants were turned into medicines. The gong rang. Sister Drum said, "It's supper time. I can't wait to see what Sojourner made."

I had learned a lot from Erasmus, but this was now a whole school in front of me.

"Sister Drum, why doesn't everybody use these kinds of herbs and healing instead of buying all the stuff at pharmacies? This seems like it's gentler on your body. Or, have I been indoctrinated by Erasmus?"

Sojourner came in. "Yes, you've been indoctrinated by Erasmus. He is a terrific herbalist and homeopath."

"He said you taught him everything he knows about herbs and healing."

"Actually, we taught each other quite a bit. But your question of why everyone doesn't use herbs is a bit of a mystery. For many centuries, before the rise of the Industrial Age, people only used herbs that grew in their gardens. When someone figured out how to make medicine and make money, then the equation changed. At one time in the United States in the late 1800s, there were hundreds of homeopathy and herbal schools, but the mainstream doctors organized and closed down many of these schools. As they say, follow the money."

"Shouldn't all this stuff be free? Like what you do by helping everybody in this area?"

"Yes, this knowledge is priceless, and for anybody who wants to study with us it's free."

"I know we've just met, but can I come back and study? I don't mean to be pushy."

Sojourner said, "I feel you're going to be an incredible herbalist and healer. Whenever you're ready to come back, the door is always open, and there's always a home for you."

The next morning, we rose at six. We went out to the meadow where Sojourner and Sister Drum began the day by drumming and chanting. There was a group of about six women who lived up here, and others lived nearby with their families.

At breakfast, Sojourner said to me, "Try the shake. It's quite yummy."

"I don't want to be ungrateful, but it looks like something on a pond. But if you're sure, I'll give it a try."

The day was going fine until about eleven o'clock when I felt woozy and realized that my period was starting. For most girls, it's not a problem, and after a few days of bleeding, you're done, but mine was like an avalanche of darkness. Erasmus had given me sepia and herbs, but I had forgotten to bring them. Damn, I had been having such a good time.

I said to Sister Drum and Julia, "I'm sorry to bother you. I'm starting my period, and I'm falling asleep. I need to stop for a little bit. Sorry to be a pain."

Sister Drum said, "No problem, let me help you. Julia, take over and finish the rest of the herbs."

She looked into my eyes and said, "Stick out your tongue. Now let's check your pulse." She took my wrist, nodded, and said, "I think I have a few herbs that can help you."

"Do you have any sepia as well?"

"Fabulous idea! We also make a great herb potion." She reached for a bottle that said *Earth Momma Love Formula* and gave me a tablespoon. She took me to the hammock under the chestnut tree, laid down a soft plastic foam pad, and covered me with a blanket. "Don't worry about us. We'll have plenty of time to work later. When you have your period, the important thing is lots of fluids, electrolytes, herbs, and rest."

"Thank you. I'm sorry to flake out on you."

"No need to apologize. Here's a bell if you need anything, and we'll check on you in an hour."

To my surprise, I heard the yap of Socrates. He leaped into the hammock. It must have been two miles from Dignity. How did he find me? Did he know I was here? When I was sad or blue he would always give me one of those doggy kisses that made me feel better.

Looking over the Blue Ridge Mountains, Mount Mitchell, or as Sojourner called it in the original Cherokee, Atulla, I was mesmerized by the vista and the mountains stretching out in front. The lavender fields were in bloom and there was a hint of jasmine. The cardinals and blue jays darted nearby, and as the hammock swayed ever so gently, Socrates and I fell asleep.

I fell into a dream, and I was in dark, inky waters. Normally, I was afraid of swimming, but I had a sense of profound peace. The water was warm, and I was a mermaid swimming playfully toward the light. Erasmus was swimming towards me, and our hands touched. He took me up to the surface and said, "Jake, you know how to swim. It's okay. You don't need me. All the people we've met on the road are angels to guide you. I can't always be with you, though I wish I could." We swirled around each other, and as he took my hand, we broke through the surface of the water, and then he faded away. I was terrified that he was leaving, but I realized I was okay.

I opened my sleepy eyes to the late afternoon light. Socrates was lying beside me and women were making herbs.

"Good afternoon, sleeping beauty," said Sister Drum. "We thought you'd sleep all day. We didn't want you and Socrates to be alone, so we brought our work outdoors. Here's a cup of tea."

"How long was I out for?"

"A little bit, but no one is counting. More importantly, how are you feeling? You must be starving. We made lunch."

"I'm voracious, and I'm sure Socrates can also go for a treat. I hope I didn't inconvenience you. Usually, when I get like this, I bleed, have lots of pain, and fall asleep, but I feel good right now."

As soon as I stood up from the hammock, I saw that I had bled on the mattress. "Damn, let me clean the mattress first." I was embarrassed. "I'm sorry that I made such a mess."

"Don't be silly. Periods are normal and natural, and there's no need to apologize. Let me help you to the shower, and don't worry about the mattress and the pad. We'll spray it off with the hose."

Julia helped me into a hot steaming lavender bath. She bathed me with a sponge. "I'm glad to help. When I first came here, my periods were as bad as yours. I could soak in this tub for days with herbs and juniper. Your body is trying to sort out your hormones. Have some more of this iron tonic."

When I was clean, I was dressed in a terry cloth bathrobe. Erasmus had left me an extra guitar, and I sat on the porch practicing what he had taught me. The bath with the lavender and Epsom salts seemed to have soaked into every pore.

"How is Erasmus?" I asked Sojourner when she returned.

"I brought some herbs to Dignity Village, and he and Roshi looked like they were having a great time building a new garage together and fixing up your RV. He'll be back up for you in another couple of days."

Over a lunch of a big bowl of beets, carrots, brown rice, tempeh, and a big dark green smoothie, I told the ladies about my dream under the water and meeting Erasmus.

Julia said, "It's probably a healing reaction. Between the sepia and the herbs, it helps your body regain balance."

"Is there something special tonight?"

"Yes, it's a propitious time for you to be here. We always have a celebration in the meadows on a full moonlit night. Tonight, Sojourner would like you to be part of this as we initiate you into our circle of women."

I thought about this for a minute. "Does this mean I'm going to be a witch like you?"

Sister Drum threw a pillow at me, and the ladies cackled and screeched like witches. "Yes, we're going to make you into the good fairy princess you are, but we won't turn you into a frog."

At 6 p.m., Sojourner called out, "Jake, come, it's time to eat!"

Sojourner's cabin was lit with candles, and there was a long table with dinner. The house was decorated with ribbons. The women had cleaned the porch and brought logs out for the Moon Dance bonfire.

After dark, several girls and I were invited to the sweat lodge made from willow branches. Maria, a thirteen-year-old girl, Tanya, who was Sister Drum's granddaughter, and I were brought in. Sister Drum and Julia took off our thin cotton dresses and began to wash us. "Juniper to cleanse. Meadowsweet to heal. Motherwort to bring you to the circle."

Julia said, "This is a perfect alignment for you with the moon and a celebration to honor your womanhood."

We were enveloped in a fog of steam, more water was thrown on the steaming rocks, and we drank a bitter tea and were led out into the cool evening dressed in long white cotton robes to three places in the circle with pillows.

Sojourner called out, "Welcome Jake, Maria, and Tanya to the circle of women. In this ancient circle, we invite you to celebrate the moon goddess within each one of us. We dance in honor of Athena, the goddess of wisdom, and Asclepius, the god of healing. We call on healing forces from the four cardinal points, the blessing of the new day from the east. From the west, the calm of the setting sun. From the north, the rains, and from the south, dreams of memory and time. This is the celebration of your new moon and who you are and will become as women. The moon is a celebration and a bonding for all of us."

The large drum called Mother Earth was struck. The bonfire was lit, and the orange and yellow flames leaped skyward. A circle of about two dozen women and girls drummed around the fire.

Sojourner said, "This circle has been the drum circle of women since the beginning of time, as all of humanity is joined by this umbilical cord of mother to child. We women are united in maternal love, which is selfless compassion."

Long after midnight, we danced, sang, and played music in the meadow. I was exhausted but incredibly happy and fell asleep in the hammock swaying gently and watching the moonlight. I had found my tribe, and I was becoming a woman.

At dawn, Sojourner brought me a cup of tea and said, "Jake, you look radiant and healthy. How was the drum circle last night?"

"I don't have words to describe this. All these years, I had been this poor girl growing up at the bottom of Black Mountain with people who had lost hope, and then I found my way to Erasmus and finally you. It's like I've been reborn."

Sojourner stroked my head. "You are an extraordinary woman, Jake. Come, let's walk to the mountain top."

We walked up the winding trail to the promontory that overlooked the entire valley. It was one of those moments in life where you realize you can't go back. The old Jake Meadows was gone. Sojourner raised her arms wide and started chanting to the evening sun, and I joined in.

"Sojourner, can I ask you—what made you, you?"

"Meaning?"

"Here you are this inspired teacher, wise woman, healer, and awesome friend. What made you Sojourner?"

"Teachers, angels along the way, and a star."

"A star?"

"Actually, Stella was my great love, and I knew it from the first time I saw her. She worked in Guatemala with the people in the mountains during the civil war." Then she was quiet and looked towards the sunset. "I could have gone with her, but I had to finish work here. I was on my way to live with her and then I found out she was killed protecting children from the government soldiers."

"I'm sorry to hear that. Did you stay in Guatemala?"

"I worked there briefly before I finished medical school, but by the time I finished school, I realized my true passion was the herbs and medicines of the Cherokee people. I was lucky, I realized this was my gift and my passion. In my work, I'm inspired by my great love – Stella. Stella is always the inspirational angel and starlight that guides my life. Come, they're waiting for us below."

I spent the day with Sister Drum and the other women, making herbs and potions. I filled up a box with new herbs for Dignity Village, restocked their emergency kit, and added some herbs to our kit in *Emma Goldman*. The evening was peaceful. I played guitar and sang with the women. I could stay here with my Sojourner and my new friends, but I needed to continue with Erasmus. Before bed, Sojourner said, "Remember Jake, we always have a home here for you."

"Thank you. I do feel at home, but now, I need to go with Erasmus. Though it may sound odd, I think he needs my help."

The following morning, we returned to Dignity Village to deliver herbs. I felt like a jigsaw puzzle being slowly put together again, but the pieces were still a jumble of past and future. When we came down, Roshi

Kanji and Erasmus were by *Emma Goldman*, and she was washed. As soon as I saw Erasmus, I ran across the field and whooped, "Erasmus!" He took my hands and swung me around like I was a little kid. Then we fell and rolled in the grass laughing.

"I missed you! I hope you didn't fall apart without me," I said.

"Of course, I was totally dysfunctional without you!"

"Really?"

"I'm only playing with you."

Roshi Kanji folded his hands in a bow. "Jake, we missed you."

I folded my hands and bowed deeply to Roshi Kanji.

CHAPTER FOUR

Leaving Dignity on the Way to New Orleans

Exhausted! Happy! Gone to another planet, I wrote in my diary the next morning. Today, we were leaving Dignity and heading to New Orleans. Though we *sort of* knew where we were going, surprises and detours always appeared. This was the magic of Erasmus and as he said, "Life is a journey, and you never know what or how things will present themselves."

Black Mountain seemed as if it was another life. My world had changed from the first moment I met Erasmus, Alice, Rumi in Cleveland, Phil the Tinker, and all the hobos and gypsies. Then meeting Roshi at Dignity, and my mother, my sister, my…wow! Sojourner and her circle of women friends. Plus, my friend, and travel buddy, my fluffy Socrates, who comforted me when I had the blues, made me laugh with doggy kisses, and guided me through the woods.

The last few weeks had been surreal. In the beginning, I could barely write, let alone know what surreal meant. I still hear his voice guiding and inspiring me. "You can do it, Jake! Be a bit more patient! Come on, Jake, it's time for swimming!" I went from a pimply-faced girl to a clear-skinned strong young woman who could almost keep up with

Erasmus. In our *Summer of Love*, I lived an extraordinary life, though we only had those few months. Was I bitter or angry because we didn't have more time? Hell no! He reminded me always, "Carpe Diem," seize the day. "Live each day as if it were your last."

Dignity was a place I could have stayed at for a long time, but we had a plan and we were heading to NOLA. Mist rose from the Great Smoky Mountains and cardinals, blue jays, and woodpeckers were in a glorious chorus.

Roshi said, "You know I never say goodbye. I always say, 'Hasta la proxima'—until the next time. Man, Erasmus, I love you," he said in his gravelly voice. "As always, it was a cosmic blessing and joy to see you and your awesome apprentice hobo." Jim leaned over and kissed him on both cheeks, enveloping him in his strong arms.

Roshi bent down and gave me the gentlest of hugs. "Thank you, dear Jake! Welcome to the Noble Order of Hobos and Saints. Here's a small gift to remind you of us."

It was a small greenish-bronze brass bell with strange writing on the side. I asked him, "Roshi, what does the writing say?"

He squatted down and looked at me directly. "This is Sanskrit and the heart of Buddhist teaching, 'Behold the jewel in the lotus.' Without getting all fancy on you, it means to always stay awake to your true nature and the possibility of what you can become."

He placed it around my neck, right next to the amethyst from Alice. "The bell always reminds us to be awake and present in the moment. Though it may be a wee hard to hear, ring it when you need help." Then he kissed me on my forehead. It was gentle, but I felt a zing that went right to my toes. Tears of gratitude rolled down my cheeks.

"I love you, Roshi," I said.

Then Louis walked over. "I'm sorry I lost it last week and haven't been well, but I also wanted to say goodbye."

Erasmus reached over and hugged him. "Nothing to apologize for, Louis. All of us have a bad day. You are a dear soul!"

Louis said, "Thank you, Erasmus and Jake. I wanted to give you something I made." He took out of a black cloth sack a dreamcatcher so exquisite it looked like it could catch a rainbow. It was made from branches of willows and oaks woven with fine thread, turkey feathers, and tiny crystals. "Jake and Erasmus, I hope both of your dreams always come true. You both inspire me. God bless you in your journey."

These are some of the gifts that remain with me today. These gifts and the most important gift, the time with Erasmus, have endured for over twenty years.

Erasmus, Roshi, and I embraced Louis. I never realized that crying could happen this easily. I could stay here forever with Erasmus and Socrates.

In these weeks that I'd been with Erasmus, I'd found people who wanted me to be part of their family. Besides loving yourself, one of the most important things in life is finding your tribe.

Erasmus said, "I love you, brother."

"And as always, I love you too, my brother," said Roshi Kanji.

I said, "Knock it off, guys! I'm going through too many damn tissues watching everybody say goodbye! It's making me feel like warm oatmeal."

Erasmus laughed. "Everybody, did you hear what Captain Jake said? Warm oatmeal! That has to be the funniest thing I've heard in a long time!"

As we stepped into *Emma Goldman*, Socrates leaped into the front seat with me. "Goodbye, everyone. I know we'll see each other very soon. I love you all." Those words "I love you" now seemed to roll easily from my tongue.

I heard a voice singing in the distance. Sojourner stood on the rocky outcropping high above Dignity, her arms stretched out towards the morning sky, and her voice soared throughout the valley. It was a song without words, a chant filled with love and healing. Her blessing touched my soul. I didn't have to say goodbye, or I love you, to Sojourner. She knew. She always knew.

We were riding down the steep road near Celo Valley. I had been writing notes furiously, afraid to lose these insights. I look back on this time and remember one thing that Erasmus always told me. "Even if you can't spell or write it correctly, it's important to get the idea down." Even though his penmanship was meticulous like calligraphy, he often reminded me how many of his first drafts looked like chicken scratch. "Sometimes even I can't figure out what I was trying to say." He always gave me the confidence to accept myself despite my faults, and always left the window open to see the possibilities ahead. I learned over the years this is called *unconditional love,* the rarest love of all.

We came down a steep mountain pass, and a red Camaro raced up behind us.

"Damn idiot!" said Erasmus. "They're going way too fast for this road, and from what I can see, it's probably a kid." Erasmus beeped as he extended his hand out to slow them down. Then there was a pickup truck flying down the mountain behind the red Camaro and gaining on the car.

Erasmus put on his blinkers and gently guided *Emma Goldman* to the side of the road. Though they didn't have much room, the vehicles zoomed past us. Erasmus was angry. I rarely saw him get angry, but he stopped and breathed to slow himself down. "I know what's going to happen, and it ain't pretty."

"No, 'Rasmus. I'm sure it'll work out," I said with cheery optimism, but I had no idea what I was talking about. I just didn't want to see him upset.

The rain started to pour down in sheets, and we parked by the side of the road and chatted about our time with Roshi and Sojourner until the rain abated.

"I know this sounds strange, but I don't have much to say about Sojourner and the circle of women. I'm still processing it."

"Was there anything wrong? I thought you said it was a fantastic experience?"

"It was incredible. Besides meeting you, it was the most important meeting in my life, but I need time to let it percolate in my bones. Isn't that how you say it? Time to percolate in my bones."

As the rain let up, the evening sun appeared. He said, "If we go about another fifteen miles, there's a nice camping spot down by the river on the other side of Celo Valley. Let's aim for there tonight. Then we'll start making the long haul to New Orleans, and I'm hoping we can be there in another week or so."

Erasmus was driving slowly down the mountain, and the Smoky Mountain sunset had dark thunderclouds on the horizon. We saw that the guardrail had been ripped down at the last hairpin turn. "Damn! I was afraid of this! They must have spun out of control. Let's get to work!"

We pulled the car over to the nearest flat section of the road. "Jake, put the blocks under the tires, and get out the emergency medical kit and the flashers. Also, I'll need some of the mountain rescue pack, the one with big rescue ropes and harnesses. You do that, and I'll see what's going on below. Put some of these flares about fifty feet up from where we are and light the fuses in the road."

Erasmus looked down the steep ravine towards where the red car was. The silver truck was implanted in a boulder further down the embankment. I was scared. He anchor the rope to the guard rail, clipped the other end to his harness around his waist, and grabbed the backpack with medical supplies.

"Jake, I'll be okay. Stay with *Emma* and Socrates. If a car comes by, flag them down, and tell them to get a rescue truck and an ambulance here as fast as possible. Don't be afraid."

He slowly let out the rope slide through a metal rescue eight as he descended down the ravine. I heard people crying in the red car, which was scrunched up like a paper ball. A girl was crying out, "Help! Help!"

"Hold on! I'm coming!" Erasmus quickly got to the side of the car. There were two girls inside.

He called out to the girls in the car, "My name is Erasmus, and I'm here to help you. I'm going to break the back window to get you out. Cover your eyes with your shirts." He swung a little bit closer with the rope still in one hand. He broke the glass with a small hammer, and the girls screamed. "I'm sorry. Don't move! I'll take you out one at a time." He reached inside the car. I wished there was something I could've done besides stand by and watch from above. I don't know how he did it, but he gently extracted one of the girls from the car and slung her over his shoulder.

She was sobbing. "Stop! I'm in so much pain."

He said, "I have to get you up to the road. It will only hurt for a little more." With the girl strapped to his back, he climbed up to where I was waiting. "Jake, she's in shock, and I don't know what's broken. Look for any bleeding. Elevate her feet, get her some blankets, and clean off the blood from around her face."

"What's your name?" I asked the girl.

"I'm Kate. My sister? How is she? Please get her!" She was sobbing hysterically.

Soon another car came by and stopped. I told the drive what had happened. "Go to the next town and get an ambulance."

"Sure, what else can we do?"

"Pray a rescue truck comes soon."

The man said to the woman with him, "Carmen, stay with this girl and help her and I'll go to Burnsville to get an ambulance. I'll be back as soon as I can."

Carmen said, "I'm an R.N., and I can take care of Kate. You help your friend." She was calm and tender, both with me and Kate. "Kate, we're going to get you to the hospital."

I gave Kate some aconite under the tongue for the shock. We wrapped her in blankets and gently lifted her inside the RV. "I know you're hurting, but as soon as Erasmus comes back with your sister, we can go to the hospital," I told her. "Who were the people chasing you?"

"Some rednecks. We had stopped for gas, and they were hassling us, calling us Mexicans, wetbacks, and immigrants, but we're Americans. Why are people crazy racists?"

Socrates stayed with Kate. I went back outside and turned on the big flashlight to see where Erasmus was.

"Erasmus, how are you?" I shouted out.

"I'm okay, but I'm having trouble getting Maria out of the car. Can you come down?"

"Sure. Hang on!" I had been running up and down the hillside of Black Mountain for years without ropes, but I tied a thick rope around my waist and rappelled down.

"Great work, Jake. This is going to be hard. I'm afraid this girl is in worse shape," he said quietly. "Give me a hand. I'm going into the car to put a sling around her."

He pulled away more glass. "Hold on, Maria. We're going to get you out of here." Erasmus's arms were cut from the glass, and though it was a cool night, he was sweating. "Come over here, Jake. Put on my gloves. If the two of us work together, we can pull her out gently. I think her legs are broken and maybe more."

"Erasmus, I can do this. I'm skinnier than you are," I said.

"You're right, but the car may slip at any time. Hold onto the rope, don't worry about me."

He reached into the car and pushed the front seat forward. The car started to slide a bit more down the slope. "Hold onto the rope, Jake!" The girl was sobbing. "Maria, we're almost there. This is going to hurt as we get you out. I'm afraid this is the roughest part, but the car is on the edge of rocks." Despite the glass and twisted metal, he reached around Maria and put a harness on her. "I know you're hurting, but I have to get you out."

"Please, I don't want to die! I don't want to die. What about my sister?"

"Your sister is up above and safe. Jake, wrap this rope around the tree next to you and make sure your footing is secure. We've got to get her out before this car slides any further."

I pulled on the rope to bring Maria out of the car. She was free, but unconscious. I took her in my arms and guided her in the harness up the hillside, but Erasmus was still in the car as it started to slide.

"Hold onto her, Jake! The car is starting to tip!" Everything happened quickly as he spoke these words, and the car slid down the hill.

"Erasmus!" I screamed. "Get out!"

The car rolled down the ravine. I looked to my right but didn't see him. I was trying to hold onto Maria, who had fallen unconscious. "Erasmus! Where the hell are you?" I shouted.

There was only silence as the car tumbled down and burst into flames.

A booming voice called out from above, "Jake, hold on! I'm coming down!"

It was Roshi Kanji! He rappelled quickly down the hill.

A voice further down the ravine called out, "Jim, get the girl and Jake! I'm okay." It was Erasmus.

I had cinched my rope around the tree and had Maria over my shoulder. She was safe. But I couldn't pull myself and the girl up.

"Roshi, get down here, now!"

Amid this insanity, with the car burning below and blue police lights flashing, I heard Erasmus holler, "Captain Jake, don't make me laugh. My ribs are killing me! Get the girl up to the top."

In a few moments, Roshi Kanji was next to me. "Jake, I'm going to ascend with the girl, and then I'll come back for you. Watch Erasmus. He looks pretty beat up."

"You take Maria. I can climb up on my own rope, and don't take all day about it."

"Yes, ma'am!" he said with a laugh.

It was a huge relief when he took Maria off my shoulders.

Roshi said, "Maria, I've got you now. Hold on!" The girl was draped over his shoulder like a rag doll as he slowly pulled himself up the side of the ravine. The guardrail was destroyed, but the post was holding as we inched the injured girl up the hill. When he reached the top, he said, "Easy with Maria. She's pretty beat up, but she'll be okay." As soon as he got the girl into the waiting arms of the police and firemen, he called out, "Erasmus! I'm coming down!" He rappelled down to about a hundred feet and, in no time, was standing next to Erasmus, holding onto his rope and perched on a rock.

"Saints alive! 'Rasmus, you look a mess!"

"Took you long enough to get here, Jim. Let's get out of here. How's Jake holding up, and the other girls?"

"Man, that Jake is tough! The girls are safe and on top. The cops are here."

"Jim, I'm afraid you have to help me. I think I broke some ribs and got more than a few cuts." The car below was in flames and rolled over again.

"Let's go, man! Like the old days. Come on, little brother!" Carefully as possible, he leaned him over his shoulders. "I've got you, man. We're going up."

With his massive arms bathed in the blue spotlights of the police car, he slowly lifted himself and Erasmus up the side of the ravine. I was too pumped with adrenaline to be afraid and cried with relief when Roshi lifted Erasmus into the waiting arms of the people on top. Kate and Maria were safe.

When we got to the top, the blue police lights were flashing. Several men from Dignity Village were there, and Sojourner was helping Kate.

I was confused. How did they get here? Where did all these angels come from?

Erasmus shakily stood up, covered in blood, his forearms cut. "Thanks, Jim. I think I owe you another one!"

I rushed over to Erasmus and wrapped my arms around him. "I was so damn worried. I thought we had lost you."

"Jake, easy on the hugs. I may have broken a rib. I'm glad you're safe."

Roshi said, "Strangely, when you left, I was feeling quite happy. I said to Sojourner, let's go into town to pick up a few things. When we drove down and saw *Emma Goldman*, we were scared about what we would find, and as always, you get yourself into some fine messes."

"Kate!" The two girls were on gurneys and crying.

"Maria!"

"Who brought them up?" asked a man who walked over. "I'm the EMT, Tom Daniels. Those are the luckiest girls. They might've tumbled over the cliff if you hadn't gotten them."

Erasmus said, "I think we're all lucky. Unfortunately, the people in the silver truck didn't make it." He saw the tow truck coming alongside the guardrail. "Jake, let's follow the ambulance to the hospital."

"Are you okay?" I looked at his arms and his shirt, which were covered in blood from the accident, and the scrapes and cuts on his face. He looked dazed and shocked.

"Jake, before we go. Wash the blood off of you."

"No, Ras, I'll wash the blood off of *you*. Sit down and drink some water."

Roshi said, "Erasmus, she's right. Your shift is over for today. I'll drive with Jake to the hospital. Louis and Sojourner will drive you in our car. You're in no shape to drive anywhere. Damn, Erasmus, I can't believe what you did! It was like someone with Green Beret training leaped down and got those kids. You always make me proud. Let's get you and the girls to the hospital."

"Thanks, but it was a joint effort with Jake. She was incredible. Don't you need to get back to Dignity?"

"This is the Dignity we need to be at now," said Sojourner. "I am grateful everyone is safe. You need stitches and lots of arnica, comfrey, and calendula. Man, you're a mess!" She leaned over and gave him some arnica pellets.

When we got to the hospital, Erasmus looked worn out and pale. They wheeled him into the emergency room, and I followed. I was scared when I realized how hurt he was, but he never complained and only asked about the girls and me.

"Miss, I'm Doctor Mohammad, and you can't go in," said the doctor who rushed over to see Erasmus.

"Like hell, I can't. I'm his granddaughter. Get him fixed up!"

Erasmus looked at EMT Daniels and Doctor Mohammad, and said, "I would never argue with her. It might be dangerous." He smiled and winked at me. "Get me sewn up, Doc. We've got places to go. What's the status of the girls?"

"We got them stabilized, but one girl has a ruptured spleen and her legs are broken. The other girl is already sewn up and in recovery."

Erasmus said, "Please, make sure their families are called, and my friends Sojourner and Roshi Kanji will take care of anything else they need."

"Thank you, Mr. Hobbs, but you need to be quiet now and let other people help you."

"Erasmus, quiet? Hardly," I said.

Erasmus needed forty-six stitches and had three broken ribs. When he left the ER in a wheelchair, Louis, Sojourner, and some other guys from Dignity were waiting.

"Remember, Erasmus," said Tom Daniels. "With your condition, you need to slow way down! And rest! Got me?"

Roshi came in and introduced himself. "Doc, hello I'm Roshi Kanji. My people can help you find the parents, and we'll stay with the girls as long as we need."

Sojourner smiled. "We have a home nearby, and Kate and Maria can stay with us until their parents come."

"In the meantime, let's all get some rest. I'm beat!" said Roshi. "There's a nice motel next door, and the owners are my friends, so we can stay for a few days. Do you hear me, Ras? You need to rest."

Erasmus looked up at him and smiled. "Aye aye, captain." This means 'I hear, understand, and obey.'

By the time we got into the Pine Lodge Motel, it was almost 3 a.m. Sojourner, Louis, and Roshi stayed in the room next door. I was exhausted, but I was more worried about Erasmus. He looked awful.

"Ras, I know you're a stubborn SOB, but anything you need tonight, bang on the wall and we'll be here? Got it?" said Sojourner.

"Yes, ma'am!" he said weakly with a laugh. "Don't worry Jake is with me."

Erasmus fell back on the king-sized bed and let out a huge sigh. "Do you mind if Socrates and I slept with you tonight?" I asked.

"Sure, kiddo! It will be nice to have company."

I slipped on my shorts and a t-shirt, and Socrates leaped into bed. "Ras, remember. No funny business!"

He said, "Don't make me laugh. It hurts too much."

With Socrates between us, I held his hand. I didn't want to let him go. I breathed a sigh of relief and fell into the deepest sleep.

In the morning, we were awakened by the booming voice of Roshi. "Good morning, my lovely sunflowers. Rise and shine!" He walked in with a tray of orange juice and a breakfast of French toast with whipped cream and berries.

Erasmus was slowly waking up. "I feel like I've been run over by a truck."

"It's almost noon, but we thought breakfast was still in order," said Sojourner.

"Coffee! Double strength. I think I have a body hangover," said Erasmus. "Every bone in my body hurts!"

Roshi and Sojourner gently propped him up. His arms were bandaged, he had cuts on his face and neck, and his face was bruised. The whites of his eyes were yellowed.

Erasmus said, "That was one hell of a reunion. I was hoping for something more pleasant. Man, I couldn't believe all the insanity yesterday. How are the girls?"

Roshi said, "Maria has two broken legs and some internal injuries, and her parents will be here later today. Kate's in better shape, but the shock of the accident will take time to heal. Sojourner is helping her, and Louis and our friends are sitting with the girls now."

Sojourner said, "I've been giving the girls some homeopathic remedies and herbs, and we told the parents that they could stay with us at Dignity. Maria will have to be in the hospital for at least this week and then she can rest with us. Damn, the universe must've been looking out for them. Erasmus, if you and Jake hadn't come when you did, the car would've rolled off the cliff with them inside. The universe moves in such mysterious ways."

"We were incredibly fortunate to come by, and Jake was astonishing. I didn't know she could move so fast. It was like watching a goat race down the hill." Then he looked at me. "Jake, you kept totally cool! You didn't panic and knew exactly what to do."

"I didn't have time to panic. It was all adrenaline."

Roshi said to Sojourner, "Did you hear how tough Jake was? She said to me before I took Maria topside, 'Take the girl, and don't take all day about it!'"

"Did I really say that? Damn, I can be a real bossy pants!"

Erasmus was holding his ribs with a pillow. "Stop! Stop, the laughter hurts."

I turned to Erasmus and said, "It's okay! Man up!"

Roshi exploded with a bellow of laughter. "I love Jake! She's scary and precious! Did you hear that? Man up! That's terrific. I'll have to use that."

Did we laugh so hard because of all the pain in the last twenty-four hours? The laughter seemed to absorb it and made it fly out the window.

It was peaceful that afternoon, after the tremendous rush and pain of the accident and all the chaos. We sat outside by the brook and played music. I was grateful we were safe, even though Kate and Maria were injured and Erasmus was absolutely beat.

Louis and I folded up the ropes and the harnesses and put away all the extra gear we took out of *Emma Goldman* last night, but Erasmus only had to sit and supervise. He was moving very slowly today. We made a fabulous dinner of stir-fried tofu and black beans and invited the emergency room staff and hotel owners to join us.

While we ate, Doctor Mohammed said, "When I came to the United States from Yemen, I was a malnourished orphan adopted by a Quaker family. They looked at me and said, 'Welcome, son.' They didn't care where I was from or whether I had a different religion. They found a mosque a half hour away, and the Imam became a family friend. This kind of unconditional love was the light that has always inspired me. It was natural for me to become a doctor. Eventually, I'll return to Yemen and set up a clinic there."

Sojourner said, "Yes, that is the paying forward of the higher love. Perhaps that's what joins us at this table, all of us have experienced trauma and turmoil in our lives, but we seem committed to helping others."

"Amen!" everyone said in unison as we raised our glasses of lemonade.

I turned to the hotel owners. "What about you, Elijah and John? What brought you here to this part of the Carolinas?"

Elijah said, "We had fallen in love with each other when we were young before we really understood what gay was. But we knew we loved each other, and when we tried to talk to our families about it, they disowned us. We left Arkansas and traveled to a place that would accept and welcome us. Our adopted kids Gene, Clara, and Michael are exactly like us, queer kids with no place to go, and any kid who is gay, transgender, or in between will always find a place with us. As soon as we moved here, we became close friends with Sojourner and Dignity Village. Between our motel and Dignity, we help a few people find their way. But we're just innkeepers. Ain't nothing fancy about us. We're two guys who love each other and their kids very much."

A couple of months ago, I had never met gay or transgender people. I'd never known people who lived their lives simply to help others. In my poverty, all I thought about was surviving from one day to the next and I didn't understand why you would help somebody if you weren't going to get something in return. The only fantasy I had was of getting out of

Black Mountain. I changed from seeing the world as black-and-white to a world of color and hope. The color of hope is infinite possibilities, something I could never have imagined.

The big pots of vegetables, rice, and tofu stir-fry quickly vanished. That was surely the best medicine. Erasmus sat on the side and played his classical guitar quietly, attentive and enjoying the big party.

Roshi said, "Sojourner and I are going to the hospital to bring some food to Maria."

Louis said, "I can clean up, but Erasmus—you are under orders to chill out!"

"Right!" said John. "Erasmus, you are to do nothing for the next forty-eight hours. Understood?"

I said, "Socrates and I will help you clean up as well."

"Wow! That's a lot of bossy people," Erasmus said with a laugh. "Let's sing a little before we break up the party." We sang some of our favorite songs, like "Freight Train," and everyone joined in.

I felt like I had taken a long cool shower of love. All the pain I had felt in life slipped away. Surrounding me was an army of angels.

By the next day, Erasmus looked perky. He was up at dawn and made tea for all of us. As I slowly got up and had my tea, I said, "Ras, I'm glad you're feeling much better. I was really scared for you the other day. When the car started to slip away and you were still inside it, I thought it was all over. But it was like watching a movie. You were holding onto the rope and suddenly flew out of the car like Superman."

"I couldn't have done it without you, Jake, and of course, all the other people who were there to help. We had an army of angels with us that night."

"I want to ask you about something you said to Doctor Mohammed at the hospital."

"About my condition?" Erasmus looked away from me. "Let's take a break and chat for a moment before breakfast. I could lie to you and tell you everything is fine, but it isn't."

"You said you wouldn't lie to me. That was one of the ground rules."

"I have to be upfront with you."

He looked at me with his blue-green eyes and even with the bit of yellowing, they were lovely. He put his hand on my shoulders and said, "Remember I have prostate cancer, and the Agent Orange stuff and hepatitis C. It isn't getting better. That was one of the reasons I came back to Dignity. Not only to reconnect with Roshi and my tribe there, but I also needed medical help from Sojourner."

"I am so goddamn mad. This ain't fair!"

"Easy, Jake. I'm not dying yet. There are options. We're going down to New Orleans so I can see some specialists. When I met you several months ago, I was traveling south and out to New Mexico to get help. I wasn't planning on meeting you, but you're the best medicine I could've ever asked for."

"So, what is this prostate cancer? Can we fix it? Can I give you one of mine? Or something like that?"

"I wish you could give me a spare, but it doesn't quite work like that. The herbs and the other medicines from Sojourner have helped me immensely. The main thing for you and me is to enjoy our time together now. I'm okay, but the car accident knocked the wind out of my sails. I'm sure I'll be ready to head down toward New Orleans in a few days."

He looked at me with his eyes filled with tears. "I love you, but like a grandpa loves his granddaughter."

I said, "Grandpa or not, I'll be with you for as long as you'll have me."

I believed he would get healthier with my love and care, and the cancer and hepatitis would simply go away.

During the week at the motel, he was getting stronger. Sojourner gave him herbs, Roshi Kanji gave him massages, Socrates gave lots of love, and I was making all his favorite dishes — tacos, tofu and veggies, grilled cheese sandwiches, veggie burgers, and hobo brownies. I was happy to see him stronger. Though he never complained about anything, the accident took a lot out of him. Whenever I asked how he was, he would say, "It's only a trifle."

One minute we were driving, ecstatic after Dignity Village and looking forward to New Orleans, when suddenly—the accident. It's strange how everything transformed after that. My relationship with him deepened, and it dawned on me what a profound moment this was and how fragile and impermanent life was. Living in the hollows of Black Mountain, life was fragile and crazy. It was chaos, never knowing if there would be something to eat or if we would be evicted, but I never saw this as abnormal—simply, it was life, and life was chaotic. However, with Erasmus, even living in the RV with him, Socrates, and our ever-changing adventures on the road, there was a certainty and a peace I'd never had before.

Erasmus and I had already done our yoga this morning and were drinking a cup of ginger tea by the riverside in the shade. Erasmus said, "Ah, this is the moment of grace. When we realize we are blessed, even when things are bad."

"Huh? Can you make that plain English for the less erudite like myself?"

Erasmus threw a pillow at me, and Socrates jumped on my lap. *Erudite* was one of Erasmus's favorite words and tossing it back to him was good.

"Grace! Kismet! Without getting fancy, it's a moment of chance and fate."

"Like something good?" I asked.

"No, neither good nor bad. It's duality. It's a mutable event. For example, the car accident was very bad in one way, but if we only look at it as bad, we miss the point and the learning. We spoke about this last week -- you can't stand in the same river twice."

I said, "As you had said last week, 'Heraclitus, no man ever steps in the same river twice because it's not the same river, and he's not the same man.'"

"Big bravo, Jake! Now apply that to grace and kismet."

"Bad things ain't always bad? Like when I first met you, I was lost, freezing cold, hungry, and I had nowhere to go."

"Yes, exactly. Sometimes things are awful, and I am not sugarcoating it. There's tragedy, death, and poverty, and you can't rationalize any of it. However, there is wisdom and peace in this moment of grace, even if we don't know nor ever understand. I was in Calcutta, India, many years ago at a train station. It was hot with swarms of people, more than you can imagine. It reeked of humanity. I didn't have a place to sleep, I was hungry and recovering from Dengue or some bug. However, I had a moment of grace and insight that it was all perfect in the middle of being lost."

"It sounds awful and frightening. I'm not sure what I would have done."

"Here is the beauty in that mess. I saw a family of four poor skinny people, on a small square piece of cardboard outside the train station enjoying dinner. They had only a bowl of rice and some vegetables for the mom, dad, and the two children. They were laughing and playing with each other. I was dumbfounded. How could people who were this poor have such happiness? The dad looked at me and pointed for me to join them.

"I folded my hand in gratitude and declined, but then he gave me a papaya from a cloth burlap bag. I took out my knife, peeled it, cut it up into five sections, and shared it with the family. It was the most delicious fruit I had ever eaten. Though I only had a little money, I tried to give it to him as I was about to leave. He smiled with his perfect white teeth and graciously declined with folded hands. I was profoundly touched by his humility. He gave me a mango as I was leaving to make it even more extraordinary. It was one of the most precious gifts I had ever received. This impoverished man and his family were my saints. I learned more about the philosophy of kindness at that moment than I had from any other saint I had met in India."

"Ras, that's amazing! I hope I'll go to India one day. It reminds me of the first day I met you, and you gave me dry clothes and fed me a bowl of hot oatmeal."

"Yes. We have all been touched by grace. That is why I always fold my hands in gratitude before eating. It reminds me of the train station in Calcutta and the many acts of kindness I've experienced along the way."

"But no God?"

"That's a deep question before breakfast. Perhaps there is or isn't a god, but I've found my church in the action of kindness we create every day. The prayer I seem to offer the most is gratitude!"

A voice boomed in front of *Emma Goldman*, and it was Roshi. "I'm grateful if you can join us for breakfast instead of all this yakking."

It was funny seeing Roshi inside *Emma Goldman* because he had to bend down, and though the RV had a lot of room, he was simply big.

"Jim, we're slowly getting up and about, but we wound up getting caught in a long conversation about India."

Roshi plopped down on the floor and stretched out. "Yeah, Ras and I were there after Vietnam, and we met in Khajuraho, the erotic temples. We were two lost souls wandering around the enormous mystery of India."

"Yes, I remember. Man, I can't believe all these decades have passed. How could I forget how you towered above the entire crowd in a market?"

The breakfast bell rang. Sojourner called out, "Let's eat!"

Erasmus said, "This is the thing about karma. I lost touch with Jim after India. I was shocked when I was in California, five years later."

Roshi said, "Ah, this lovely reminisce will be continued, but Jake, thank you again for what you did with those girls. You were astonishing. I didn't know you were this courageous mountain girl. Wow!"

"Actually, you and 'Rasmus did the hard work. I just made sure you didn't take all day about it!" I winked at him.

"Sassy!" said Roshi as he threw a pillow at me.

"'Rasmus says sassiness is the best part of my personality!"

Socrates, who was nestled in my lap, barked.

"He agrees!" said Erasmus. "Let's continue this over breakfast."

"Let's eat, all this philosophical philandering is getting me hungry!" said Roshi.

Sojourner and Louis had made my favorite almond pancakes and blueberries.

"Man," I said. "There is love in every bite!"

"I think Jake will be my new guru," said Roshi. "I need some of these *Jakeism*s in my life and dharma talks. What did you say when we were saying goodbye at Dignity? 'Stop all the love stuff. I'm feeling like warm oatmeal.'"

We all laughed at my *Jakeism*s.

"Roshi and Sojourner, don't you have to go back and take care of Dignity? We have this covered, and we can handle everything with Maria and Kate," I said with my usual naïve optimism.

Sojourner smiled and hugged me. "We need to be here this week. There has been a huge storm of craziness with the crash, and we need to help you, Erasmus, and the girls."

At sixteen, I was overflowing with my certainty of ignorance, but quickly, with the help and guidance of Roshi, Sojourner, and Erasmus, I was learning to keep my mouth shut and observe. Boy, did I have a lot to learn.

We spent the next few days taking care of Maria and Kate. Maria was slowly getting better with the herbs and homeopathy from Sojourner, and the bruises were fading. We found out that the boys in the other car were both drunk and not wearing seatbelts when they flew off the mountain. The coroner said, "At least they didn't suffer. They died immediately. Cars, alcohol, and teens do not mix."

"I would say cars, alcohol, and anyone do not mix," I said.

Erasmus looked at me, nodded his head, and smiled.

Kate and Maria's parents, Miguel and Rosie, came as soon as they heard, and the hotel owners graciously offered to put them up for free. Miguel declined the offer. "All of you have been incredibly gracious, but we can afford it, and we'll stay until Maria is strong enough to travel."

Maria was sitting in the dining room in her wheelchair and said, "I feel like I sailed off a cliff and landed in a cloud of angels. I'm grateful for all you did for us."

Roshi said, "You did sail off the cliff, but I am not sure of the cloud of angels."

Sojourner playful slapped him on his shoulder. "Hush up, Jim. She's trying to pay us a compliment."

"Sorry, Sojah. You're rough on me sometimes."

"Not as rough as I need to be." She tickled him.

I loved seeing Sojourner and Roshi playing with each other like two kids.

The real collision came when the other parents came to the hotel. Jack and Augusta McCoy drove up in a beat-up red Chevy truck, the fender tied on with a rope, and the windshield cracked. Jack was a gaunt man about fifty years old, his face weathered, and he had a limp when he walked. His wife Augusta was a heavy-set woman with bleached blond hair and wore purple spandex pants and a halter top. Jack knocked on the door of the hotel office, at first timid, and then pounded on it. "Where the hell are you?"

Roshi and Sojourner came out of the office. Roshi stuck out his hand and said, "My name is Roshi Kanji, and this is my friend Sojourner. Can we help you?"

Augusta said tearfully, "We got a phone call that our boys Mathew and John were killed. We came as soon as we could borrow a truck."

Roshi said, "We know about what happened. We were there at the accident. We're here to help you as best we can. We're so sorry."

Jack McCoy burst out in anger. "Sorry? I'm beyond sorry. We lost our boys and our only car was destroyed. I lost two days of work, and I'll be fired if we don't get back. I don't know what the hell to do. This is the worst day of my life, a life that's had too many bad days." His face was flushed from drinking. He was like a deer caught in the headlights—dazed.

Roshi said to Jack, "I know you're in a lot of pain. I lost my brother in a car accident a long time ago. Let me get you some water, and let's sit by the river and talk."

Over a foot taller, Roshi gently put his arm around Jack and led him to two chairs by the riverside under the shade. I saw them talking and heard Jack sobbing. Jack cried and raged, and Jim was totally at peace.

Sojourner was with Augusta. "Come with me, Augusta. I'm sorry to hear about your sons. Tell me about them."

Sojourner spoke to Augusta for more than an hour. Augusta also cried and screamed. Sojourner held her and listened.

I watched as Roshi and Sojourner listened to these two parents as if they were the most important people in the world.

Erasmus was talking to Miguel, who was a mechanical engineer. Miguel said, "I deal with all this pain and loss by working. I'm happiest when I'm fixing a machine and have grease under my fingernails. I need something to take my mind off this craziness. Erasmus, this Airstream is a dream to work on, and since we have to be here until the girls are ready to come home, this is perfect. The engine has about 250,000 miles, so we'll have to change timing belts, filters, tire rotations, tune-up, and flush the entire engine. How's that sound?"

Erasmus said, "I'll definitely need your help. If Jake is free, she's a terrific helper too!"

Rosie said, "Keep Miguel busy! If he's not fixing something, he gets stir-crazy. I'll stay with the girls, and Sojourner is teaching me how to gather and make herbs. Before this, I thought chamomile only came in a little tea bag."

"Me too," I said. "Until I met Erasmus and Sojourner, I didn't realize all these weeds were medicines. I lived in West Virginia, and we made teas when we were sick, but I never realized there was a whole pharmacy in nature."

Next to the motel was a large field of chamomile, lavender, and St. John's Wort on the periphery. All these healing herbs were perfect for what ailed the soul. By harvesting the herbs, I felt better and happier. Rosie and I spent the afternoon harvesting while Sojourner was helping Maria.

Jack continued to talk to Roshi. "We were the white cracker kids who grew up picking tobacco or cotton or doing any kind of work. We thought there was hope with our boys. We thought our family's luck would turn around. Now, this. We're back to where we were before, but now, we're more broke and don't even have a decent truck to get us home."

Before supper that evening, Miguel and Rosie agreed to talk to Jack and Augusta, with Sojourner, Roshi, Erasmus, and me. It was tense and I was afraid. Roshi said, "I know there is a lot of pain and hurt now, but can we take a few minutes to close our eyes, pray, and breathe?"

Miguel and Rosie were too furious. "Jack and Augusta, how could you have let your sons do this? Look at our daughters!" Maria was in a wheelchair in a corner, and Kate's arm was in a sling and bandaged up.

Jack and Augusta looked sheepishly down. Sojourner and Roshi sat next to them.

Augusta was crying, and she said, "Everyone, we're sorry. We didn't know our boys stole the pickup truck. We still owe ten thousand dollars on it. We're totally screwed. We lost our two boys, I'm unemployed, and Jack barely makes enough money. We can't even find the words to tell you how sorry we are."

Jack lit a cigarette and took a sip of Wild Turkey with his shaking hands. "Sorry ain't a big enough word," he drawled. "We're grateful the girls are alive. I wish we could pay you back for all this damage and hurt." He turned to Kate and Maria. "We're sorry our boys did such a terrible thing to you."

Maria said, "The boys were really angry. They kept harassing us at the store and we had to leave. I'll never forget how awful this was, and then watching their truck roll off the cliff."

Miguel and Rosie sat next to Kate and Maria, and Rosie said, "I am grateful Maria and Kate are safe, but this did not have to happen."

Miguel spoke to Augusta and Jack. "I'm still angry for this craziness and pain that John and Mathew caused, but I'm sorry you lost your boys."

Rosie said, "We need to be alone with our family. We can talk tomorrow, and I'm grateful but profoundly sad. We accept your apology, but it's really going to be a long while before we can forgive this."

Jack unsteadily got up on his feet and walked over to extend his hand to Miguel. "Again, I'm sorry for the hurt our boys caused you and Katie and Maria."

Miguel said, "Thank you, Jack and Augusta. We'll talk to you tomorrow."

Erasmus and I slept in *Emma Goldman* that night, and he said, "Man, I liked the motel, and I'm grateful for the hospitality, but I love being back home. What a day this was with the families. I'm happy Roshi and Sojourner were there."

"That was painful today. I felt badly for Augusta and Jack, and of course, Miguel and Rosie, and the girls. It's the same kind of crazy stuff in Black Mountain, parents not around, people not taking responsibility. Yet, you, Roshi, and Sojourner made it all go away."

"No, we didn't make it go away. Seeing the boys' parents take responsibility was a first step, but their lives are shattered. None of this is over, but it's the beginning of forgiveness. There is so much pain there, and we're just beginning to find some reconciliation."

"Ras, I haven't figured this out. How do we find forgiveness? And maybe I can forgive my mother for her craziness?"

"Jake, I've spent a good part of my life on this question of forgiveness. I wasn't a good father, nor was I much of a husband. I was too consumed in my pain from the war, my excuses, and my self-righteousness. I am still learning what forgiveness is about."

Then he was silent for a long time before saying, "I didn't mean to lay this onto you, but in many ways, this is the best part of my life."

"How do you mean?"

"I've learned to forgive myself, make amends with my son and my ex-wife, and the people I've harmed."

"Erasmus, don't be this hard on yourself. What did you teach me? Every saint has a past and every sinner a future?"

"Maybe you'll be my new Roshi. I think Roshi Jim has some serious competition."

"The only value I'm afraid I have is my beginner's mind, as Roshi calls it. In other words, I don't know squat," I said.

"See what I mean? That is more profound than some of the best teachers I've heard. I love how you're open, Jake. I wish I had met you years ago."

We had supper that evening. Sojourner, Roshi, Augusta, and Rosie made a huge salad, eggplant zucchini lasagna, and garlic bread.

When we sat down, Sojourner said, "Roshi, can you say a blessing?"

"Jake, please say grace," said Roshi.

"Okay. Let's all say it together and hold hands. *Yum! Yum! Yum! Tummy love! Amen!*"

The trays of lasagna quickly disappeared, and despite the insanity of the last few days, everything seemed to lighten a little.

Roshi spoke to Jack and Augusta while we were cleaning up. "If you like, we can have a funeral service for Mathew and John at the little church nearby. We'll take care of the expense. Is that okay?"

"Mr. Roshi, I don't know what to say. Despite all the hurt that John and Mathew caused, you, Sojourner, Jake, and Erasmus have been incredible. Augusta and I are grateful to everyone. And of course,

Miguel and Rosie. Thank you all." Jack reached over and shook hands with Roshi. "Thank you."

"Jack, I know you've been struggling with work. We have a small farm at Dignity and could use an experienced farmer, and Augusta could work with Sojourner. But the only condition is no alcohol. We are a sober community. How does that sound?"

"This would be a huge step, and, yes, if you can help me stop drinking, that would be a blessing. But can I keep smoking?"

"The smoking we can handle," said Sojourner. "I'll make funeral arrangements for Mathew and John at the little church down the road. I'm afraid your truck might not make it back home, so take mine. It's got a lot of miles, but it's in better shape than yours. We'll take yours back to Dignity. How does that sound?"

Augusta and Jack looked at Sojourner and Roshi. "Thank you. We never met people who were this kind. We don't know what to say."

"We know how hard this is, and if we can help you, we're happy to do that."

The small service at the West River Church the next day reinforced how fragile life was. Jack and Augusta sat in the front row. Sojourner, Roshi, Erasmus, and I were behind them. Erasmus played "Hallelujah" on his classical guitar. The door to the chapel opened as Rosie and Miguel came in with their daughters, Maria in the wheelchair and Katie pushing her. They wheeled up to the first row, and Miguel sat next to Jack, and Rosie sat next to Augusta and held her hand. After the caskets were placed in the graves, we sat under the immense oak tree and had iced tea and lemonade.

"Roshi and Sojourner, if you'll give us a try we would like to take that job on your farm. I ain't perfect, but I'll try," said Jack.

Roshi said, "Welcome. Dignity is about second chances."

Miguel and Jack embraced as they left. Miguel said, "Good luck to you both. I know there is a long road ahead of you and we'll keep you in our prayers."

We helped John and Elijah clean up with their family, and the following morning after breakfast, it was time to head to New Orleans again. I said, "Roshi, don't get all soggy saying goodbye to us again. I didn't bring my tissues."

Roshi said, "I love you, Jake. You're precious! I know we'll see each other soon."

Sojourner said, "Remember the new herbs I gave you for Erasmus. Make sure he takes his medicine and goes slower."

"I don't think he'll ever slow down. I love you, Sojah. I have a feeling we'll see each other soon," I said as I hugged her.

"Remember, Jake, any time you want to come back to Dignity, we always have a home for you," said Sojourner as she held me in her arms.

I said, "Okay! Stop it, guys. You're making me feel like warm oatmeal."

They laughed. Socrates barked and leaped up into my arms. It was time to go, and everyone from the hospital, Elijah and John and their kids, and, best of all, Kate and Maria walked out to say goodbye.

"Thank you, Jake and Erasmus, and Socrates," said Jack. "We're going to stay with Sojourner and then go home. We are so grateful for all your love and care. Thank you."

"Good luck to you both with Sojourner and Dignity Village."

It was time to start our journey south again to New Orleans. As we looked in the rearview mirror, everyone was still waving.

What a marvelous way to start a day.

CHAPTER FIVE

The Hard Lessons of Patience, Forgiveness, and Not Smacking the People Who Annoy You

With all the pain and tragedy over the past few weeks, our emotions were worn thin and we needed to recover. We were exhausted! Even Mister Gregarious himself, Erasmus, was tired of people, and so was I. With all these experiences, I was like a hummingbird darting quickly between the bright, succulent flowers of life and drinking it all in as fast as possible.

We left the tragedy of the car accident and were shell-shocked as we drove south. My life was always scary, with my mother's crazy boyfriends, not enough food, her addictions, and always living on the edge of eviction. But I said to Erasmus, "I never really understood the true fragility of life until we were getting the girls out of the car."

"Yes, it's like the poem from William Blake, 'to see a world in a grain of sand and a heaven in a wildflower. Hold infinity in the palm of your hand.' When we were hanging on the rope over the cliff getting Maria and Kate out of the car, I was reminded how fragile life is too."

"When I saw you climb into the car and get the girls, I never thought I'd see you again."

"Jake, you were amazing, and focused and leaped down the hill like you'd been doing that all your life. Remember the book we've been reading, *Zen Flesh, Zen Bones*? I love the story of the guy trying to escape the tiger."

"Yeah, and then he sees the cliff below, realizes he has no choice, and leaps. Then on the way down, he grabs a vine."

"And remember? What's next?"

"A damn mouse is nibbling the vine! He looks below, and there's the biggest bear. He sees a strawberry growing next to him and eats it."

Erasmus laughed. "So, what do you think it means?"

"Boy, Erasmus Plato Hobbs! You're slow today!"

"Smarty pants. So, what does it mean?"

"Carpe diem!" I said and then added after a pause, "Don't eat day-old fish."

"I get it, Jake!" It woke Socrates up, and he barked. "Maybe Socrates was an Epicurean?"

"Okay, now who's the smarty pants? I give up. What's this epicution thing?"

"Epicurean. Epicurus believed that when the world was falling apart, you needed to taste that strawberry and savor the moment. Jake, read me the story of the mice, the bear, and the lion again."

I got my reading glasses and opened *Zen Flesh, Zen Bones*. In the margins were notes in his neat handwriting. I still read slowly, but Erasmus was patient. When I would mess up a word, he would smile and help me.

"'Rasmus, where did you learn all this stuff? Did you go to a lot of schools?"

"My mother, who studied philosophy in college, read philosophy and poetry to us as kids. We lived on a small farm in northern Vermont, the winter nights were long, and she would read to us by the wood stove. The land was rocky and hard to farm and we called it Hardscrabble Farm.

My dad was a farmer who only finished ninth grade because he had to help support his parents. He was smart in his own way and could fix any machine and made more money fixing things than milking cows. My brother Henry David didn't care for school or books. He said, 'I'm a Vermont cow-shit farmer, and there ain't anything better.' But I took to books like a frog to a pond. No matter how hard my life got, I always had books as my refuge. I liked poetry, and one year I took a trip to New York City and met Moondog, a blind poet dressed like a Viking who sang his poetry in Washington Square Park. Who needs boring poetry classes when you have a poet like that?"

Poetry, stories, and philosophy were part of our life as we drove across America in our enchanted chariot *Emma Goldman*. I would read a stanza or a few lines of poetry, and then he would recite the next section from memory.

He said, "I like how you read the poems. Poetry inspires the mind, slows the tongue, and quickens the imagination. We read too fast!"

"Except me."

"Every day your reading is getting better. Soon you'll be ready to take your GED."

"Thanks, Ras. With my new glasses, everything is coming into focus. No pun. Last week when you showed me how to build the wooden steps, I couldn't believe geometry was that simple and I only needed someone to show me. Why do they make learning so hard in school?"

"You're right, Jake. For me and you, the Hobo College is our finest teacher."

We drove past Asheville and Erasmus said, "I need less stimulation. Lake Junaluska is not too far, named in honor of the Cherokee chief who saved General Andrew Jackson. Then Jackson betrayed the Cherokees. Cherokees who had lived here for hundreds of years were forced to move to Oklahoma, and all their lands were given to white settlers. Junaluska's wife and family died on the Trail of Tears. The Trail of Tears of 1834 is one of the most shameful parts of American history."

"Erasmus, why don't they teach this important stuff in school? I remember the stories about George Washington and Thomas Jefferson, but not that they were slaveholders, or that Jefferson had six children with a slave woman Sally Hemming. Why don't they teach us about this Chief Junaluska or Emma Goldman? Or how to change the oil on an Airstream or any other useful stuff?"

"Most of what they teach in school is to give you the illusion that you know what's happening. Suppose they taught the real history, the genocide of Native Americans, the deportation of Mexican American citizens, all the lies that start wars, and all the lies of the American dream myth? In that case, people might get up off the couch and start a revolution, but most folks are too lazy, and all they want is their McDonald's, TV, football games, and they're happy."

"Damn, that's harsh. McDonald's was a special treat for my mom and me at Christmas! Growing up in Black Mountain, it wasn't that we didn't have a future. I just didn't see hope. We lived at the bottom of a coal ravine, and hope seemed as far away as a trip to the moon."

When I first met Erasmus, I quickly realized how poor we were in Black Mountain, but as we traveled I learned that some people had it even worse. Traveling throughout America, I saw all the homeless in parks and broken cities and told him I couldn't understand why we let that happen.

"Jake, you're right. This is insane. How can we allow people to sleep on the streets, old people looking for food in dumpsters, and somebody as smart as you without the chance of a decent education? Let's walk along the lake. I need a little quiet after all the excitement."

We slipped into the parking lot by Lake Junaluska. Socrates leaped out, but Erasmus got out slowly. The accident had taken a lot out of him, though he wouldn't admit it.

"Take some of the veggie loaf and salad for a picnic. I need to forget about the cares of the world for a moment. How about you, Jake?"

"Absolutely! I need to dance in the sun!" I danced about with Socrates leaping next to me.

We walked for a half mile. The day was serene, and the breeze rolled across the lake to make diamond-like ripples. All the cares and worries of these past few weeks faded. We came to the picnic area and sat down. Then I heard a commotion and arguing.

A big man was screaming at a woman. "Emily, you're worthless. I don't know why I ever married you. Worthless!"

She said, "Please, Jason. I didn't do anything wrong. I didn't make you lose your job, and you can find another."

He turned and smacked her across the face, and she fell to the ground.

"Damn crazy stuff!" said Erasmus. "Let's help her."

The guy was about to kick the woman. "Get up, you lying faker. I didn't hit you hard. If you don't get up, I am giving you something to complain about!"

"Stop it!" Erasmus jumped in front of the man, bent down, and huddled over the woman, who was sobbing. "We're here to help you. I'll get you someplace safe."

"Get away from her, you old bum. She's my wife and I'll do what I want with her."

Socrates was growling and barking at the guy. "Get away, mutt." He tried to kick him.

Erasmus stood up and said to the guy, "Stop this craziness! Can't you see what you've done to her?"

The big hulking guy lunged towards Erasmus with his fists balled up. I didn't think. I leaped up and punched him in the nose. I heard it crack. He bent over, and his nose was bleeding. He was like a raging bull and stormed after me, but he was in too much pain and didn't know where he was going. "I'm going to get you, little bitch!"

I was ready to smack the big bully again, but Erasmus shouted, "No, Jake! Leave him alone! The police will be here in a minute. Let's help this woman. Hold her and let me help this guy."

"Goddamn! I'm going to get her!" the man shouted.

"No, you're not! Let's stop your bleeding, and we'll get your wife to the hospital. Sit down. Let me get you some water." Erasmus took his bandana and water from his canteen and sat the man on the bench.

I wanted to smack the guy with the biggest club, but Erasmus was patient and talked him down. The bleeding bully was crying. I was too damn mad. The last thing I wanted to do was talk to him.

After Erasmus calmed him down, the man said, "I'm sorry. I don't know what came over me. I lost my job this morning, and I was so goddamn mad. I didn't mean to take it out on my wife."

The police arrived and Erasmus said, "We'll go with his wife to the local hospital. Please help him, his nose is broken."

It dawned on me what I'd done. Me, Jake Meadows, one hundred and thirty-five pounds, punched a grown man and broke his nose. I was shaking. Adrenaline was pouring through me. What was I thinking? I never hit anyone. We'd only wanted some quiet time, and then suddenly we were in a hornet's nest.

Emily, the woman who had been beaten, woke up. The left side of her face was already turning black and blue. "What happened? Where's Jason?"

Erasmus held her and said, "The police have taken him away. We need to get you to the hospital now." He gave her our phone so she could call her family.

As we drove to the hospital, she said, "This is it. I've been hit and beaten too many times. I'm done with it. I'm done with all this pain." She sobbed, and I held her as we drove to the hospital. When we got there, her sisters were waiting.

"Emily! Are you okay?" they asked as they held her.

Emily turned to us and said, "Mister, thank you and your granddaughter for helping. I'm not sure I would be here if it wasn't for you."

"We were glad to help."

We went back to the picnic area by the lake.

"Jake, now I understand that I shouldn't piss you off," said Erasmus with a smile. "Man, you pack a mean punch. It's not that Jason didn't deserve a little love tap, but that was a love slug. Damn!"

"I'm not sorry I smacked the dumb SOB, but the beast leaped out of me. I wasn't thinking. I only reacted. I thought of my mother's boyfriends and how mean they were, and I didn't think about it." I started to cry when I realized how angry I had been.

Erasmus held me and said, "Jake, I also wanted to punch him out, even though I don't punch people."

The throbbing of my hand reminded me of what I had done. Erasmus gave me an ice compress. I said, "I know it was wrong, but he was a mean son of a bitch and…"

"No, you still didn't have the right to hurt him. No matter what he did. I could have talked him down." He looked at me, not in anger, but with compassion and care.

He was right. Erasmus could talk a vulture off a funeral cart and he could calm anyone down, even me. "Damn, Erasmus, I hate it when you're right. I'm sorry. I made a mistake. You always remind me of compassion for all beings. To be honest, I know it in my head, but I can't have compassion for the bastard. I'm sorry."

"Jake, don't beat yourself up. I'm still trying to figure out compassion as well. I was also damn mad at this guy. But I was that guy at one time. It's taken me years to learn to hold back and not hurt people. Though I never hit a woman, I was selfish and cruel. Which do we choose in life? Coming from our pain and anger, we try to rise above. Like when Louis at Dignity was having a breakdown, do you remember how everybody dealt with him with love and compassion?"

These words sunk into me as we drove to Chattahoochee with an ice bag on my hand. People never hurt their hands punching in the movies, but mine was sore and swollen. Though I agreed with what Erasmus said, part of me was grateful to have slugged Jason. We were quiet, Socrates sat on my lap, and he and I fell asleep. Erasmus put on some classical guitar music, and before too long, we were at Chattahoochee Park.

"Jake, you'll like this place. It has spectacular petroglyphs. They're stone carvings from hundreds of years ago, and a part of the forest has remained untouched. It's the oldest virgin forest. I hope we meet my friend, Sequoyah, a full-blooded Cherokee Chief who lives in this forest with his family."

"I thought all the Cherokee had been wiped out or moved to Oklahoma with the Trail of Tears? How did they survive all those years when Native Americans were being hunted and killed?"

"Like the Seminoles in Florida and many First Nations people, they blended into places so remote no one could find them. But you're right.

Over four thousand people died in the forced march to Oklahoma. Still, the remaining Cherokee fled to these mountains, like Sequoyah's family. If we meet him, he'll tell you more about this shameful history. His family has been caretaking these woods for generations, and some have been able to reclaim their land. Others like Sojourner learned the wisdom and herbal traditions."

We drove up an old dirt logging road. Erasmus downshifted, and we easily climbed it, twisting around the mountains. Everything was quieter, and the oak trees, birch, and ash were huge. The road narrowed. I wasn't even sure if *Emma* would fit, but we made it and found a clearing in the woods with a view to the north. It was breathtaking and quiet. Erasmus knew all these secret sanctuaries, far from other RVs and people.

"Let's take a few days here. I need some quiet time. Years ago, I was lucky to meet and spend time with Sequoyah and his family in this forest. I'm going up to the mountains tomorrow. Can I leave you with Socrates?"

"Sure, but are we okay?"

"We're fabulous. I'm proud of you and how well you did with Sojourner and at Dignity. Both Roshi Jim and Sojourner said, 'Any time she wants to come back, she's always welcome.' Let's go for a walk. I have a wonderful surprise for you."

We walked up the trails through the thick forests of oaks and maples to the petroglyphs. "These petroglyphs tell the story of the many people who have been here, Cree, Cherokee, and tribes we don't even know. Look at how extraordinary they are."

I walked around these carvings on the rocks, with all their swirls and patterns.

"What do they mean?" I asked.

"I'm not sure exactly, nor does anyone else, but with a bit of imagination, we can guess."

I started to draw the figures in my book. There were things that looked like birds soaring, writing, and carvings of animals, circles, and spires that swooped upwards. "Kind of like an abstract painting, it makes sense and then doesn't? I love them, even though I don't understand them."

"Yes, like the sky. We don't need to understand the chemistry of the sky to appreciate how awe-inspiring it is."

We had a picnic underneath the rock ledge and ate a scrumptious dinner of rice, beans, and tortillas. I could imagine people hundreds of years ago eating in this sacred space. We didn't say much. I was chattered out. I had been talking, listening, and learning so much lately. I lay down underneath the sheltering ledge as a light rain began to fall. I imagined all the people who had been here for thousands of years.

The rain tapered off at twilight, and we returned to *Emma Goldman*. I'd started to think of *Emma* as a comforting mother who held me close with her smell of sandalwood, colorful quilts, and handcrafted wood. Erasmus played his classical guitar and I read a book, *A People's History of the United States*. Afterward, I nestled in the back with Socrates, and Erasmus folded out the bed in the front. "Goodnight Jake. Sueños con angelitos."

"Goodnight, my sweet Erasmus." Funny, even to this day, twenty years since I last saw him, when I close my eyes I still say, "Goodnight, my sweet Erasmus."

At dawn, he was up and playing his guitar. I soon discovered a world of serenity I had never imagined. Erasmus made a yummy breakfast of oatmeal and fruit, and he said, "I'm going up to the mountains and I'll be back by tomorrow. I'll leave Socrates with you. Okay, Socrates?" Socrates looked at Erasmus, leaped up, and gave him a big doggy lick. "I'll be back tomorrow, so take good care of Jake."

He packed a canteen, guitar, a small day pack, and a walking stick. "This area is safe and remote, and Socrates will protect you."

We hugged goodbye, but I didn't feel abandoned.

"Don't let the door hit you on the way out!" I called as he turned to leave.

"Wise guy!" And with that, he disappeared up the mountain trail.

I felt lazy as the sunlight poured through the window and I fell back asleep with Socrates. When I woke, I finally dragged myself outside and did my morning yoga. Even Socrates followed along, and when I did the downward dog, he was right there with me. I felt stronger and healthier than I'd ever been. I still ate voraciously, but now I ate mostly vegetables, nuts, and fruit. Though Erasmus said he didn't mind if I ate meat, I had lost my taste for it.

The woods were filled with Kentucky and prairie warblers, and the red-headed woodpeckers were tapping the oaks. I missed Erasmus's laughter and guitar playing, but I was happy. I read and studied for two hours to get ready to take my GED. Once I hated reading, mainly because I couldn't see, but now, I'd discovered reading was fun. When I didn't understand something, Erasmus would patiently sit with me and help me figure it out. The difference with a great teacher is that you never feel dumb. An extraordinary teacher reminds you that the glass is always half-full. Finding out I needed glasses and someone patiently teaching me how to read and do math transformed my world with confidence.

I started cleaning the RV, and before I knew it, several hours had passed. Though we always thoroughly cleaned *Emma Goldman*, I wanted to do an extra special cleaning today. I started in the back underneath the bunks, the back closets, and the tool closet. Though Erasmus was a simple man in many ways, he had a ton of stuff stored in nooks and crannies. How many people drive around with a chainsaw and enough tools to build a house? After cleaning the inside, there was a stream nearby, and I gave *Emma* a good bath and washed the solar panels on the top. She glowed with her bright metallic yellow shine.

After all the adventures, traveling, and excitement, thoroughly cleaning *Emma* was a joy. Even Socrates helped by fetching tools, sponges, and rags. After lunch, I napped by the stream and listened to all the cardinals, wrens, starlings, the flicker of the yellow finches, and orioles, and I came to know all the sounds of the woods. Once I awoke, I drew a picture of Erasmus playing the guitar with one of his charcoal pencils. I wish I had been more productive the rest of the day, but I chilled out, read, and was sublimely happy with Socrates.

I went to bed early and at dawn, I heard the whistle of a warbler and knew it was him. I had slept for eleven hours! He came back sounding chipper with a big basket of blueberries. "Good morning, Jake. It's almost 7 a.m. You looked like you had a great snooze! And no wonder you're tired. You cleaned the inside and outside of *Emma*. Man, even the shine on the window is polished. Thank you for doing the extra love, the TLC!"

One of the many things I learned from Erasmus was the gift of appreciation. This made him extraordinary, how he appreciated and valued people.

"Yeah, I got a little carried away cleaning. I'm glad you like it."

"So much so. I'll make you blueberry pancakes. Freshen up!"

"I missed you, but not really. Wait, that sounds snooty. I did miss you."

"I missed you too, my fresh girl! We also have guests this morning. Sequoyah and his granddaughters are coming by. Wait, I see them by the edge of the woods."

The two girls with Sequoyah were about sixteen and eighteen.

"Hi, I'm Adsila, and this is my sister Ahyoka. You must be Jake. We live in the mountains just beyond the petroglyphs with my grandparents, Sequoyah and Elisi. We met Erasmus on the mountaintop the other day near the sacred caves, and we were surprised at how much he knew about the forests."

Sequoyah was as tall as Erasmus, and his long grey hair was neatly braided. With a big wide smile, he said, "Osiyou. Welcome to this forest, our home."

Sequoyah and his granddaughters brought more berries to the table. They looked like Sojourner, with light coppery colored complexions and high cheekbones. Over breakfast, Sequoyah and his granddaughters told us how this forest was created by the god Ye Ho Waah.

Adsila told the story in Cherokee with Ahyoka and Sequoyah, then translated it into English.

"The god was Ye Ho Waah and the whole world was covered in water, and from the waters, an island arose. Over time, he created trees and plants, but the thing that was the most special was the creation of the land. A water beetle helped create more land, and with more lands, the earth was gradually covered with forests."

We spent that day and the next with them and learned more creation stories. The girls showed us their fields, the herbs, and the trail leading to their home deep in the forest. Adsila, the older girl, said, "Though

I am happiest here in these woods, I have to finish my schooling, and then I'll study medicine."

"How old are you?"

"I'm twenty-one and I'll start medical school at Duke University in one month. My sister is at Emory studying law. We want to help rebuild our nation, and part of what we need to reclaim is our forest. Loggers, farmers, and trappers have done a great deal of damage for too many years. My great-great-grandfather was Sequoyah, like my father. He gave the Cherokee people their alphabet and fought for our rights."

Ahyoka said, "We Cherokee, Cree, and other Native Americans have been here for centuries. We had our land stolen, and our dream is to work with others to reclaim it."

I was astonished by the boldness and courage of these girls. They knew their destiny. I wished I knew mine.

After breakfast, Sequoyah and his granddaughters took us up the trail to their home. The path disappeared, and soon we walked into the oldest part of the forest, with massive oaks, maples, and dense firs.

Sequoyah said, "These forests are our heritage and hold the spirit of our ancestors. They were the lifeblood of our nation before they were cut down by loggers. Native Americans have always been stewards of the land, but the greed of the White people has done a great deal of harm. But despite the logging, we managed to save as much as possible," he said while resting his hand on a massive oak. "These trees all have spirit and hold the history and the songs of our people. Adsila and Ahyoka will continue the fight and carry on our legacy. "

Erasmus nodded. "Thank you, Sequoyah, Adsila, and Ahyoka. I'm grateful for what you've done and what you will do."

We spent the afternoon gathering elderflowers, echinacea, turkey tail mushrooms, and rishi. They pointed out the sounds of the birds and could tell each one by their call. They noticed things that I never would have on my own, like the difference between the songs of the bright yellow hooded warbler, the scarlet tanager, and the chestnut-sided warbler.

Erasmus said, "That is incredible. Every time I come back here, Sequoyah teaches me about more birds and their songs. I often feel like I know so little."

Sequoyah began to whistle different kinds of bird songs, and his granddaughters joined in. It was a symphony, and I joined with the rap tap of the woodpecker.

I saw and heard this forest in a way I never had imagined – it was alive with thousands of birds, frogs, and flowers galore.

We stopped by the waterfall to drink in a grotto with the petroglyphs. I asked Sequoyah, "Can I ask you, how do you see the difference between the Cherokee and non-Cherokee? Is there a difference?"

Sequoyah said, "Our legends tell us that we are all one people, all streams from the one main River of Life. To be a Cherokee is to be aware of the world and to see it as alive. In our four hundred years since European colonialism, we've survived the destruction and loss of our land, and our people are strong and proud of our heritage."

"Doesn't it make you angry about what happened to the Cherokee and the other Native Americans?"

Sequoyah said quietly, "Not angry, but resolved to restore our land, our rights, and to pass on our culture to the next generation."

Adsila said, "Grandfather taught us the wisdom of the forests and these lands, but our father turned away from the tribe and refuses to speak Cherokee. Too many of our people have forgotten our language and our songs are only heard by the wind. In my generation, we'll not only reclaim our memories, but we'll reclaim our culture."

Ahyoka spoke first in English so I could understand and then in Cherokee. "Yes, we are the people of the land, we are the children of the forests, the bear and eagle are our kin, these rivers run through our veins, and the sky and heavens are our dreams. We will endure as long as we remember who we are and the dreams inside our souls."

Sequoyah said, "Thank you, Adsila and Ahyoka. You will bring the legacy of our people forward and make our people proud."

"I wish I had that sense of place and people. I don't have a history. I'm a mutt, Irish, Scot, and whatever. I don't have songs or history.

Until I met Erasmus, Sojourner, and you, I didn't know the names of the plants. I only knew I lived at the bottom of Black Mountain. I was told the original name of Black Mountain was something like Wohali.

"Wohali is the Cherokee word for eagle," Adsila told me. "Long before the colonialists came, the Cherokee nation stretched north and south to Florida. Perhaps there is some Cherokee inside of you?"

I looked at her and her sister. I was surprised and immediately thought of Sojourner. "I think I'm a mutt, and I only know a little about my grandfather, a coal miner, and the only thing he left me was a locket with a picture of his mother, but it's sealed shut."

Erasmus said, "That little silver locket? Let me see if I can open it." He took out his penknife and gently pried it open. "Jake, look here."

It was my great-grandmother. The picture was black and white and faded, and she had high cheekbones and long braids.

Erasmus said, "She does look like you, and possibly Cherokee. Maybe that explains why you instinctively seem more at home in the forests."

"Grandfather, what do you think of the name Halouna for Jake?"

Sequoyah said, "The fortunate one? That is perfect. Halouna."

I said, "I never believed I had fortune nor much of a future. Now, with Erasmus, Socrates, Sojourner, Sequoyah, Atasula, and Ahyoka…I am Jake Halouna Meadows."

Sequoyah carved a small piece of wood with Halouna written in Cherokee, and Atasula and Ahyoka braided grass together to make a necklace. "Welcome, granddaughter. We've been waiting for you."

A crow called out from the oak tree near us. I fell to my knees in the grass, held my name in my hands, and the wind blew through my hair. The whole family surrounded me. At last, I knew who I was.

The next morning, Sequoyah and his family came by again. Sequoyah said, "I have a feeling we'll see you again soon. Safe travels, and now that you know the forests and trails, you know how to find us."

Ahyoka said, "We have a gift for you." It was a dreamcatcher woven like a spider web. In the center was small clear quartz, surrounded by bluestone and feathers.

"It's incredible and lovely! Thank you."

"The stone in the center is from these mountains, the blue is to remind you of this river, and the web is to hold all your dreams," said Adsila.

Ahyoka said, "It will also remind you to come back here and see us soon."

I have always kept that dreamcatcher with me, and we hung it in *Emma Goldman* above the dining table.

Erasmus said, "We have a small present." He took out his drawing pad, and unbeknownst to them, he had sketched Sequoyah and his granddaughters in charcoal pencil.

"Erasmus, this is incredible. It will be in the center of our house over the fireplace. Thank you."

At each place we had been, I felt like I had found more of my tribe, and I knew I would see Adsila and Ahyoka again. We turned to say goodbye one last time, but they had already vanished into the woods.

We returned to *Emma* in the evening, and we were heading south to Birmingham and then to New Orleans. Our bags were filled with mushrooms and herbs from our walk over the past few days. "Erasmus, I feel I know so little about these forests."

Erasmus reminded me, "It's called Zen Mind, beginner's mind. Learning should teach us humility, and we have to empty our minds of all our clutter. My mind in particular."

We left the campsite early and cleaned up everything.

"We'll head down to New Orleans, but we'll stop in Birmingham first. Liz and Marty, and their family, are expecting us."

Over the next few hours, we made our way down Route 53, Socrates on my lap. Erasmus looked better, though the car accident had taken a lot out of him. Still, after our time at the Chattahoochee, he had his old spunk back.

We stopped in Rome, Georgia at the home of Major Ridge, the Cherokee chieftain who was also a slaveholder. According to many, he betrayed the Cherokee nation by signing *The Treaty of Echota*. Erasmus, Socrates, and I sat under an old oak for lunch with our salad, rice, and bean bowls. An older woman walked by, and Erasmus invited her to join us. She had long silver hair tied in braids and a peaceful presence.

"My name is Ama Ross. This was the house of the man who tried to destroy the Cherokee nation, Major Ridge. This bitter legacy remains, though it has been over a hundred years. Major Ridge owned over two hundred and thirty acres and hundreds of slaves."

We ate lunch with Ama as she told us the story of this Cherokee chieftain, the four thousand Cherokees who died on the Trail of Tears, and the hundreds of thousands who lost all their property.

While driving south again, there were long stretches of empty roads, and Erasmus said, "I need a break from driving. This is a pretty flat stretch of road, not too much traffic, and you can do like you've done before driving *Emma* around the campsites."

"Erasmus, I don't even have a driver's license! I'm only a kid!"

"It's easy. We won't go fast, and I'll be beside you."

I slid into the driver's seat. It was one thing driving *Emma* around a campsite or a parking lot, but this was a seismic change. In his casual way, Erasmus talked me through everything, adjusting the mirrors and reviewing the safety checks, and soon we were off. I felt like I was driving a boat. It wasn't hard. We were cruising at about forty miles an hour. For the next hour, we stayed steady, as *Emma* was quite drivable and easy.

"That's it, Jake, and ten miles ahead is a little rest stop on the other side of the state line."

Sweet Home Alabama said the welcome sign. I saw a cop ahead at the roadside, and instead of panicking, I smiled and waved at him. One of Erasmus's many quotes that stays with me is, "You catch more flies with honey!" In other words, when you see a cop, wave hello.

"That's terrific, Jake. You drive *Emma* like you've been driving all your life!"

"I learned from the best!"

Though I drove for many more hours in *Emma Goldman* in the years to come, I never forgot that first moment of driving on the road. I looked over to Erasmus, and he was smiling. He was proud of me. That was a big difference in my life, having someone who was proud of me. I never had someone appreciate or value me as much as Erasmus.

We had a few more hours to Birmingham. I was concerned about Erasmus as he took a long nap after lunch, but he was perky and chatty again afterward. He took the wheel, and I got a crash course in the history of Birmingham and civil rights, and the powerful poems of Langston Hughes.

"I can tell you a lot about those crazy times in the 1950s and 1960s when African Americans were denied their basic rights as citizens. You'll understand why it was so unbelievable when we walk through the Civil Rights Museum later today. I still find racism and bigotry unbelievable, though I've seen it many times."

Then, from memory, he recited the poem by Langston Hughes, *Birmingham Sunday.*

BIRMINGHAM SUNDAY
(September 15, 1963)

Four little girls
Who went to Sunday School that day
And never came back home at all–
But left instead
Their blood upon the wall
With spattered flesh
And bloodied Sunday dresses
Scorched by dynamite that
China made eons ago
Did not know what China made
Before China was ever Red at all
Would ever redden with their blood
This Birmingham-on-Sunday wall.
Four tiny little girls
Who left their blood upon that wall,
In little graves today await:
The dynamite that might ignite
The ancient fuse of Dragon Kings
Whose tomorrow sings a hymn

The missionaries never taught
In Christian Sunday School
To implement the Golden Rule.
Four little girls
Might be awakened someday soon
By songs upon the breeze
As yet, unfelt among
Magnolia trees.

"The girls were killed while they were in Sunday School? That's insane. Why would people throw dynamite at a church? Why do people do such crazy, evil things?"

"I wish I knew or understood. There is no rationality to hate. To my mind, hate and racism are a disease, and it's next to impossible to get them out of your soul, but there are still many stories of how people transformed their hate. There is the story of CP Ellis, a Ku Klux Klan leader. He went from being a hate-filled man to eventually working with Black leaders in the community for civil rights."

We drove to the Civil Rights Museum in Birmingham, and I had a hundred questions percolating in my brain. It was difficult to believe this city was the scene of such hatred and violence.

Socrates, Erasmus, and I sat in the park before strolling to the Sixteenth Street Baptist Church. We sat in the back pew and meditated for the girls who were killed: Addie Mae Collins, Cynthia Wesley, Carole Robertson, and Carol Denise McNair.

Erasmus put his arm around me as we sat in the back pew. I was flooded with all the stories of courage, heroes of civil rights, incredible hatred, and then reconciliation. So many things that Erasmus had been teaching me over the past few months became clear, including how people can rise from their hatred and pain and find their way to forgiveness. Only years later would I realize how much I had truly learned in these few months, far more than I had learned in high school.

We drove out of town and found ourselves a camping spot by the river. A large man with a lantern came over and spoke to Erasmus in a thick drawl I could barely understand.

"Sir, this ain't a good spot to stop. It'll get wet here by morning and ya'll be stuck in the mud. Come over by my farm and there's a good place to put your RV."

Erasmus said, "Thank you. We'll be over and not get in your way."

"Please, be our guest tonight. My wife is making supper, and we always have a place for guests."

His name was George Jones, and his family had farmed the fields for generations. We met his grandmother, his wife Emma Mae, and his sons Moses and Samuel. Erasmus said, "Jake made some brownies for dessert, and we have a big basket of blackberries we picked."

We bowed our heads and the grandmother, Lorna Mae, said grace. "Kind and heavenly Father, we are thankful for this food, and bless us all. Amen."

Though the family had chicken, we ate the homegrown collards, yams, rice, and vegetables.

George and Lorna Mae told us of the bitter times of Jim Crow. George said, "We were all scared. Scared of the Klan and the terrible injustice. We almost moved up north, but this farm has been in our family for over a hundred years. Our boys Samuel and Moses will be going to high school in Birmingham. We'll miss them, but their future is not this farm. As a boy, I could never imagine attending a properly integrated school."

Moses said, "I'm a science nerd, and there aren't schools here for my brother or me. Samuel is a whiz at math, but we would never get a chance at our local school."

After dinner, Erasmus played his guitar. At the same time, Lorna Mae led us in singing songs like "Wade in the Water," "When the Saints Go Marching In," and then my favorite, "Goodnight Irene." Definitely, this was "Sweet Home Alabama," just like the song.

When it was bedtime, Erasmus said to me, "Thank you for another fantastic day. Tomorrow, we'll be in New Orleans. Sueños con angelitos."

I woke up later than usual. When I peeked out the window, I saw Erasmus with Moses and Samuel fixing an International Harvester truck.

Erasmus said, "I grew up with these trucks on our farm in Vermont, and though I'm only a fair mechanic, I think we can fix this."

Moses said, "I couldn't turn over the engine yesterday, I think the spark plugs are fouled."

Sam said, "Let's regap them and sand them a little to see if we can get a better firing."

I drank my tea and watched Erasmus working with the boys. After some tinkering, the truck was purring. George said, "It sounds better than brand-new!"

There were high-fives all around, and at the breakfast table, we dived into a stack of pancakes and blueberries.

George said, "If you and Jake want to stay here awhile longer, my family would like to have you. You're a terrific mechanic, and Jake is a great singer."

Erasmus said, "We'd love to stay, but our friends are waiting for us in New Orleans. Jake and I have a gift for Samuel and Moses." He gave them a brown package with three books, *Zen and the Art of Motorcycle Maintenance*, *Small is Beautiful*, and *A People's History of the United States*. They were our three favorite books.

"Thank you, Mister Erasmus! Thanks, Jake. We don't know what these books are about, but I bet they're special."

When we left, Grandma Lorna Mae gave us a basket of cornbread. "Thank you both for coming by and gracing our home."

George and Erasmus shook hands. Erasmus said, "Thank you for your kind hospitality. We will definitely visit on our next journey."

We waved to the family as we drove out of the farm.

"Erasmus, they are such good people. I definitely understand why you could call it *Sweet Home Alabama*. I could have spent a lot more time here."

"Maybe we can come back in the future, but today we'll reach New Orleans by the afternoon."

"No matter where we go, we run into such good people, almost like you're a magnet."

"It's the law of attraction. Though it doesn't always work, putting out positive, loving energy will attract good people into your life. You have a natural talent for that, Jake."

As we approached New Orleans, the clouds darkened, and lightning stabbed the sky. The wind was blowing against *Emma Goldman*, but Erasmus wasn't nervous. "Don't worry, if it looks bad, we can pull over, but I think we can beat the worst of the storm."

"Do the words *overly optimistic* have any bearing on this conversation?" I asked with a smile.

"Bravo, Jake! Well-spoken! I will curb my optimism 'til we cross the Pontchartrain."

The sky turned blacker in the early afternoon as we reached the bridge. Lake Pontchartrain looked as wide as the ocean, and lightning danced on the water's edge. We were listening to the music of Arthur Lee and Love. It was surreal, and we were driving at a crawl of forty miles an hour. Waves were splashing on the bridge. I was afraid we were about to get swept away.

"It's okay, Jake. *Emma* is a heavy RV, which means she stays low enough to the ground, and because of the Airstream design, it doesn't get knocked around as much."

We had to slow down to twenty-five miles per hour, and the Arthur Lee music almost seemed to be playing in time to the lightning flashing in the sky and striking the water.

After what seemed like an eternity, we reached the other side.

"Welcome to New Orleans, Jake. Laissez le bon temps rouler! Let the good times roll!"

CHAPTER SIX

Laissez le Bon Temps Rouler

Erasmus put a CD in and "House of the Rising Sun" played. I couldn't believe we'd finally made it to New Orleans. "Man, this is an amazing city."

"As they say, you ain't seen nothing yet. I've visited New Orleans for many years, and I'm still astonished by it. Most times, it's a pleasant surprise. You never know what you're going to get here. It's a city with a thousand stories, secrets, and sorrows spun every minute."

Socrates was leaning on the dashboard, surveying everything in front. We wound our way around the city through the French Quarter and drove down Esplanade with the massive oak trees covered in Spanish moss dangling like a giant cobweb as sunlight danced through the shadows. There were old elegant houses from the 1800s painted in pinks, blues, and yellows with wrought iron railings. Vibrant purple bougainvillea graced the old wooden houses that bent and sagged with the weight of time and age.

In the distance, I heard the slow creaking of freight trains and a foghorn from the Mississippi. The roads were more broken than mended, with potholes everywhere, but Erasmus drove with ease and care as *Emma Goldman* bounced along, though her springs groaned in protest.

"Jake, see the sign on the side of the road? That's one of the most famous and important sites. It's where Homer Plessy was arrested for riding a train in 1892 that was supposed to be only for White people."

"I don't understand."

"In New Orleans, like with so much of the history with African Americans, it's complicated and racist. Home Plessy looked like a White man, but he had one great-grandmother who was African American. According to the segregation laws of that time, that made him Black. What's bizarre is that he was so fair, he had to tell the conductor he was a Negro and refused to go to the section of the train reserved for Negroes. This led to a huge civil rights struggle and a Supreme Court decision."

"That's crazy."

"Racism is crazy. Even though New Orleans is one of the most culturally diverse cities in the USA. That's one of the reasons I love this city, it's almost three hundred years old, and every place you go, every street from the French Quarter to the Lower Ninth, has an incredible story. There's a house in Treme where the Voodoo Queen Marie Laveau lived in the 1800s and people still make a pilgrimage to her grave and offer gifts for a favor. How can you not love a city like this?"

There were old warehouses on either side, the train whistle blew, and I felt the humid air off the Mississippi. The church bells rang from Francis Xavier Seelos, the grand red brick church with stained glass windows. It was named after a priest who helped victims of yellow fever in 1867.

Coming up the street was a rickety green pickup truck selling vegetables and a Black man with a grey beard in overall bib jeans and a tattered straw hat was calling out his wares. "I have mango. I have spinach, yellow squash, and corn on the cob," he'd chant from a PA system attached to the roof of the pickup. "I have eggplant, I have onion, and I have garlic."

"My friend, Mr. Okra!" called out Erasmus. "Now I really feel I'm back in New Orleans."

Mr. Okra waved at him with a smile. Erasmus stopped and shook his hand. Every Wednesday, Mr. Okra drove down Dauphine to the Lower Ninth Ward, and at the end of the day, whatever produce he had left, he would donate to the Church of Love. There were too many poor places in the city, like the Lower Ninth Ward, without supermarkets.

Mr. Okra stopped and said, "My grandpa sold vegetables and fruit in a horse-drawn cart."

Erasmus said, "These buildings around here are called shotgun houses. You can shoot a gun from the front of the house to the back in a straight line. Fortunately, I don't keep a gun, as you know."

The shotgun houses in Bywater were nestled tightly against each other in yellows, blues, purples, and chartreuse. Every home had a front porch or a stoop and wrought iron railings. I could be happy spending a day doing nothing but sitting on the front porch of one of them and watching the parade of people passing by.

Erasmus said, "We're almost there." The potholes and broken roads were rough on *Emma Goldman's* springs. "The Bywater is broken into wards, including the Lower Ninth Ward, one of the poorest parts of the city that was almost destroyed by Hurricane Katrina."

Across the street from Francis Xavier Church was a sign over the entrance to a building painted in rainbow colors:

Church of Love: No Religion. ONLY LOVE.
Step One: Love.
Step Two: Take responsibility for your life.
Step Three: If you can't! Ask for help.
Step Four: After you have help, take responsibility.
Step Five: Go back to step one and repeat.

Erasmus beeped his horn. Men and women were in the parking lot, elderly, young, Black, White, and Latino cleaning up the yard and planting flowers along the edge of the fence. A thin older man with a straw hat and a woman with grey hair tied back in a ponytail turned around and looked at us. They smiled and walked over.

"Hey, everyone! It's Erasmus!"

We parked in the shade and stepped out of *Emma Goldman*, and Socrates leaped out. The couple bent down to greet him. "Our very handsome friend, Mr. Socrates."

Erasmus and the couple hugged. "Marty and Liz, you look great, and I've missed you immensely. I want to introduce you to my very good friend, Jake."

Liz said, "Hi darling, Erasmus told us about you and what fun you're having."

"Great to meet you, Father Marty and Sister Elizabeth. Erasmus told me about your work here."

"Call us Marty and Liz. The Church decommissioned us, and we're now free to do our own thing. At the Church of Love, we welcome everyone, even hobos like Erasmus and yourself," he said with a smile.

Later I would find out about Liz and Marty's history as a priest and a nun, getting arrested repeatedly for protesting the military, getting married, and their evolution into this homeless shelter.

Liz said, "Erasmus said you were one of his favorite travel buddies and helpers."

"That must be a full-time job and a half," Marty said.

"It's far more than time-and-a-half work." I smiled at Erasmus. "But he seems like he's worth the trouble. Sometimes it just takes a bit more effort to keep Erasmus in line."

"So, Jake. You keeping me in line?" said Erasmus with a big laugh.

Marty and Liz walked us over to a table and said, "Please sit, have a cold lemonade, and meet our crew. We've missed you, Erasmus. We thought you would come back last year."

"I would have come back sooner, except I was in Spain for about five months working with a refugee project, and if the stars align, I'd love to go back. Right now, I'm happy traveling with Jake and Socrates." He looked at me with the sweetest of smiles as his blue-green eyes sparkled, and I blushed.

This was the mystery of Erasmus. I'd had no idea he had been in Spain. So much of who he was and where he had been was revealed slowly to me.

"Erasmus, you look fabulous and always seem to be doing good work," Liz said. "We got postcards from you in Majorca and Granada. I wish we could travel too, but as soon as we plan a trip, one thing or another comes up."

"Marty and Liz, your best travels are your journeys to the heart that inspire many people."

"Erasmus, you do have a way with words."

While they were gabbing, I walked over to a group of little Black girls who were jump roping. I learned that their family had been evicted and now lived at the Church of Love. Jamila, Mary, and Esther were four, six, and eight years old and showed me a jump roping style from New Orleans called Iko Iko. The girls clapped, double Dutch jumped, and sang, "My grandma and your grandma sitting by the fire…" The men working nearby soon took their garden clippers and shovels and tapped out the beat. One man had a glass bottle and, with a nickel, was tapping along.

This is New Orleans, where a party can happen at any time. Over the next few weeks, I would get to know these girls and more of their stories.

"Jake," Liz said. "We have a little bedroom up in the tower."

"A tower? Like I'm Rapunzel?" I said, loosening my ponytail, and my long brown hair flew in the wind.

"Maybe that should be your new name?" Erasmus said with a laugh. "Rapunzel Jake! Rapunzel Jake, let down your hair!"

"That sounds like fun, but would I take a bed away from somebody who needs it? We could sleep in *Emma*."

"Jake, that's very thoughtful, but I have a nice room picked out for you. We're happy you're here," said Liz. "We could certainly use some more help around here. Marty and Erasmus will be so busy gabbing we may not get anything done for a few days."

I said, "As much as I love Erasmus, you're right. It's astonishing how much work gets done despite his gabbing."

Erasmus playfully threw a pillow at me. "I think it's debatable who gabs more! Jake can talk more than all three of us!"

Liz said, "We're going to have a lot of fun even though, as always, we have a lot of work."

Liz and I walked around Bywater towards the Rainbow Bridge. She said, "We're happy to have you here, Jake. Let me tell you a little about our story. Marty and I fell in love about twenty years ago when Marty was a priest and I was a nun. You're not supposed to fall in love when you're a priest and a nun, but as soon as we saw each other, it was like a thunderbolt and we immediately knew we were meant to be together. We saw that St. Francis Church owned this run-down warehouse but wouldn't do anything with it. With friends, we took it over and made it into a community."

"What did the Church do?"

"They threatened to evict us, and through some small miracle… the more noise they made, the more our support grew. Carpenters, plumbers, poets, electricians, and ordinary folk transformed this into our community. Since then, we've become good neighbors with Francis Xavier Church and have reached an accord. We don't technically own this building—we expropriated it."

As I was to find out later, it was close enough to legal, and in New Orleans, close enough to legal is more than you need.

"Like many places, it's not what you do, but who you know. That's why New Orleans is known as the Big Easy. If you know the right people, it's easy enough to get things done," said Liz.

"This sounds like something Erasmus would do. If he sees something that needs to be done, he does it without asking. Like cleaning up a park, planting flowers, or rebuilding a stone wall."

"Yes, we're in the same mindset. Sometimes, it's better to seek forgiveness than to ask for permission."

"Do you know Roshi Kanji and Sojourner?" I asked while we walked up the rusty bridge over to the Mississippi.

"Sojourner and Roshi are part of the family we call the *Noble Order of Hobos*, nothing formal, just noble and kind individuals who come together to help people. Sojourner was here a few months ago to visit and restock our herbal pharmacy and give workshops. Roshi Kanju brought a dozen people here last year, and we built a new annex. This work is our rent for living on the planet."

That night as I was going to sleep, I was writing in my journal and thinking about how humbled I was to have met these people who were committed to helping others.

Then I heard a ping on the window. It was Erasmus from the ground floor.

"Goodnight, Rapunzel Jake. Sueños con angelinos."

"Goodnight, my darling Erasmus."

Socrates was next to me and barked down to Erasmus.

At dawn, I walked down Dauphine before anyone else had woken up. I walked across the rusty iron bridge to the Mississippi with Socrates and watched the sun rise over the old broken docks. According to Erasmus, these were major docks for slavery and the cotton industry. This was the contradiction of New Orleans, a beauty built on the horrid foundations of slavery.

I loved this time in the morning by the river watching the city come to life as I wrote in my journal and drank my coffee. Though I liked traveling around in *Emma* with Erasmus, I soon learned to love the spontaneity of New Orleans, the parties and fun that happened at the drop of a hat, the music in the streets, and the easy friendliness of people.

After breakfast, I helped the girls, Jamila and her sisters, with schoolwork. Initially, I wasn't confident I would be much help, but with all that Erasmus had taught me over the past months, I was surprised at how easy it was to help them with their math and reading. I felt at home as I looked around our classroom at the Church of Love.

Erasmus saw me from a distance and smiled and winked. It was his way of saying, *Great job!* I've kept these little *Erasmusisms* (as I called them) with me all my life.

After lunch, Liz and I walked down to the Country Club, the local swimming pool. I loved the names of the streets along the way, like the intersection of Piety and Desire Street. Someone said there was a brothel on the corner here, but like most things you hear in NOLA, there are a lot of tall tales told with a wink and a grin. Every inch of the city has a story or a fable. Personally, I love the idea of a brothel at the intersection of Desire and Piety – even if it ain't necessarily true.

The Country Club was a gracious house from the 1800s with a big front porch. As you walked in, disco music played and a gaggle of drag queens in purple and gold sequined gowns were at the bar. It was like nothing I had ever seen in Black Mountain or anywhere else.

Liz smiled and called out as we walked towards the ladies at the bar, "Good morning, ladies. You all are the picture of loveliness!"

"Sister Liz, who is this darling creature with you?"

"This is Jake, who's helping us. She's a teacher."

I didn't realize I'd been promoted, but I appreciated the nod.

I walked into the dressing room to change into my swimsuit and to my shock there were half-naked men and women. "Oops, I'm sorry." I was beet red. "I thought I was in the girl's dressing room."

A naked Black woman with a big Afro smiled and said, "Honey, don't worry, we're all God's children."

Liz said, "Everyone, give a shout-out to my friend Jake."

Soon I was enveloped in hugs from a room of half-naked people. That was NOLA! Everything was spontaneous and madly delightful. Anything goes! I never felt like a stranger because no matter how strange you are, there's always someone stranger in New Orleans.

The small swimming pool in the back had people of all kinds hanging out. Boys with boys, girls smooching with girls, old people, and me, Jake Meadow from Black Mountain, West Virginia. The Country Club was the hub in NOLA of straights, gays, lesbians, and every stripe of person in between. I felt like a fish out of water, but soon I was laughing and playing with many new friends.

My bathing suit strap broke and I was trying to fix it when a rainbow-haired man said, "Dahling, don't worry, I have my sewing kit with me. Come over here to the poolside." In a minute, he had fixed the strap. Then he looked at me and said, "You're so cute, I could almost be a straight man, but that ain't gonna happen. One more thing." Then he fixed my sagging halter top with a quick stitch.

"Huh? My tiny boobs got a face-lift!"

The pool was bubbling with people drinking, and one couple looked like they needed a hotel room, but it was all good fun. Despite the crazy brokenness of the city, with the cavernous potholes, shady politics, and the huge divide between the rich and the Lower Ninth—the Crescent City knew how to have fun! We would come back here often to the pool, and in the mornings, the security guard let me in when I wanted a swim without the party. Quickly, I felt at home in Bywater and the Big

Easy, despite its reputation as the dark underbelly of crime, hopelessness, drugs, and sin—most times, I felt safe. Everyone was looking out for me.

We had supper with everybody at the shelter. I looked around the room and then at Erasmus.

"We seem so at home here in New Orleans. Truth be told, I like it here too. Can we stay?"

Erasmus looked at me, smiled, and then turned away. He seemed lost in thought for a long time. "It's like my favorite song, 'Time in a Bottle.'" He reached for his guitar and sang the song. I didn't realize how poignant and true it was. He said, "That song is for you. I wish I could take every moment with you and always hold it close. I've enjoyed traveling with you, even with all your sassiness."

"My sassiness? I thought it was you who was the sassy one!"

"See? My point exactly!"

I told him about my day walking over the Rainbow Bridge at dawn, teaching the girls, and swimming at the Country Club.

"Yup, that's what I love about New Orleans. It's spontaneous and crazy, and you meet many fun characters daily."

After dinner, Erasmus said, "Let's walk downtown. The market on Frenchmen Street is open, and there is a jazz show at Preservation Hall."

Erasmus dressed in his dapper green felt fedora, blue sports coat, and his best jeans. I put on the frilly dress that Alice from Cleveland gave me months ago and a dash of makeup and lipstick.

We walked up to Frenchmen Street and to Jackson Square for beignets from Café Du Monde. Beignets and hot chocolate, the powdery burst of deliciousness, made me want to eat a dozen, but I restrained myself.

Erasmus said, "I've been so busy with Marty and Liz. Sorry I haven't been having much fun lately. I love all the tutoring you're giving the girls."

"Not to worry, I'm up to my ears in fun and discovering New Orleans. I hate to sound rude, my dear 'Rasmus, but I've hardly missed you!"

He said with a chuckle, "If you weren't so pretty in your dress, I'd throw a beignet at you!"

The evening sun lit his silvery beard and twinkling green-blue eyes. It was a cherished memory of him.

The Preservation Hall had a Dixieland jazz band with big brass trombones, clarinets, washboards, and drums. When they started playing "Iko Iko," Erasmus and I danced as we sang with the band.

"Iko Iko," Erasmus explained, "is like a jambalaya stew of languages with Indian words, French phrases that have been turned upside down, and people's inventions. The word Iko, some have said, means in Cajun *ecoutez* or *listen*."

My feet couldn't stop dancing, and Erasmus looked happy and healthy. We had many perfect moments during our *Summer of Love*, but this was one in particular that I cherished.

We stepped out into the cool evening air. A guitarist in a silver glitter jumpsuit on rollerblades glided down the street playing an electric guitar, a jazz band played in Jackson Square, and a fire eater was performing on the steps to the river. It was always a huge party everywhere. With the chaos, noise, and the sweetest jazz from the street musicians, I could live here a hundred years and never tire of the city. While walking through the streets, Erasmus would tell me all the stories of the past, of how the Native Americans, the Spaniards, the French, the enslaved African Americans, and hundreds of other cultures came here to create this phenomenal city.

Jackson Square was filled with tourists, hustlers, fortune tellers, artists, the homeless, and a mob of madness and fun. We walked down Chartres Street and in the shadows, I saw a girl who looked familiar. She was smoking a cigarette and wearing a black leather mini-dress, a sheer white blouse, fishnet stockings, and three-inch heels. A car stopped and sped off.

"'Rasmus, I can't believe it, but I know this girl. I got to talk to her."

I walked over to her and said, "Hi, are you Mandy? Don't you recognize me? I'm Jake from Black Mountain."

The girl turned away and took another drag of her cigarette. "I don't think so. My name is Lana, and I'm from New Orleans. Piss off. I'm a working girl."

I persisted in talking to her, and a big man with a scar across his cheek wearing a shiny grey suit said, "Girl, get out of here. Lana's busy."

Erasmus looked at her and me and quietly said, "Time for a strategic retreat. We need to refigure this. There's nothing we can do."

He walked over to Mandy and said, "Lana, this is the card of where we're going to be. It's the Church of Love down in Bywater."

She looked at Erasmus. "Yeah, I know where it is. But beat it! Whatever you do, don't get Stanford mad."

"Lana, if you need anything. Anything at all. Call me." I wanted to take her away, but I was angry and confused. Why was she here and working as a hooker? It didn't make sense. "Mandy, we can help you."

She said, "Scram, kid! I'm trying to make a living."

Then I saw that the man she was with glared at her and put his finger over his mouth as if to say, 'Not another word.'

We walked up the block away from Chartres. I sat on the church steps and cried, and Erasmus held me.

The bright lights and laughter of the city faded away. A drunk guy was peeing in the middle of the street, a disoriented homeless man was begging, and frat boys were screaming and guzzling beer. I hated the stupidity, drinking, drugging, and Mandy on the street corner. The brokenness, the beauty, and insanity made New Orleans the Big Easy, but there was hardly anything easy about it.

"Come on. Let's go for a walk and talk." Erasmus took me by the arm, and we stopped on a bench by Café De Monde. I was in a daze. I was scared.

"I can't believe what I saw. This could have been me. She's barely eighteen. How did Mandy get here?"

"Jake, we can keep an eye on Mandy, but as you said, she's eighteen. It's her choice."

"Being a prostitute is a choice?"

"Sometimes, but we can see if she needs help. Marty and Liz have a lot of friends and they always know what's going on. How do you know her?"

"She was a year ahead of me. I remember her as being smart. I thought she would find some way to escape and maybe even go to college."

I was angry, frightened, and shaking. "It's the goddamn Black Mountain! No one gets out of that hole. No one gets anything. I could have been Mandy on the street corner!"

"Come here, Jake." He put his arm over my shoulder, and I cried. I was in New Orleans having a great time until I was reminded of Black Mountain. Worse, a girl smarter and prettier than me wound up as a hooker.

"It ain't fair. It just ain't fair!"

A good cry and a great friend can soothe a troubled soul.

"Don't worry, we'll figure out something. Marty and Liz know everybody in this neighborhood. Let me brighten a sad day for you. An old friend of mine, Germaine Bazzle, is playing at the jazz club Snug Harbor tonight. I think it would be fun."

Though shaken by what I'd seen, good music always eased my cares. When Germaine Bazzle took the stage, all my cares fell away entirely. She was singing "All of Me," and I was humming along. She looked at me and smiled.

"Sorry, Ms. Bazzle. I didn't mean to interrupt you."

"Not at all. I liked your humming," she said with a smile.

At the break, she said, "You remind me of one of my granddaughters. Do you know how to sing Summertime?"

"Yes, ma'am. I can't sing like you, but I like to sing, and my friend Erasmus has been teaching me.

We sat on the stage together. She hummed a little, and I began to sing. I closed my eyes, and the bass, horn, and drums started.

Germaine said, "Sing with me!" I forgot I was on stage and when I opened my eyes people were applauding.

Germaine said after the show, "I loved your singing. We can sing together some more, and I can teach you. You've got talent."

"Ms. Bazzle. That would be awesome. Thank you."

Erasmus said, "Germaine, thank you very much. I drew this picture for you." It was a pen sketch of Germaine and me.

It began to rain, and Erasmus said, "I know a song – 'Singing in the Rain.'" Then he began to sing and dance.

I'm singing in the rain.
Just singing in the rain.
What a glorious feelin'
I'm happy again.

I laughed with glee watching him tap dance and sing, and an older Black man in a stylish purple suit, a bowler hat, and a pink satin tie joined him. The two of them skipped and tap danced down Frenchmen Street. A kid took out his harmonica, and another guy was tapping a beat on a glass beer bottle. This is New Orleans, where anything can happen at any time of the day. Even tap dancing in the rain.

Going to sleep that night, I had a huge grin as I thought of Erasmus and that man dancing in the rain.

Erasmus said, "Goodnight, Jake. Sueños con angelitos. We'll figure out something with Mandy."

"Thank you. I love you, Erasmus P. Hobbs," and then I paused. "Of course, like a granddaughter loves her grandpa!"

Socrates barked as he snuggled beside me. "And, yes, I love you too, Socrates."

Everyone in the world should fall asleep with laughter on their lips and a heart filled with love.

My days were filled with fun, teaching the little kids and them teaching me how to dance and jump rope. My favorite thing was sitting in a park like Jackson Square or hanging out at the Country Club pool and watching people.

Two days later, Marty got a phone call from the hospital. "Do you know a girl named Mandy Taylor who calls herself Lana?"

"What happened?" I asked.

"Mandy's in the hospital, and we can go downtown in my car," said Marty.

"Let's go, Jake!" said Erasmus.

We raced to Marty's beat-up Chrysler convertible. Marty took out a blue police light and stuck it on the dashboard. "I'm a chaplain with the police department."

Despite the evening rush hour, we flew down to the hospital. I was in the backseat, the sky and the city above me. I saw the prostitutes on Canal Street, the cars slowing down, and I thought of Mandy. The city lights flashed before me. A motorcycle cop saw Marty, and I thought we would get a ticket. Instead, he gave a thumbs-up, turned on his siren, and took the lead with flashing lights. I felt like I was in a parade, and in a few moments, we were at the Emergency Room, and Marty slipped into the clerics' parking.

When I went into the Emergency Room, I didn't recognize Mandy. Her face was bruised, swollen, and covered with dried blood, her arm was in a sling, and she was hooked up to an IV. Her lips were swollen. Her long brunette hair was in a tangle of blood.

"Mandy!" I screamed. "What the hell happened? Who did this?"

"Jake, shh! She can't talk now. Let's sit with her and pray," said Marty. "That is the best thing we can do."

"Mandy, I'm Erasmus. I'm a friend of Marty and Jake. We'll help you until you're out of here, and we'll find somewhere safe for you."

I got a basin of warm water and a washcloth to wipe off the blood, and even asleep, she smiled.

Looking up at me through her swollen eyes, she said, "Thanks, Jake."

There was a commotion in the hallway. People were yelling, and a man over six feet tall with a long scar on his cheek stormed into the hospital room. "That's my girl! I'm in charge of her. Everyone out! I'm taking her out of here right now."

A five-foot Filipina nurse walked over and confronted Stanford. "We'll take care of Mandy, but out of the room right now!" She reached up and pointed her finger right at his chest. "Now! Out!"

Stanford backed up, and the motorcycle cop walked into the room and looked at him. "Stanford, also known as Sonny Boy, Big Mac, and also known as the meanest pimp on Canal Street? I have only one question: should I arrest you now or wait until I get testimony from Mandy?"

"I love her! She's mine!" He started to cry. "She was my best!" Then he was handcuffed and taken away. Stanford had enough arrest warrants to keep him in jail for a long time.

Erasmus, Marty, and the nurse stood before Mandy's bed. Mandy had several broken ribs, her face was bruised, she had a concussion, and a fractured arm. I couldn't believe someone would do this to such a pretty girl. This could have been me.

Liz came into the room. "She'll stay with us for as long as she needs. We have a nice room for her until her parents come."

I said, "She doesn't have anyone but us. Her mom ran off years ago. Her father died when she was four and she lived at her cousin's house when she disappeared."

"Did anyone try to find her?" Liz asked.

"We're from Black Mountain. If you've gone missing, we hope you found a better place than our holler."

We visited every day, and on Sunday morning, we went to the hospital to pick Mandy up. Though the bruises were better, she still looked dazed and shocked. It would take time to heal all the pain from working on the street and the terrible beating by her pimp.

Mandy stayed with us at Liz and Marty's place. We had spent the previous day painting her room, which overlooked the garden, lilac-colored. I heard the tugboats on the Mississippi when I opened the window. The fog horns sounded like plaintive calls, a low moaning in the morning.

Mandy looked up. "Jake, I never thought I'd see you here. I'm really embarrassed and angry."

I didn't know what to say. I leaned over to hug her, and she said, "Easy, my ribs are still sore. I need to get out and check on Stanford. I bet you he missed me."

Liz closed the door to the room. We were all shocked. Erasmus spoke, "I don't usually tell people what to do with their lives, but I will tell you this, your life with Stanford is over. He's as mean as a junkyard dog."

"But he still loves me!"

"He beat the hell out of you!" I shouted.

"I deserved it. I shorted him twenty dollars so I could buy a new dress. All I wanted to do was to look pretty for him."

"Mandy, this is crazy. He's in jail for beating you up."

"I ain't pressing charges, and he'll be out soon. We'll have a baby together, and everything will be okay."

I couldn't believe what I was hearing. It was crazy.

Erasmus looked at Mandy. "I'm sorry, but he's one mean guy. He has a long list of warrants for assault and battery, drug possession, and he's on his way to prison for a long time."

Mandy sat on the edge of the bed and sobbed. "He loves me!"

"No, Mandy, he didn't love you," said Liz. "The only thing he loves is the money you make for him. He's an evil pimp and he nearly beat you to death. You're staying with us. It isn't a discussion. Do I make myself clear?" She crossed her arms, and I don't think anyone would dare to argue with her.

Mandy said, "How long do I have to be here?"

"You'll stay here 'til you're better. Clear?"

I thought Mandy would be grateful, but she was angry, and though she had been nearly beaten to death, she thought she still loved Stanford. Every day there was a little more brightness in her spirit, though. I could see the light coming back into Mandy's eyes, but the emotional bruises would take a long time to heal.

At the end of the week, I wanted to go out to the Quarter to listen to music. I asked Erasmus, "I want to go to Jackson Square for music. Would you like to go?"

"Jake, I'm a little worn out today. Liz can go with you for a bit. Or do you want to go for a walk by yourself?"

"You're right! I can go myself. It's only a short walk across the railroad track. I shouldn't be back too late. Is that okay?"

I put on my pink dancing dress and sandals from Alice with a touch of lipstick, and this girl was ready for New Orleans.

Erasmus smiled and said, "Have fun, but not too much fun!"

It was Saturday night, and the French Quarter was alive with music. As much as I loved being with Erasmus, it was great to have the freedom to walk around the city on my own. A little jug band played in Washington Park, and soon we sang fun songs like "Jump in the Line." Some boys had a bottle of wine, and I saw no harm in a sip or two.

One cute boy, Tyler, with long brown hair, and his friend Paul took me down to the Blue Nile. "Don't worry," said Tyler. "I know the bouncer. We can get you in."

I felt all grown up! At sixteen, I felt sexy and free. We danced to this great rock and roll band, and I was throwing back shots of Hurricanes. I lost all track of time. It was my first time drinking and going out by myself. I was free and happy, my head was swimming, and these boys threw off their shirts and danced with me.

I found out later that at the Church of Love, Erasmus had said to Marty and Liz, "I'm worried about Jake. It's 10 p.m. and she's not back yet. Do you know where she might be?"

Marty said, "Let me get a few people together and make a few phone calls. I know she likes Frenchmen Street, and we can look in the clubs."

Marty, Erasmus, Liz, and a handful of people from the shelter fanned out up Frenchmen Street and started looking in the clubs. Erasmus and Liz walked into the Blue Nile. I was dancing with Tyler and Paul in the middle of the dance floor when I saw Erasmus.

"Uh oh! What time is it? Erasmus, join us for a drink! I met these boys, and we sang, played music, and then found our way here. Great club, don't ya think?" I asked.

"It is if you're twenty-one, but you're sixteen."

One of the boys confronted Erasmus and said, "Hey, Grandpa! You can't break up the party. Scram!"

Erasmus looked at the kid, who was very drunk, and pushed him back. "You jerk! She's sixteen! The party's over."

"Sixteen? Are you kidding me? Damn, we were going to take her home with us. I'm sorry, Mister. We didn't know."

I said, "Erasmus, come on, lighten up! Have a drink with us! The Hurricanes are great!"

Then I stumbled into Erasmus. All the music, lights, and people on Frenchmen Street were a blur as Erasmus threw me over his shoulders. "Party's over, Jake!" I blacked out.

I woke up when I got into the cool night air and realized I had made a monumental mistake. Erasmus put me down near Marty's car, and suddenly all the booze came up and I puked over my pretty pink dress.

Erasmus took out his bandana and wiped my mouth. "Jake, if you have to puke, lean your head out of the car. We'll get you home in a minute."

I lay back in the convertible, and I didn't remember anything after that.

"Wake up, Jake, it's noon!" When the curtains were opened up, I realized what I had done.

Mandy stood there with a tray of oatmeal, coffee, and water. "I never bring anyone breakfast in bed, but given that it's noon, I think it's time for you to get up."

"Where's Erasmus?" And the memory of the boys, the music, and the Blue Nile came back to me. "I am so sorry! What did I do? And, uh oh, I think I made a huge mistake."

"You sure made a mess of it last night. When Erasmus and Marty brought you in, I cleaned you up and washed your dress out."

I was caught between feeling profoundly ashamed, embarrassed, and incredibly stupid. How could I do this? How did I do this?

Erasmus walked in. "Jake, how are you doing today? That was some party last night!"

I hung my head. "Erasmus, is there a word for being more than embarrassed?"

"Human? Yes, I will admit you made a huge mistake in judgment, and I was very angry that everyone had to go out and find you. But since I am a master of occasionally doing stupid things, I couldn't stay mad at you for long. However, you need to own up to the mistake."

"I'm sorry. I thought of all the amazing, wonderful stuff that happened over these past few months, and I felt it all fall away. I am sorry, to you, and to all of our friends here. I am so sorry I embarrassed you with my incredibly stupid, atrocious behavior." I started to cry.

Erasmus and Mandy both put their arms around me. Mandy said, "Don't worry, we all mess up. Trust me! I know about monumental mistakes!"

"It's okay, Jake. Here's a tissue," said Erasmus. "We all have failed. I have failed monumentally many times before. Fortunately, there's no harm, and it only reminded you and us of how far we have to go."

Mandy reached over and held me close while I was still blubbering.

"I'm sorry I let you down," Erasmus said. "I didn't watch out for you." I could see that his eyes were already filled with tears.

I stopped blubbering for a minute. "Erasmus, you trusted me, and I let you down. The fault is mine, not yours. I'm sorry I let myself go and be a stupid kid. I should've known better. But here I was, as you say, full of my sassiness and smartness when those guys approached me and asked me if I wanted to go for a drink. Suddenly I felt like a big girl. As you know, one drink led to another, and soon I was dancing and carrying on at the Blue Nile. Though I am ashamed I let you down, from what I remember, it was fun until I realized what I did."

"Of course, it was fun! Roshi and I have gotten rip-roaring drunk and danced away more than a few nights. However, we both know where it landed us. We are both alcoholics, and we learned over a long time that the booze only temporarily masks all the pain and loss."

"Erasmus, why do you feel you let me down?"

Erasmus looked at me for the longest time, his eyes filled with tears, and said, "I should have been looking out for you. Here's a very long story that I will make as short as I can. As a boy living in Vermont in the Northeast Kingdom, I hated all the work to keep our farm and our twenty-five cows going. Up in the morning at four o'clock milking every day and at the end of the day. Three hundred and sixty-five days of the year. Even on Christmas, shovel the path to the barn, milk the damn cows, and shovel the manure. Then coming back from school and shoveling the barn...we were dirt-poor cowshit farmers. No matter how hard we worked, we always seemed behind. When you talk about not having new or clean clothes, I understand. We survived on hand-me-downs and the Salvation Army. I was lucky I had a mother and a father, but my dad, with his grade school education, only spoke a little. Mostly, a 'yup' there and a nod. The words I remember most were, 'Ras, clean the barn. Milk. Chop wood.'

"Though my dad worked sixteen hours a day and never missed a day of work, every day after supper he went to the woodshed with the pot-bellied stove, sat down with a cheap bottle of whiskey, and poured shots 'til he fell asleep. He wouldn't drink in front of us, only in the woodshop. Mother said he never wanted to burden us. He was dead by the time he was forty-five."

I had never heard much about his family farm Hardscrabble in the northeast of Vermont. I'd thought the farm sounded idyllic. I didn't realize all the poverty and the hard work to run a farm.

Erasmus said, "The day I turned seventeen, I took the bus to Burlington and joined the Army. I didn't even say goodbye to my family. I don't know why. After years and years of milking, haying, shoveling the barn, chopping wood, and all the work of making a farm run, I was fed up and wanted to escape. Only when I was in Vietnam six months later did it hit me. I was ashamed of myself for leaving. I wrote my mom and brother a letter saying how sorry I was, but it was too late."

"My mother wrote back, 'Erasmus, you were right. It was too much. So many things have changed in farming, and though we all tried mightily to make this farm work, it wasn't making ends meet, and you're right, it was much too hard. It wasn't your fault. We placed too much on you when your father died and didn't know how overwhelming it was for you. I wish we were able to talk. Vermonters keep too much inside and we don't talk about what bothers us. When you come back, and I do hope you come back soon, we're selling the farm to the Glaziers, and they're letting me stay in the farmhouse. We'll help out as best as possible, but I decided to return to teaching. The classroom is warm, and unlike farming, there's a paycheck at the end of the week. More importantly, teaching is my true destiny. The other sad bit of news I'm sorry to tell you in a letter is that your brother Henry David died in an accident, the tractor rolled over during the snowstorm in January. We laid him to rest in the family cemetery. He was so proud when you joined the Army and got out of Vermont, but Henry David said, 'For me, ain't no other place I'd rather be than on a cow farm in Vermont.' We all love and miss you. Mom.'"

Erasmus cried, "I wrote back but didn't return to Vermont for a long time. After Vietnam, like many guys, I fell apart. I had no idea what was wrong with me. All I wanted to do was drink and get high. Captain Jim and I were always drunk and miserable, but we thought we were having a good time. Then we met Sojourner, who ran a shelter and a mission for drunks like us."

I couldn't believe what I was hearing. I knew that Erasmus had struggled with alcohol and drugs, but I didn't realize all of this story. My heart opened wide for Erasmus and Jim, and my pain and stupidity felt so small.

When I looked up into Erasmus's eyes, I didn't see the man I'd thought he was, someone powerful and wise. Instead, I saw the true man –a man of humility, grace, and gentleness. I realized at that point why I loved him so much. He allowed me to see his true self. It is an enormous gift when somebody allows you to see their true self, free of pretense and what other people think.

That night, after dinner, he and I walked across the rusty bridge by the Mississippi. We didn't say much. Socrates was between us and leading the way. The sunset on the Mississippi was pink, orange, and lilac. Despite my wreck of an evening, I still loved New Orleans, and instead of feeling ashamed and embarrassed, I had to learn to accept it. "Jake, we often fall short of our goals and expectations, but, we recover and pick ourselves up. It's when we learn to love ourselves unconditionally that we can truly learn to forgive ourselves and others."

Instead of feeling like a stupid kid, I was blessed for having met Marty, the community here, for Socrates's doggie kisses that always made me feel better, and for the wisdom and kindness of Erasmus. I was ashamed, but I was held in the strength and wisdom of Erasmus, Marty, Liz, and all the people who helped me along the way.

That night I fell into a deep sleep. I dreamed I met my mother when she was an infant. I knew who I was, and I knew who she was. I held her in my arms as a mother would hold a baby. I rocked her and held her close. As I laid my mother to rest and drew the covers over her, I felt her breathe deeply and peacefully. I saw my father through the window as he smiled and walked by. None of it made sense.

I looked at the clock when I awoke. It was eleven o'clock. I had slept for more than twelve hours. How was that possible? I thought of everything I was supposed to do at the house that morning.

Erasmus came in with a cup of coffee. "Sleeping beauty! I thought the sandman had carried you away." He gave me a hot towel to wash my face.

I was disoriented and told him of the dream I had.

He smiled and said, "I had taken some Ignatia homeopathic last night and had a dream about forgiveness. It's been years since I've seen my mother and father, but last night I saw my father as I had never seen him. Happy and healthy, looking like a thirty-year-old, young farmer. We shook hands, and I realized I was his spitting image." Then he took a picture in his wallet of his mother, father, brother, and himself when he was a teenager. It was shocking to see him as a handsome young man.

"Homeopathy, it's nearly invisible, but man...does it pack a wallop."

Over three weeks had passed since we'd arrived in New Orleans. Mandy was mostly healed, though her spirits were still badly bruised.

"Mandy, what do you want to do?"

"Truthfully? I'd like to beat the crap out of Stanford. Right now, I've been talking with Liz and some of the other women here. I don't know how I'll do it, but I'm going to help the other girls who are prostitutes. I know a few of them. Most are unhappy and have been brainwashed as badly as I had. And –"

Erasmus said, "And what?"

"I got some good news. I got accepted into a Licensed Practical Nurse school with the help of Liz and Marty. Even though I'd gotten sucked into the world of Stanford, I had finished my GED, so I'm ready to get back to school. Marty and Liz, I know you have a lot of people who need a home, but can I stay with you until I get back on my feet?"

Marty and Liz stepped forward and put their hands on Mandy's shoulders. "Mandy, you are always welcome here," Marty assured her. "This bedroom is yours, and you've been doing a great job of helping babysit the kids, helping in the kitchen, and the work you're doing with the street girls—that is rent money enough."

Liz said, "We'll pay for your LPN school."

"I can't believe how kind you are," she said with tears of gratitude. "Thank you. When Jake and I lived in Black Mountain, we never really saw much hope, and now I feel like I'm bathing in a river of it. Thank you all—Erasmus, Marty, Liz, Jake, and everyone for making this possible. I love you guys."

Erasmus said, "We're proud of you, and Jake and I will pay for your textbooks."

"Thank you all for believing in me," Mandy said.

Unfortunately, in New Orleans, there were too few success stories. Many of the girls that Mandy knew had been brainwashed and believed the lies of their pimps. Worse, the businessmen and tourists who paid for sex knew that some girls were underage and coerced.

It was a Sunday morning in late July. The church bells were tolling at Saint Xavier across the street. The friends from Catholic Workers came to the Church of Love and brought bread and grape juice for communion. Then when service was over, we had a big potluck and sang gospel songs.

Afterward, Erasmus, Socrates, and I were alone. "Jake, I need to be heading west in a few days. I have to meet with some folks in Galveston, Texas, and then on to Arizona. I spoke with Marty and Liz, and you can stay with them for as long as you like."

I was shocked and hurt. "Erasmus, I thought we were a team? Like Batman and Robin. Like peanut butter and jelly."

"Peanut butter and jelly?"

"Yeah, salty and sweet. Squishy, delicious, and fills ya' up."

"Jake, you have a way with words!"

"I learned from the best. Erasmus, I want to travel with you as long as a rainbow is ahead."

"We are a team, better than peanut butter and jelly, but since you and Mandy have become such great friends and you've met many people here in Bywater, I thought you would like to stay and go to school?"

"School? The best school I've ever been to is the *Erasmus P. Hobbs Hobo College* and as far as I see it, I'm your best student."

"My best student?

"Yeah, of course, as an Apprentice Hobo."

"So, I guess we're stuck with each other?"

"Yeah, Socrates, you, and I. As long as you remember."

"As long as I remember what?"

"No funny business!"

"Jake, I think we are in the *fun* business!"

It was almost impossible to imagine that a lifetime of love, learning, and so many experiences that touched my soul could've happened in such a short time.

New Orleans was unlike any other place in the world, and in those moments in the Crescent City, my soul and spirits soared. I danced at the Blue Nile, sang at Snug Harbor, helped a few people along the way, and like many, I stumbled, but I got back on my feet with the help of Erasmus, Marty, Liz, and the indefatigable Socrates.

My *Summer of Love* was anointed with the sweetness of music, love, play, and work. And as we say in New Orleans, "Laissez, les bons temps rouler. Yes, let the good times roll."

New Orleans to Galveston

It was difficult to say goodbye to Marty, Liz, and the people we had grown close to over these past weeks. If Erasmus had been so inclined, I would've stayed. The girls I had tutored, Jamila, Mary, and Esther, came over with a package. "Jake, we have a little present for you. Open it up!"

I unwrapped the newspaper tied with a pink ribbon, and it was a small straw doll, hair made from brown yarn, a dress of patches, and little red shoes. "This is wonderful and something I'll always keep near. Thank you, girls."

Jamila said, "It's a gris-gris doll with mojo love. We added lagniappe, of extra magic and good luck. We loved playing with you and having you as our teacher. When will you come back?"

"Erasmus and I are traveling west for a bit longer, and at the first chance, we'll come back. Thank you, I will always keep this gris-gris close."

Mandy walked over wearing overalls splashed with paint. "I'm going to miss you a lot, but remember, Jake, we're as thick as thieves now. Ain't nothing ever going to separate us again. Though Stanford keeps writing me, I'm happy he's in jail and far away. "

"Mandy, I'm really happy to hear about your good news. Fabulous! Go, girl! Will you stay at Liz and Marty's?"

"They made room for me here. I feel blessed by meeting them, connecting with Erasmus, and reconnecting with you." Then she paused, and her eyes began to tear up. "I can't believe the world of difference from Black Mountain. What would have happened to us if we had stayed there?"

I looked at Mandy, almost a mirror image of myself. Two girls from a hopelessly broken town in West Virginia, a place without a future. I was proud of her for turning her life around. "Kismet! That's what Erasmus calls it. A stroke of cosmic good fortune!"

"Jake, what does the road look like for you ahead? Will you come back here or go with Erasmus?"

"Erasmus is going to see a doctor in Galveston and then he wants to head up to Sedona, Arizona. He says some traditional medicine healers will help him," I said with all the optimism I could muster.

"Jake, thanks for finding me in New Orleans. I believe there was a higher power at work when you found me down on Chartres Street. I can't believe I was working for Stanford. I felt like I had slid into some incredibly dark dungeon, and now I feel like a rose growing up from the sludge."

We hugged and held each other tight, and then it was time to go.

Erasmus was also making his rounds. "Marty and Liz, I am beyond words of gratitude for all you've done for Jake, Mandy, me, and all the people you've helped here."

Marty smiled and said, "It's like all your work, Erasmus. In our small way, we're trying to heal the suffering and pain of the world."

Liz said, "Here is a food basket of treats for the days ahead. We're very grateful for your visit. As you know, anytime you and Jake want to come back, there's always a place for you."

A line band was heading up Dauphine and playing "When the Saints Go Marching In." I wanted to stay in this always extraordinary city of the Big Easy. Erasmus looked healthier than I had seen in a long time. I was afraid the accident would've knocked him out, but like a true champ, he had got back up on his feet.

We left through the French Quarter and drove over to Canal Street. I didn't want to leave New Orleans. It felt like home, and I was just discovering all the rooms in this elegant city graced with centuries of stories, flower-filled gardens, more voodoo magic charm than one could imagine, and yes, the music that always filled the air with song and festivities.

We drove towards Houma and on to Dulac on the Gulf of Mexico. The smell of brine, salt water, and the Bayou filled my senses. The shrimp boats of Dulac were in the harbor with their nets like a ghostly spider web woven thick with the memory of a thousand journeys out to the Gulf, their mast lines and ropes snapping in the sunset breeze.

Erasmus said, "I like the peacefulness of this coastal drive on the way to Lafayette." The wide-open vista and bayous stretched to the Gulf of Mexico, and the sunset's orange, violet, and magenta colors filled the sky, reflecting a shimmering light like diamonds dancing on the water.

As Erasmus was driving, he told me this story of the Rugaroo.

"Beware Rugaroo of da Grand Calliou. Hush my children to tell the story of da Rugaroo. Ecoutez bien. Here is my story. I tell this story true. In da Bayou deep of Houma where da Rugaroo roams. He steals the bad children from home. When da mojo moon glows in the Bayou. The good children, he only nibbles their toes! Under the covers! Under the covers! Sleep tight! Sleep tight! To keep away da Rugaroo! And night, tucks low to dream soon you'll see. That creature who may be large or wee. Owls call out, *Whooooo. Whoooooooo. Whooooooo.*"

Erasmus acted out the parts of his story, and I laughed. "Where did you learn that story?"

"I wrote it based on the story of a creature from the swamp. How did you like it?"

"It's totally you, 'Rasmus!" I loved his fabulous storytelling and playfulness. He could make up a story so funny a vulture would fall off a funeral cart from laughter.

Erasmus said, "Climate experts say, the sad truth is that this will all be gone in fifty years. Global climate change, deforestation, and people living on the coast have all contributed to the terrible destruction. The loggers chopped down all the trees in the swamps to build houses in

New Orleans. Only one huge problem: when you cut down the trees in a bayou, you destroy the ecosystem. Cypress trees hold the water and earth. Then the Mississippi and all the tributaries were altered, dammed, and constantly changed by the Corps of Engineers and others. It's suicidal."

"Erasmus, why are people so dumb?"

"People may be smart, but there are a lot of greedy people who are only interested in themselves and their profits. From what you told me of Black Mountain, it's an ecological disaster. It's the same thing with places along the Gulf of Mexico. Mother Nature is screaming, but we ain't listening."

He parked *Emma Goldman* at Pat's Fisherman's Warf in Henderson, Louisiana. "Let's get some dinner, and then tomorrow we're going canoeing in the Atchafalaya."

We heard the hot sounds of Buckwheat Zydeco as we pulled up to Pat's Fisherman's Warf. In New Orleans, we had danced to Cajun music that set my feet tapping! In Louisiana, Cajun and zydeco were as common as hot sauce, and I wanted that hot sauce on my table all the time.

Pat's was an old-fashioned restaurant, and the smell of fried fish filled the air. We sat on the patio overlooking the river. We didn't often eat at restaurants, but it had the yummiest food in the area. Erasmus had wandered back into the kitchen to check out the options.

"I will admit," said Erasmus. "It's hard to stay vegan with such delicious gumbo and fish, but the chef is going to make us something special."

"That sounds fabulous. Did the cook mind?"

"He was gracious enough to whip something up."

When dinner arrived, a burly young Black man with a chef's apron and hat came over. "Mr. Erasmus, I made you and your granddaughter *Mama's Love Etouffee* with a special side of collards and Cajun spiced grits. Bon appetit!"

"Wow, this smells heavenly. Thank you! I hope it wasn't too much trouble," said Erasmus.

He said, "I'm a Seventh-day Adventist and my momma always cooks vegan. So, it wasn't a problem what you asked, and I love cooking veggie soul food."

"Please, sit down," said Erasmus.

We ate and chatted with Michael as he poured glasses of lemonade tea with mint.

I was starving and dug in. "Erasmus, how come you never cook me anything like this? This is so delicious and zingy it makes my toes laugh with delight!"

"Laugh with delight? Huh! You are the neologist extraordinaire! Even if I wanted to, I could never in a hundred years make anything as delicious as *Mama's Love Etouffee.*"

Michael chuckled. "Glad you liked it. I'd love to stay and chat, but I hear the kitchen crew calling. We have a big dinner party coming tonight. We don't get enough calls for vegan Cajun soul food! Y'all come back now, ya hear?" He gave a big jolly laugh as he sauntered back to the kitchen.

The band was setting up with the accordion, bass, guitars, and fiddles.

I went back to *Emma* and put on my pretty flouncy dress from Alice in Cleveland, a bit of makeup, and dress sandals, and tied a red satin ribbon in my hair. I looked at myself in the mirror, and for a girl from Black Mountain, I looked very fine.

When I came back, Erasmus was at a table chatting with some folks.

"Wow, Jake! You look pretty. Everyone, this is Jake, and I have a feeling she's going to dance all night long."

"Miss, my name is Antoine, and I'd be honored if you would permit me the first dance." He was a handsome elderly gentleman wearing a black suit with spangles, polished black boots, a bolo tie, and a stylish black straw hat with a small yellow feather. He gave me a bow with his hat and led me to the dance floor. I curtsied back to him. I figured I'd have to go slow with this older gentleman. Boy, was I wrong! When the band began, he said, "This is Clifton Chenier's 'Squeeze-Box Boogie.' Shall we boogie, my dear?" Mr. Antoine, born and raised here, was the zydeco dance champ of Lafayette. "Darling, just follow the beat, and let me lead you."

I ain't never seen anyone dance so fancy! I learned the steps by following him, he gave me a turn and a twirl, and my pretty pink dress was in a swirl. I looked over to Erasmus, who gave me a huge smile as he took out his harmonica and began blowing with the band. The band leader looked over and waved him to the bandstand.

My feet found the beat, and Mr. Antoine was easy to dance with. Another woman was next to Erasmus, and the two of them soon stepped out on the dance floor. The entire night, I don't think I had much of a rest, but who needed rest when there were all these great dancers? I said to Erasmus. "I hate to sound like a naïve kid, but all these old guys and gals can dance!"

Erasmus said, "So you think us old guys are slow? Well, my dear Jake, let's try a twirl on the dance floor."

We danced to Clifton Chenier's "Zydeco Cha Cha," and everyone got on their feet for the last dance. Young and old were singing and dancing, twisting and turning, and feet were tapping fast. Erasmus's eyes shined with delight as we turned around the dance floor. Whatever might make you blue or sad, listen to that music for a moment, and your spirits will simply fly. I later learned how the incredible struggles of the Cajun, the discrimination they faced, the poverty and oppression, and their emergence with a strong identity were best spoken about in dance and music.

At the end of the night, the musicians' tip bucket was overflowing, and Mr. Antoine came up to me and said, "Miss Jake and Mr. Erasmus, adieu, merci bien por fait la dance. Thank you for the dance."

I turned to the people we had been dancing with and said with a small curtsy, "Merci bien por vous."

Chef Michael said, "Tout le monde! Lache pas la patate." Which is a Cajun expression of pride meaning, "don't hold the potatoes." I wasn't sure what it meant exactly, but everyone stood up, cheered, and also called out, "Lache pas la patate!"

It must have been well past midnight when we got back to *Emma*. Socrates barely stirred, opened his eyes, and fell back to sleep. Erasmus massaged my feet with arnica oil. "Jake, my dancing zydeco queen." I don't even remember getting undressed. I fell asleep as Erasmus put a comforter over me and said, "Dormez bien."

I remembered the applause and cheers in my head as I went to sleep.

The birds chattering woke me up from a deep sleep. It was still dark out, and I looked at the clock to see that it was 8 a.m. Socrates was snoozing next to me. He had the cutest little snuffling snore.

Erasmus was cooking up front on the stove. "Good morning, sleepy! Man, you were one dancing girl last night! You didn't sit down once! You must be starving."

Like always, once he said food, I was immediately hungry and sang to him, "So, hey good looking what ya' got cooking? How about cooking something up for me?" Even before I had my first tea or washed my face, I was humming one of those great zydeco dance tunes from last night. My feet were sore, but I was happy.

"Grits, fruit, and papaya juice should get you started. You were everybody's favorite dancer. They want you back. After you learned the steps Antoine, Captain Jacque, and everyone wanted a dance with you. I spoke with Captain Jacque last night and he left us a canoe to paddle on through the Bayou. Freshen up and let's eat! I'm ready for a paddle!"

We sat outside while the morning light was creeping up on the Bayou. The birds were chattering and it was like a heavenly choir. Light came through the canopy of Spanish moss and the cypress trees loomed overhead. On the riverbanks, herons and egrets were already on the hunt, and the great blue heron rose up in the morning, her wings spread in a fluttering flight of blue. A gator appeared, sleepily swam along, and opened its big yap for breakfast.

Though my feet ached, I managed to do some yoga and stretches. Erasmus, limber as always, did his half hour of hatha yoga and played guitar. I could have easily stayed in this little sanctuary. Everywhere I turned the world was alive with the sounds of the Bayou. A dove was cooing above, a pink bird with a snout like a huge spoon was in the shallow waters, and the spectacular painted bunting was nearby. I took out my camera and snapped a picture so I could draw it later.

"Look at her blue, red, yellow, and green. I've got to paint her."

"Let's go canoeing! I'm going to leave Socrates here. I don't want him to be a tempting target for gators."

I was grateful to be in a canoe as my feet ached. It was an ache tempered with all the joy of having danced with the finest dancers in southern Louisiana. The stately cypresses loomed above us with their drape of Spanish moss. Erasmus paddled steadily, his strokes barely disturbing the water. I was supposed to be helping, but he was good enough at it that I was basically along for the ride and only occasionally paddled. We headed into the heart of the Atchafalaya. The sunlight broke through the thick bald cypress trees, and butterflies in bright orange, yellow, and blue dashes of color danced above the waters. Swamp snakes slithered along the water's edge, the silent assassins swiftly devouring their prey.

We came to an old fishing shack with a rusted tin roof, worn grey siding, old pirogues by the side, and Spanish moss growing over the house. The Atchafalaya was alive with light, color, sounds, and stillness. A gangly man with a long scraggly white beard, a deep sunburned brown face, and a mat of grey-white hair appeared. He looked up and seemed startled to see us.

I said to Erasmus, "I hope we didn't bother him."

Erasmus whispered, "I was told by Captain Jacque that these Cajuns in Atchafalaya are part Cajun, Cree, Black, and White. They've lived in the swamp for generations and have their own language. Yes, we should pass on by, we don't want to impose on him."

The man waved us toward shore. I was afraid and thought he looked dangerous, but then he smiled a toothless smile through his long white beard. He was standing over a big boiling pot and stirring. We tied up to the grey broken-down dock.

Erasmus called out, "Bonjour! Ca va, Capitaine?"

The man nodded, pointed to the boiling pot, and mumbled something like, "Gumbo, bienvenue." I couldn't understand him, but he gave us two beaten metal bowls and poured a heap of gumbo, gave us a chunk of bread, and soon we were slurping down delicious Atchafalaya gumbo.

He joined us and I said, "Monsieur c'était très bien!"

He looked up, nodded his head, and smiled. "Mais, oui."

His blue eyes sparkled when he smiled, and his long white beard reminded me of Santa Claus. A Santa Claus of the Bayou!

I said, "Monsieur, une chanson pour vous?"

He nodded and I sang, "Iko, Iko jocko Mo feena nay nay."

He took his metal spoons and tapped out a beat on his knees and on the blackened metal kettle. Erasmus brought out the harmonica in his pocket, and in that Bayou afternoon, we were rocking the woods. Shyly, two small children looked out of the cabin door and were soon dancing. "Alons-y!" the little one called out.

"Mes petits, allons-y," said the grandpere. "Come, my little ones."

Then he began to sing "Sont Pas Sale!" *Snap beans without salt.*

A thin barefoot Black woman came through the door with a little accordion and soon we were dancing and playing music. Grandpere took out his frottoir, a washboard with bells and a whistle, and it sounded like a proper zydeco band.

The mother, Maria, later told us, "We had lived in Baton Rouge, but the city became too poor and dangerous, so I brought my girls to live out here with my grandpere. He doesn't speak much English, and his Cajun is from Atchafalaya—and Cajun folks from Lafayette can hardly understand him. He doesn't know much about the outside world, but he taught my girls and me how to hunt, cook, and use the medicines that grow here in the swamp."

"This sounds like my friend Sojourner. She knows all the medicinal plants in the mountains of North Carolina."

Maria said, "My grandma, before she died, was called the Cajun Vodun, because she took care of all our people here, and my grandpere also knows all the plants. See here, this is *le sureau* growing next to me, good for breathing problems. I don't know what it's called in English."

I said, "This is Sambucus, or elderberry. It's an antiviral and good for infections. You can make a tea or a compress."

Erasmus looked at me. "Jake, how do you know elderberry is Sambucus?"

"Besides you, Sojourner and the herbalists were fantastic teachers. Look at this plant over here and tell me what it is."

Maria held the leaf in her hand and said, "Lozeille sauv, but I don't know the English name."

Erasmus said, "This may be yellow dock."

"Yes, it's Rumex Crispus, now you're catching on, Erasmus," I said with a wink.

"I thought you were only having fun with Sojourner. I didn't realize you downloaded an encyclopedia of herbs. Impressive!"

I blushed and said, "It was only the first chapter. I'll go back one day and keep working with her, but my first task is to take you to Galveston and then to the Navajos to get you better."

"Aye aye, Captain Jake!"

When we left, Erasmus gave Grandpere his favorite harmonica. Grandpere looked at this fine fancy harmonica and blew a zydeco tune. Maria said, "My grandpere wrote this song. It's called 'Mes Cher Amis.' The lyric in English is, 'You are my dear friend. You see me through troubles. You see me through joy. You are always my friend.'"

Grandpere looked at Erasmus and gave him some kind of medicine. "Pour votre santé, une cuillère deux fois par jour."

I wondered, did Grandpere know about Erasmus's health problems and what was the medicine he gave him?

Erasmus shook his hand and said, "Merci bien."

I took off my earrings and gave the girls one apiece. They giggled as they put them on.

We slipped back into our canoe, Grandpere, Maria, and the girls waving to us. "Bon voyage."

A morning canoe ride in the swamp that was supposed to be an hour or two had turned into an adventure into a new world. I had heard hundreds of bird songs and the sounds of fluttering butterflies, and the taste of yummy gumbo lingered on my lips.

Before I went to sleep Erasmus sang me a song. "Dor, dors, p'tit bebe – Sleep well, sleep well, my little baby."

Erasmus said, "My grandmother was French Canadian, and many had migrated south into Vermont and New England. The Cajun mothers would sing, 'Dor Dor Petit Bebe.'"

In the morning, I was laughing to myself, thinking of all the fun we had at Pat's two nights ago. I was the dancing queen as Antoine, Pierre, Jacque, Erasmus, and others danced me silly and my feet still delightfully ached.

I made a pot of grits with berries and chicory coffee for us. After many months of him serving me, in the small ways I could, I wanted to serve and help Erasmus. Little did I realize in the coming weeks, I'd have demands on my emotions and hardships that would rattle my soul.

I rarely spoke of what it was like to live inside *Emma Goldman*, our Airstream 310 modified and transformed one summer a long time ago by Lake Memphremagog. I always wanted to visit this lake with the huge name, which simply meant "big lake."

Our home, *Emma Goldman*, was a thirty-foot-long work of art, with teak handmade cabinets, granite countertops, and bookcases of polished yellow pine. *Emma* always gave me a sense of peace and welcome. When I first stepped inside as a frightened, soaking-wet kid filled with tears and anger, I simply wanted to fold myself into a blanket and disappear. In this womb of carpets, hand-woven blankets, and dozens of books I found my sanctuary.

The captain chairs were made with luxuriant fabric from Guatemala. There were Berber red, gold, and black carpets from Morocco. The silk pillows on the couch were from Thailand. Erasmus once said, "Though I don't like to shop and collect things, each one of these carpets and weavings are from a special place that I love." Above the couch, he had a charcoal portrait of his father entitled, *Dad—Irascible James Hobbs*. He also had portraits of his mom as a young woman, Angela Hobbs, his brother Henry David, and his son, who was also named Henry David after his brother. To the right was a charcoal portrait of me with my straw hat with the pretty pink ribbon and underneath he wrote, *Jake—My Fellow Hobo*. It showed up one morning and I had been startled to see it. I was honored to be included in his constellation of family and friends. There were other portraits throughout our home of Sojourner, Roshi, Marty, and Liz.

In our *Summer of Love*, it became *our* home, a home that smelled of comfort and sandalwood and spoke of Erasmus's journeys around the world.

He told me the story of what he called *The Creation of Galatea – Emma Goldman*. When he first met *Emma Goldman*, she was an old Airstream 310 sitting in a friend's barn and his friend said, "If you want her, take her."

Erasmus said, "In an instant, I fell in love with her. As you remember, Emma Goldman was a revolutionary anarchist. My mother's aunt was in Emma Goldman and Ben Reitman's circle of friends and regaled us with tales of their crew of anarchist free-loving radicals.

"My friends said, 'Erasmus, it's a fool's mission, but since foolishness and Erasmus go hand-in-hand so well, it's perfect for you.'

"Friends and family came by and the project became known as 'Erasmus's Folly.' I took over an old barn in Newport, Vermont. The goal was to figure out how to make it lighter. Generally, an RV weighs in at seven thousand pounds, and every ounce counts. Eventually, *Emma Goldman* weighed in at a sleek four thousand pounds.

"I was restoring a house at the same time and we ripped out the teak floorboards and used them for the cabinets. With friends, we took everything down to the bare bones. Every loose screw was fixed. From step to stern, all the wiring was replaced. This was my university. Many things I didn't know how to do, but in Vermont, we figure things out or ask a friend.

"One day Sojourner and Captain Jim showed up in downtown Newport. I had sent them postcards in California. I was two miles from downtown, and someone came and said, 'There are two people downtown looking for you. One is a Black man about six-foot-five, and the gal is a tall woman who looks like an Abenaki.'

"When I heard that, I immediately knew who they were talking about, but how did they find me? I washed up and hopped in my jeep, and sure enough, it was easy to find them.

"'Jim! Sojourner! How the hell did you find me here?'

"'We got this postcard from you last month saying you fell in love with a lady by the name of Emma Goldman, and you said she was one of the loveliest creatures you had ever laid eyes on. So, Jim and I were itching for a road trip and there isn't a more lovely place on the globe than Vermont. We wanted to see who this incredible lady was who swept you off your feet.'

"I smiled. 'Come, I'll show you this lovely lady, but you may get jealous.'

"Sojourner said, 'I love the smell of Vermont, cows and horses, and skies that stretch forever. We missed you in California!'

"'Yes, I have to come back to Vermont to recharge myself periodically and visit family and friends. Come with me. Are you ready to meet *Emma*?'

"They stood in the barn with the ghosted shell of a thirty-foot Airstream RV, with the interior splayed out on the floor and benches. To the side on a sheet of plywood was a big hand-drawn diagram. On a sheet of aluminum was a drawing of the revolutionary Emma Goldman dancing accompanied by her most famous quote in large letters: *If I can't dance, I don't want to be part of your revolution.*

"Jim looked at Sojourner and then at me and burst out laughing! 'So, this is the love of your life?'

"'Yeah, you got a problem with it?' I asked.

"We laughed hard and fell into the pile of hay as we looked at the bones of *Emma Goldman*. Sojourner said, 'I knew you would find the love of your life.'

"It was early August and with Jim, Sojourner, Phil the Tinker, a bunch of friends, and family, we created *Emma Goldman*."

Erasmus said, "I had met Sojourner in Venice Beach. She was an herbalist and a healer, and saved our lives. When Jim and I were still drinking she kicked our butts and got us sober. She was a physician in California, but I found out in rebuilding *Emma* in Vermont she was also a terrific self-taught mechanic and engineer.

"When we were rebuilding *Emma,* she was a woman possessed. She looked at the engine on the Airstream and started to mumble. She took out a notepad and as fast as most people type, she wrote out calculations and, on a chalkboard, made a diagram of the engine.

"Sojourner said, 'Yeah, I know this beauty. You boys can help, but I have an idea for this diesel engine, and I read about a new design where we can use just about any fuel to run the engine. Our friend Phil the Tinker is also a terrific mechanic.'

"She walked around the Airstream, mumbling, taking notes, and finally said, 'Boys, we're going to have a lot of fun in the next month. However, you're going to have to get your lazy butts in gear.'

"The next morning, Sojourner woke us up with two coffees. 'Boys, let me show you what I worked out last night while you slugs were snoozing.'

"On big rolls of paper, she had drawn out the engine, the driveshaft, and the entire mechanical, refrigeration, electrical, and solar systems for the RV. It was an almost flawless hand-drawn schematic. She said, 'I hate to be picky, but who's the dummy who designed the drain and the septic? Here is a more efficient way. Also, by recalibrating the engine and tinkering with the heads, we can make it even more efficient. The wiring from the Airstream is old and there's a better way.'

"Jim and I were in a state of shock. Sojourner, our healer, herbalist, spiritual cheerleader, and awesome drummer left us speechless. 'How did you learn to do all of this?' I asked.

"'Necessity is the mother of invention. I had some of old cars and no money, and I needed to figure out a way to fix them up and sell them to help pay my way through medical school. Drink your coffee. I made some waffles, and you're going to need them as we have a lot of work ahead. I wish I could have talked with the Airstream engineers. I don't know what they were thinking when they designed this refrigeration. We're going to make *Emma Goldman* sing like the beautiful lady she is.'

"True to her word, Sojourner kicked our butts. Jim and I would have worked a few hours a day and then gone for a swim and a hike, but she was a woman on a mission. She was the Chief of the Works, with designs, schematics, and work schedules laid out. She was a force of nature and many people stopped by and wanted to know how she tweaked and modified the RV. How was she able to get it to run on diesel and vegetable oil? Rumors started to fly, and people came by with their motorhomes. She said, 'I'll help you, but the cost is we got to get *Emma Godman* ready to fly before the first snow.'

"Welders, sheet metal fabricators, solar panel electricians, and ordinary folks were tickled by the idea of transforming a rundown, nearly busted RV into a small palace on wheels. Soon there were a dozen trailers parked outside as people heard about this Airstream mechanic and wanted her help.

"While Sojourner and Jim organized the volunteers, I had a small woodshop in the corner and fitted the cabinets, milled the floors, made the benches and storage, and made the floors and ceilings from leftover lumber. I lined the inside walls and ceiling with spruce-fir lattice. Vermont is a land of innovation and invention. We didn't have a lot, but if I needed wood, someone had it lying around in a barn. My cousin the electrician suddenly showed up with all the wiring for the refrigeration, cooling, showers, stoves, and lights. Phil the Tinker helped with the wiring and engine rebuild.

"Originally, I wanted a simple upgrade, but no one argues with Sojourner. What would have taken me over a year or two of dawdling, diddling about, and such—she had the Gantt chart on the walls with the timelines and worked with the efficiency of an OCD project engineer.

"Something magical was happening! It was like a barn raising in Vermont. Dozens of people come together with food, drinks, tools, and a lot of sweat, and made *Emma*."

Erasmus said, "The reason I'm telling you this, Jake, is that when you look at *Emma Goldman*, I know you see a lot of the beauty. But I want you to know about all the sweat, fun, arguments, failures, and help from many people that went into her. And of course, Jim and Sojourner, who hung in with me until the first snow at Thanksgiving. I knew they wanted to go back to California, but we needed to finish it.

"Jim said, 'Sojourner and I want to talk to you about an idea that has been in my head. I want to have a community where I can work on my Buddhist practice, and a place for recovering addicts. My uncle in western North Carolina just died and left me a hundred acres, with a broken-down house and a barn. We're going to California to tie up loose ends, but Erasmus, would you like to meet us in the spring in North Carolina and maybe we can fix up the place?'

"I said, 'Let's get *Emma Goldman* up and dancing like the elegant lady she is, and then we can definitely plan for this Dignity Village.'

"Sojourner said, 'Dignity Village? Why did you call it that?'

"'It just rolled off the tip of my tongue. I'm not sure where the name came from. Maybe it's an homage to you, Sojourner? You helped Jim and I reclaim our dignity and got our lives back on track.'

"'I agree with you, Erasmus!' said Jim. 'I had this dream last night and it had to do with dignity and reclaiming our identity. Like our journey when we first met in Venice Beach. Talk about serendipity!'

"This was the start of Dignity Village, with a house that had more mice than nails and was more broken than mended, but it was a perfect place to start. Sojourner, Roshi, myself, and many hundreds of volunteers worked to create the sanctuary.

"In the last weeks, the mechanicals were finished, the water and waste systems were installed, and solar panels were put on top of the RV. The wood still smelled like it had been freshly milled and polished with Tung oil, and the dovetails and miter joints were as smooth as a baby's bottom.

"It was serendipity that guided the transformation of *Emma Goldman*. It was like the story of Pygmalion creating Galatea, the statute that came to life with the guidance of the goddess Aphrodite. Our *Emma Goldman* hummed along in her 145 SAE horsepower, with an astonishing efficiency in weight and power for such a venerable lady.

"Caleb, a ceramist who had worked for NASA, happened to be strolling around downtown Newport and found his way to our workshop. Sojourner was talking to him about the problem with the aluminum aircraft coating, and then the two of them disappeared into a technical mumbo jumbo that was lost to Jim and me as we were finishing the last folding bed and installing the solar panels.

"Caleb said, 'When I worked at NASA we had a similar challenge, how to create a lightweight heat-resistant shield to protect the spaceships. I have friends in Burlington with a ceramic and paint studio, and they would love to take this on.' True to his word, a rainbow-colored bus rolled up the next week and the paint crew was ready.

"Five workers in spray masks and suits had brought gallons of a special light ceramic paint that had been mixed up in a chemistry lab at UVM. The volunteers meticulously cleaned the exterior, and at last, the layers of this light yellow ceramic paint were applied. Then we waited overnight to see what she would look like in the sun.

"The following morning as the sun rose, we all took the tape and wrapping off of *Emma*," Erasmus said. "I was afraid it would turn into some disaster, but with Sojourner and Caleb at the helm, it was perfect!

"We gently wheeled her out to the meadow as the last shroud and wrapping were taken off. Sunlight bathed *Emma*, and it was a golden yellow with sparkles of the glass coating and splashes of purple, orange, and dashes of emerald. Everyone gasped as the sunlight bathed our beauty.

"I would have sprayed automotive paint, but truly no words can describe this. It's not too bright to blind the other drivers, but a golden hue with many splashes of sunlight. With help, we painted the outline of Emma Goldman dancing on the side, along with her famous quote, 'If I can't dance, I don't want to be part of your revolution.'

"Thus," said Erasmus, "this was the start of a love affair with dear *Emma*."

"Wow, Erasmus that is some story!"

"We're still an hour from Lake Charles. Why don't you drive?"

Although I had driven *Emma Goldman* on the road once before this was still a terrifying proposition, but Erasmus's confidence quieted my doubts. I did all the things I was supposed to do like checking the mirrors, and soon we were rolling.

Erasmus said, "Keep going. You're driving like a champ."

Lake Charles passed in a haze. The smell of the refinery with its thick black clouds of sulphur hung in the air and I felt like I was breathing heavier. We rolled up the windows and turned on the air conditioner.

"This is Louisiana at its worst intersection of racism, pollution, politics, and the insatiable greed and collusion of the oil and chemical companies," Erasmus said as we drove along the highway that he called "Cancer Alley."

"This is one of the poorest parts of the state, with all these chemicals pouring out of the smokestacks. Terrible things like chloride, benzene, dioxins, and all the residue from the refineries. I sometimes feel hopeless about humanity when I see this crazy stuff."

I said, "It's like Black Mountain with all the chemicals polluting the water, the sludge from the mines, and the land barren."

We drove through Lake Charles. I wished we could take all the people away from this misery. Refineries were to my right with flames coming out of the gas stacks. Poor broken-down wooden shacks surrounded them.

Yet, within a few miles of the refineries and plants, the Gulf of Mexico and the beaches beckoned. This is the paradox of Lake Charles. It has beautiful bayous, rivers, and the Gulf, but the factories and refineries keep pouring out this toxic brew.

Despite the horrible pollution, it was smooth sailing across the Louisiana line into Texas. Another first for me, reaching Texas. Erasmus took out his guitar and started singing "Deep in the Heart of Texas." Socrates was between us snoozing contentedly.

Galveston welcomed us with its wide sunny smile and warm sultry breezes. I wanted to jump in the Gulf and swim all the way to Mexico, but I would settle for a splash in the water. We came down to the waterfront and parked in the shade. I loved the sound of the Gulf and the palm trees swaying by the oceanfront.

Though it wasn't quite the ocean, I had the feeling I was swimming in the Pacific. I hoped when Erasmus felt better, we would find our way to California. He often spoke of his time there with great fondness and sadness.

We had some burritos and roasted corn by the pleasure pier. Erasmus said, "Let me tell you about how Roshi Jim and I met Sojourner." With Socrates nestling between us, Erasmus told me the story.

"Galveston reminds me of Venice Beach where Jim and I were lost until we found Sojourner. She was a strikingly lovely lady with dark brown hair tied with ribbons, sitting on a bench and drumming. Jim and I were walking past. She said, 'What took you boys so long to show up?'

"'Miss, I think you have us mistaken for somebody else,' I said.

"She looked up at me. 'Take off your sunglasses, open your eyes, and remember who you are.'

"In Venice Beach, you meet many strange people. Jim said to me, 'You don't know her. Do you?'

"'No, but she seems familiar. We've been drinking a lot, but I would've remembered somebody as beautiful as her. I'll meet you back at the apartment, I want to go back and talk to her.'

"I walked back to where she had been sitting, but she was gone. The next day and the following one, I showed up at the same spot at around the same time, but I couldn't find her. I looked all the way from the pier down to Venice, and the longer I looked, the more I knew I needed to find her.

"Jim said to me, 'There are plenty of other women around. Why would you get hung up on this one? She's pretty, but I think she's stuck up. Let's get some weed and light up for sunset.'

"'No, I'm going to look for her.'

"Finally, after a week we found her again. She looked at us. 'Are you two ready to begin?'

"Jim said, 'What do you mean, begin? Like to drum, or should we go out and party?' He winked.

"'You boys have been boys for long enough. It's time for you to live your true dharma.'

"Jim asked, 'What you mean, dharma? I heard of the book *Dharma Bums*.'

"'You're lost and need to find your real path. Are you ready?'

"The wind shifted and storm clouds rolled in from the ocean. It started to rain, and she covered her drum with a tarp. 'My name is Sojourner. I'm a drummer and a healer. I have a small house nearby for yoga and healing. I've been waiting for you two. Something told me that I need to help you both get back on the path. You have far more important things to do in life than drinking, drugging, and being party animals. Are you ready?'

"I was shocked as I looked at her and her lustrous brown eyes. It suddenly hit me as if somebody had slapped me upside the head that she was right. Suddenly, I found myself sitting beside her and crying. She held me close.

"Over the next month, Sojourner helped Jim and I get sober. Every morning we would meet on the beach in Santa Monica at sunrise, do yoga, and run."

I said, "I still find it almost impossible to believe that you and Roshi Jim were such…derelicts. Yes, that's the word. You two were bums. Drunken and stoned bums wandering. It's nothing like you two now."

"This was the weirdest damn thing. You're right, Jake. I felt like some cosmic intervention suddenly came down and woke both of us up, and that divine intervention was Sojourner. How she found us and how she knew we had another destiny -- is still beyond me."

"I feel the same way about Sojourner. She has an incredible wisdom and kindness."

Erasmus said, "Yes, that is all true, but she also has a toughness and steely resolve that transforms everybody around her. But there is nothing ostentatious in the way she does it. Like when we started Dignity Village, her vision, skill, and wisdom brought it forward, and she had the sweat and guts to make it happen. Too many of us have a dream of what we would like to do, but most times it never materializes. She has the true mystic calling—feet rooted in the earth, and spirit in the heavens."

"I don't get that, Erasmus. What do you mean?"

"She has ancient Cherokee wisdom and a very pragmatic way of making things happen and she is incredibly smart. A visionary may have an idea, but it's a very rare person who can take that idea and make it real. In a way, she made Jim and me. We were these broken-down veterans, wallowing in our pity and pain, and somehow, she saw through this. Many of the people you've met like Marty and Liz have also been touched by her grace."

"How so?"

"Through a long and strange journey, they met Sojourner years ago in New Orleans. This is how the story gets really strange according to Liz.

"Liz told me that she and Marty were by the broken-down pier where a woman was drumming at sunset. They didn't pay any attention, since there are so many musicians in New Orleans. She stopped drumming and said to them, 'Hello, please sit with me and enjoy the sunset.' She drummed and finally as the sun was setting into the Mississippi she said, 'You two seem like you're ready to take the next step. What do you think?' Marty and Liz looked at each other and knew at that moment what they needed to do. All of their attachment to their religious vocations, and most importantly their fears, simply vanished. They turned and asked her, 'What should we do next?'

"She took out a small mirror from her bag and held it in front of them. 'The answer is quite clear. Isn't it?' They wrote their resignation letters to the Catholic Church.

"They found an empty warehouse across from Saint Francis on Dauphine Street. The Church was furious with them for leaving and tried to cut them off without money, but Marty and Liz were in love. Nothing could stop them, but they couldn't find Sojourner again. A year later she walked into the place that became the Church of Love. She had a van full of herbs, potions, and such. She said, 'If you like I can make a small herbal pharmacy and show you how to use it.'

"Marty and Liz had never heard of plants as medicines, but Sojourner made the herbal medicines in Dignity Village and would come down with apprentices every six months to teach and restock the pharmacy."

That evening we hung out by the waterfront in Galveston. We found a food truck with vegan burritos and sat down to watch the sunset with Socrates. The next day, Erasmus had to see a specialist, Doctor Swamivinda, but tonight it was only the three of us watching the enchanted evening sunset.

Erasmus took out his guitar and we started playing near the burrito truck. I had a tambourine and I was singing all of our favorite songs. I put my hat down on the bench and after a few songs, it started to fill up with money. "Jake, since we made all this money, go over to Juan at the burrito truck and give it to him for those homeless people sitting over there."

A homeless man, woman, and child were sitting nearby and after Juan brought them the food that we had paid for, they walked over to us. "Thank you, Mister, we appreciate your kindness," the man said. "We had been renting our house for a long time and a new owner took over and before we knew it, we were out on the street. We have our van and some friends we're going to stay with in San Antonio. Your kindness of dinner and song lifted our spirits. Can I play a song for you?"

Erasmus said, "Sure thing. Play us a song."

He sang folk songs from Mexico like "La Bamba." The hat filled up again! We gave more money to Juan and he said, "There are no more homeless people who need burritos tonight. You keep the money."

I said, "Sadly, there will be more homeless people who will need food. I know that you give what you can, but Erasmus and I want to give you some extra money to cover your cost."

"Miss, if more people were as kind as you and Erasmus are the world would be a far better place."

That evening we met many people from Nicaragua, Chile, and Mexico to teach us songs. I felt like this kind of night would last forever.

A man with a cowboy hat and long braided grey hair walked by in the shadows. He said, "I know a song, can we sing? It's called 'Crazy,' the Patsy Cline song."

He took the guitar from Erasmus and sang "Crazy" with a twangy rusty voice.

Erasmus said, "Man, you sound just like Willy Nelson, only better."

The man faced Erasmus under the streetlamp, smiled, and said, "You think so? I'm glad I sounded better than Willy."

Erasmus looked at the man and said, "For once in my life, I am truly lost for words. Willy, please, one more song."

Willy smiled and said, "I'd love to stay longer and play, but I have a show in San Antonio and the tour bus is about to leave. Thank you for keeping the music alive. You and your granddaughter are a joy."

They shook hands, and I said, "Thank you, Mr. Willy."

Our hat had a crisp fifty-dollar bill in it and on the back, he had written, *Thank you, Willy!*

We taped that bill over our dining room table, put our guitar and tambourine in *Emma*, and strolled along the pier of Galveston. We walked over to the Ferris wheel and the amusement park that was set up by the waterfront. Erasmus said, "Come on! Let's hop on board."

Socrates, Erasmus, and I were soon aloft. Socrates was yapping, standing up and mesmerized by the city lights below. The wheel took us around. It stopped at the top and for a moment I was afraid, but Socrates and Erasmus were next to me, and with them I was fearless.

When the sky burst open with fireworks, it was almost as if this special show was just for us. In the cool evening air of Galveston, suspended above, the whole world with the circus lights whirling around beneath us, the two of us were swaying in our private dreams. This was the best moment of my entire life, and these were the two that I wanted close to me: Erasmus and Socrates. Probably Sojourner and Roshi would've been ideal too, but the Ferris wheel cart might've gotten a wee bit tight.

The next morning, we woke up in the campground by the cottonwood trees, and the sunrise was glorious over the Gulf of Mexico. We had to meet Doctor Swamivinda at ten and drove up the coast, following a map drawn on paper, like a treasure map. We reached a thickly forested grove and there was a mailbox with a sign, *all welcomed!*

I knew we would find the answer.

CHAPTER EIGHT

By Fate and Fortunes Chance - We Dance

We arrived at the garden of Doctor Swamivinda near the Gulf of Mexico.

"Erasmus, are you sure this is right? This looks like a huge tropical garden." Monkeys were swinging in the trees, parrots flew above, and a peacock passed before us, his feathers rising in a glorious burst of colors.

"This is the direction I got, and besides, even if this is the wrong road, I love this garden."

A quarter mile down the road, there was a large stucco house with a gold dome and a fountain with the Indian goddess Shiva in the center of its courtyard. A man wearing a red turban appeared at the doorway. He folded his hands, bowed the way Roshi Jim bowed, and pointed to a parking spot. Erasmus was moving slowly, but we had been moving so fast these past weeks. A little slower was better.

"Welcome, Namaste," said the man. "I am Gurudev, an assistant to Doctor Swamivinda. Come in, let's have some tea, and the doctor will join us."

We walked to the interior courtyard where parakeets flew, pink flamingos splashed in the pond, and several small spider monkeys swung above us. We sat on large bright orange cushions, and a young woman with an Indian dress brought us ginger tea.

Erasmus said, "Sojourner recommended this Ayurveda doctor and I am looking forward to seeing him."

I had stepped outside of Texas and landed in India. I felt better without even meeting the doctor, although I was nervous and afraid of what he would say. I had seen my grandpa die from black lung, unable to breathe and slowly suffocating from emphysema. Though Erasmus could run up a mountain, I saw how the illnesses were making him more tired, but he never complained, and even when we rescued the girls from the car accident and he was badly cut up, he soldiered on.

The doctor was a small Indian man with a shaved head, a long, flowing white beard, and the pearliest smile I had ever seen. "Welcome, Erasmus and Jake." Doctor Swamivinda asked about our trip, then turned his attention to Erasmus, held his hand, and took his pulse. He looked at Erasmus's tongue and eyes. He nodded, and after an hour of chatting, he said, "My friend, you have a lot of mileage on your body, but I think we can help you. Not cure you, but help you. My colleague Gurudev will make up some herbs for you."

"But Doctor, can you make him better?" I blurted out.

He said, "Jake, I wish one magic pill or potion could help him. As you know, Erasmus is quite ill, despite his strong constitution. With cancer and hepatitis, he needs to rest. You can stay here at the clinic, but he seems determined to go to Sedona. These medicines will strengthen him, but ultimately, we are all in the hands of fate." Doctor Swamivinda bowed and folded his hands. "Bless you in your journey. Do call me in a week. We're here to help you."

Gurudev gave us the herbs and medicines and said, "The instructions are there."

Erasmus said, "How much do we owe you?"

"We only ask for donations from all our patients. Whatever you can afford is up to you. Namaste." With folded hands, he bid us farewell.

We drove slowly from this garden sanctuary and took the road to the Gulf of Mexico. It was almost evening, and we found a shady spot by the shore.

"So, Erasmus. Where do we go from here? What did you think of what the doctor said?"

He looked out to the Gulf. "I don't know how much time I have left, but I won't dwell on illness nor waste a moment of breath on what I don't have. Instead, I'll put my energy into savoring each moment, spending time with Socrates and the people I love, like you, and serving others in whatever small way I can. I have friends in Sedona from the Navajo reservation who will also help me. If the wind blows right, we'll head to California. There are many places to show you, from the deserts to the mountains, the beautiful Pacific highway along the coast, and the magnificent Sequoia trees and Yellowstone Park. Right now, our journey is toward San Antonio and onward to Sedona. How are you doing, Jake? I don't want to burden you with my illness."

Socrates woke up from his nap and gave a little bark. "He wants to be part of this conversation," Erasmus said.

"Socrates is always part of the conversation. I wouldn't change a single thing. Your illnesses aren't a burden, and I'm grateful to help you. Erasmus, you are my favorite hobo, and I couldn't imagine a better person to travel with."

He nodded his head and smiled. "We never know where the journey leads. Jake, thanks for hanging in and helping me."

We drove to a truck stop on the edge of town, heading north and west to San Antonio.

I put some diesel in, and Erasmus checked the fluids and tire pressure. It was a hot day, the wind was blowing strong from the Gulf, and as I looked towards the truck stop restaurant, I recognized a man at the entrance.

"Erasmus, do you see the guy over there with the long hair and the cowboy hat? Doesn't he look familiar?"

"Sure does! You saw him when we first met. He was the guitar-playing truck driver in Ohio."

We pulled *Emma* into a shady spot and walked into the restaurant.

"Aren't you Erasmus from Ohio?" asked the man as we approached. He had a straw cowboy hat, boots, denim jeans, a guitar slung over his back, and long wavy brown hair. To my sixteen-year-old dazed eyes, he was the sexiest man I had ever seen.

"Yes, and you're Matt!"

"Man, good to see you! And who is this lovely young lady?" He winked at me.

I blushed. "You don't remember me? I'm Jake."

"You look so different than when I saw you three months ago."

I said, "It's the friends I travel with. Despite my occasional gnarliness, Erasmus and Socrates are good company."

"Only occasional gnarliness, Jake?" asked Erasmus.

"Not any more than yours, my dear Erasmus P. Hobbs."

I had gone through a world of change over these past three months. The girl from Black Mountain, West Virginia, had blossomed into the new Jake Halouna Meadows—Apprentice Hobo.

"Matt, it's great to see you. Join us, and we'll tell you about some of our adventures. How've you been, and where have you been with the Magic Flyer?" asked Erasmus.

"You remember the Magic Flyer?"

"Yes, it's a dandy rig, and you were going to California. So, what happened? Did you make it there?"

"To California and back a bunch of times since I last saw you, but the engine for my truck is on its last legs, and I was getting a new one in Flagstaff."

Erasmus and I looked at each other in disbelief. "The world is a small, strange place. How are you getting there? We're heading out that way too."

"I was going to hitch a ride," Matt said. Then Socrates leaped onto his lap.

"You remember our trusty guide, Socrates?"

"Yes, love muffin. A very handsome fellow indeed."

We gabbed for a bit, and Matt started to play his guitar while we waited for breakfast. Erasmus and I never shied away from a song, and we soon joined him in "On the Road Again." Everyone joined us for the chorus before we got to the second verse.

I said, "That was great. How about, 'Goodnight Irene?'"

I started to sing, and an older man with a beautiful baritone sang the next verse, "Sit yourself down by the fireside bright…" There wasn't a dry eye in the house.

When the last chorus came around, the man sang acapella. Tears rolled down his cheeks, but his voice never wavered. This bustling diner was as silent as a church. When he was done, everyone broke into applause. "Bravo, Sam!"

On our way out to pay, the waitress said, "That was fabulous! We hadn't heard Sam sing since his wife Irene died last year."

"Irene?" I asked.

"Yes, this is a picture of the two of them from the 1950s when they sang at the rodeos—*Irene and Sam's Buckaroos*." It was a photo of a handsome couple wearing cowboy hats.

Sam came over and said, "Don't worry about the bill. This was the best medicine I've had in a long time. When my Irene died last year, I thought all my songs were gone, and today, I held her close to my heart. Anytime you want to come and sing at the diner, there's always a place for you. Here's a CD for you of Irene and me. Jake, she would have loved singing with you."

I gave him a hug and a kiss on the cheek. "Thank you, Mr. Sam."

We glided out of the diner on a cloud of good wishes.

"Erasmus, did this really happen? What was that word you use? I feel like I've been kissed by kismet."

Erasmus said, "Me too. I believe if we allow the possibility of magic and miracles, they can happen. Our intention matters the most. Matt, would you like to go to San Antonio and Sedona with us?"

"Perfect! I love your magnificent *Emma Goldman*. I can't believe all the fine cabinetry, carpets, and your art. When I get my rig, I want to make the sleeping compartment look like this."

"I'm always glad to make some cabinets, and Jake is also getting pretty good with carpentry. Last week we made new picnic benches and a swing in a park."

We headed towards San Antonio. Erasmus sat in the captain's chair behind the passenger seat dozing. Matt was driving, and I was beside him with Socrates. It was strange to see someone besides Erasmus or myself driving. I considered *Emma* "ours," but Matt was right at home. He was easy to talk to, and as Erasmus dozed, we headed west toward Brazoria National Wildlife Refuge. I rolled down the window to let in the fresh breeze from the Gulf of Mexico.

"My truck is my home, like you and Erasmus with *Emma*. My sister in Nevada gets my mail, and with more things on computers, it's even easier to be mobile."

"Do you ever miss having one place to call home and a girlfriend?" I was more interested in if he had a girlfriend than a home. A good-looking guy like him shouldn't be left alone.

Matt said, "Girlfriend, no, but I have special friends. I like how you and Erasmus went this southern route by the Gulf of Mexico. It's far more peaceful. As to home, I was an army brat as a kid. We moved every two years or so, which was a lot of fun. Though I missed having long-term childhood friends, I learned to get along with many different people. What changed for me was when my dad went to Vietnam. We didn't see him for more than two years, and when he got back, he was a different man and plagued with health problems."

"This sounds like Erasmus and his struggles with Agent Orange disease."

"What a strange coincidence. My dad also suffered from Agent Orange. He had all these problems with breathing, and his skin was inflamed, but the Army wouldn't believe him until he became very sick."

"We've been to a few doctors over the last couple of months who are trying to help Erasmus. He's in great shape most of the time, but on some days he looks weary."

"Jake, this must be hard for you, being around a person struggling with sickness like this."

"It's hard to see him sick, but he still has a lot of energy and vitality. On a good day, he can walk and swim much further than I can! These past few months have been astonishing, and I've learned so much from him. My school in West Virginia was awful, and even by the tenth grade

I could barely read or write, but with Erasmus's super patient tutoring, for the first time I read a book from cover to cover," I said. "I'm getting good enough to take my GED soon."

"Bravo, Jake. What was the book?"

"*Civil Disobedience*, by Thoreau."

"A perfect book to read while living in *Emma Goldman*. Erasmus sounds like an incredible teacher and a fabulous friend."

"Hey, do you see the truck pulled over with his flashers on?"

Erasmus woke up and said, "This is strange, don't you think, Matt? An eighteen-wheeler shouldn't be pulled over to the side of the road."

"I agree. Let's check it out," Matt said.

We found a clearing ahead of the truck and walked back to it. The driver looked like he was sleeping with his head on the wheel.

Matt leaped up, looked in, and said, "I don't think we can do anything. He's dead."

"Should we call the police?" I asked.

"No," said Erasmus. "Matt, make sure your fingerprints are wiped off the truck where you touched it."

I heard a baby crying from the inside of the truck. "What do we do?" I asked.

Matt said, "Erasmus, do you have something to break open the lock?"

"Sure thing. Jake, get the heavy hammer, and let's see if we can open this up."

When the truck doors were opened, there was not only a baby, but more than a dozen people inside. Erasmus told them in Spanish, "Don't worry, we're not the police. We only want to help."

We got the people out of the truck, gave them water, and tried to find out what happened.

They had been smuggled from Central America. One man said, "At the border, we gave the driver all our money, and he said he would help us, but we've been stuck here for hours."

"We can't call the police, they're refugees, and they'll be deported. They need help, and I have friends at a church about an hour from here. Let me make a few phone calls." Erasmus always seemed like he had friends everywhere, and today, we desperately needed some of them.

Though Matt didn't speak Spanish as well as Erasmus, he soon made everybody feel comfortable and promised them we would find them a place to rest. We had to get out of there as soon as we could. We had a dead truck driver in his rig on the side of the road and at least fifteen refugees and, if you include me as a sixteen-year-old runaway, we had a recipe for disaster.

"Let's hurry," Erasmus said. "Get them into *Emma*. The church said they would help, and the Quaker community in San Antonio will get them north to safe houses."

A young mother, Anna, with a baby said, "They took all of our papers and our money, and we had no idea where we were going. Can you please help us?"

Erasmus assured them nobody would be turned over to the police and said, "Come into the RV, and we'll drive to a church nearby. You're safe with us."

"Gracias a Dios." The woman kissed Erasmus's hand.

Erasmus drove, and Matt was in the back with me and the other people who filled up every spare inch of *Emma*.

Anna breastfed the baby, and I later found out she had just turned sixteen, and this was her second baby. Her first baby died last year. As she fed her, her eyes closed, and she quietly hummed a song, "Arroro Mi Nino."

"Hush-a-bye, my baby

Canción de cuna
Arrorró mi niño,
arrorró mi sol,
arrorró pedazo,
de mi corazón.

Este niño lindo
ya quiere dormir;
háganle la cuna
de rosa y jazmín.

Hush-a-bye my baby
Hush-a-bye my sun
Hush-a-bye oh piece
Of my heart.

This pretty child
Wants to sleep already
Make him a cradle
Of rose and jasmine."

Matt sat on the floor with Anna and the other mothers. He took out his guitar and played along until we heard a police siren and saw flashing red lights.

I moved up front as Erasmus pulled over, reached for his papers, and rolled down the window.

Erasmus said, "Hello, Officer. How are you? Something I can help you with?"

"We saw your license plates from Vermont and thought we would say hello and welcome you to the great state of Texas," said the cop looking at us through mirrored sunglasses with one hand resting on his gun.

"Mighty hospitable of you! And here are my papers."

"Besides the welcome wagon, we heard there are illegal immigrants in the area. We're checking all cars and trucks for any wetbacks."

I was terrified, but Erasmus was cool as an ice cube, even when dealing with cops.

"Do you mean refugees? If we see any, we'll let you know."

"Any contraband or drugs in your RV?" The cop tried to peer into the back.

"We're good. Were you in the First Cavalry? How long ago did you serve?"

"Actually, my uncle was in the First Calvary and was killed in Vietnam. How did you know?"

"I saw your tattoo. I was a medic in Vietnam and met a few of those soldiers."

I interrupted them. "Excuse me, Grandpa. Is the police officer going to get me to the hospital?"

"Sir, you didn't tell us your granddaughter was sick."

"I think we'll be okay, but where's the nearest clinic?"

"I can have a police escort go with you to the hospital."

"No, we don't need an escort, but thank you."

One of the babies in the back started to cry and then was muffled.

I loudly retched into a paper bag. "Grandpa, let's hurry! I need my medication."

"We won't keep you, sir. I hope your granddaughter is better. Good to meet a vet."

"Sure thing, Officer!"

We slowly drove away from the two police cars, and as soon as we were out of range, Erasmus burst out laughing. "Jake, you didn't tell me one of your talents was as a con artist."

"Grandpa, you know I got the *Police About to Bust Us Flu.*"

Matt explained to the people in the back what had happened. The laughter took all the tension out of the air, but it was still dangerous with the police and Border Patrol around. We came to a fork in the road and drove to Shiloh Church in a grove of cottonwoods. A dozen cars were already there, and people came to meet us.

An older man with a long white beard came over. "Hello, Erasmus! We haven't seen you in a long time. We called around to friends, and everybody is ready to help. Bring everyone inside. We have supper waiting."

Erasmus explained to the refugees, "These people are your friends and will help you to go north for sanctuary. They have dinner and a place for you to sleep tonight nearby."

In the small church, tables were laid out, and there was a place setting for about twenty people with big bowls of salad, rice, beans, tamales, and chicken. The restrooms were small, but everyone took turns washing up and then sat down for dinner.

One of the men spoke in English. "Thank you all. Gracias to Matt, Erasmus, and Jake. You saved our lives."

After dinner, several nurses treated the people who needed help and took them to a neighboring house. I was exhausted. Anna and her baby Angelina slept in the back of *Emma,* and I slept on the bunk bed in the front.

The next morning, we woke up to the sound of sirens. "Damn, I can't believe the police are here! What will happen to everyone? Anna, stay here, and we'll come back for you," said Erasmus.

I ran into the church. It was completely empty. There wasn't a single table or any sign anybody was here last night, only the pews for Sunday service.

The Border Patrol and the State Police stormed the church, but the only people there were Josiah, the elder of Shiloh, his wife Rebecca, and us.

Josiah said, "Martin, Phil, and all you boys made a terrible mistake. Whatever you heard about Shiloh Church, you're mistaken. We're a peaceable, law-abiding people. You've known us all your lives, and we only do God's work."

"Except when it comes to immigrants. We know you shelter wetbacks, and one day, we'll find out how you do it," said the sheriff.

When the police left, Erasmus asked, "Where did everyone go?"

Josiah told us, "Like the churches of the Underground Railroad, we have a safe house not too far from here. After dinner, we cleaned up the church and brought everyone there."

Anna and her baby Angelina were safe. She said to Erasmus in Spanish, "I have to get to San Antonio. My husband is there and works in a factory. Can you get me there?"

"Sure, we can help you," Erasmus said. "Josiah, thanks to you and your church for helping these people."

"We're following the gospel's message, providing shelter and help to refugees. Until this country turns around and enacts sensible immigration laws instead of endangering people, we'll continue to help them."

Matt said, "Thank you. We'll head up to the Quakers in San Antonio, and we can look for Anna's husband."

We waited until the cars arrived, and slowly, people headed to sanctuary churches up north.

Anna told me her story while we waited. "I come from a small town outside the capital of El Salvador. My father was a farmer who disappeared one day. My mother died last year. My brother survived by joining a gang to protect our family and then was killed by the police. Then Ricardo moved in and took care of us, and two years ago, I had my first baby."

"You were fourteen?" asked Erasmus.

"Yes, it was the only way we could get protection, with a husband and a baby. There is nothing in my village. It has all been taken over by drugs and gangs. Ricardo left ten months ago for the USA after our first baby died. I have this letter, phone, and an address from him."

Matt said, "I know where this is. Soon this will be over, and you'll be with your husband. You can start your life here."

While Matt drove, Erasmus told me he had once worked with refugees on the borders. "This is only a small glimpse of the horrible situation. Tens of thousands are fleeing the gang violence, drug wars, and corruption, and people like Anna and her family are caught in the middle."

"Not to make it about me," I said. "But it makes my crazy life in Black Mountain seem tame. I can't believe this girl is my age and she's been pregnant twice, crossed thousands of miles with a baby, and lost her family. This is a very scary world. Erasmus, how does anyone keep their hope?"

"This is something I've struggled with," said Erasmus. "How do we keep our faith in humanity with all the craziness?"

Matt called out, "We're almost there. This looks like the meat packing area. Let me park and see if I can find someone to help."

"Jake, can you stay with Anna?"

About a half-hour later, Matt and Erasmus came out from one of the factory buildings with a smaller man. Anna stepped out of *Emma* with Angelina.

"Ricardo! Ricardo!" She ran to him.

"Anna!"

We drove to the Quaker Meetinghouse and were met by Friends who were there to help Ricardo and Anna.

Matt said, "Thank you, everyone, but as we all know, this is the first step in a long road. There are many obstacles ahead."

"Don't worry," said a woman with long grey hair. "I'm Helen. We have an attorney to help this family become legal. We have an apartment where they can stay. Erasmus, Matt, and Jake should stay the night here too, and you can park *Emma* in our lot."

"Perfect, today has been exhausting for everyone," I said.

We said goodbye to Anna, Angelina, and Ricardo. Though I only understood a few words of Spanish, I understood their gratitude. Anna said in her best English, "Thank you."

Erasmus shook hands with Ricardo as they left, and he took money out from his shirt pocket. "Un regalo. A gift for your family from us."

He refused, but Erasmus insisted. Anna embraced all of us. "Thank you."

In the morning, the sky seemed to stretch forever with pink and orange clouds. I was the first up and made coffee. I stepped out of *Emma Goldman* with Socrates, sipped my coffee, watched the sunrise, and wrote in my journal.

I wrote -- *Everything is unreal. With all my hardships, my mother, her string of worthless boyfriends, all the abuse, and now with Erasmus and Socrates. What will the journey ahead be? I know this is only the beginning. I know we can beat this, the cancer and Agent Orange thing. I'm happy we're together, but I see how much this trip has taken out of Erasmus.*

I made oatmeal with nuts and fruits, and we ate breakfast beneath an oak tree with its limbs stretching wide. I wanted to put up a hammock and spend the day reading. "All this excitement is too much for me," I said.

"What a day it was yesterday!" said Matt. "It's awful to think this happens every day to thousands of refugees fleeing poverty, drug wars, gang violence, and oppression, and all this country does is make their lives more difficult."

Erasmus said, "America has a love-hate relationship with immigrants."

"Can we make it to Sedona in a few days?" I asked.

"Sure, as long as nothing else happens."

Almost on cue, Erasmus's phone rang. "Are you kidding? No, it's not possible!" he said.

When he hung up, he turned to us. "Jake and Matt, I got a call from someone inside Immigration, and the police are coming after Ricardo and Anna. We're a little obvious in our bright yellow *Emma Goldman*. One of the Quakers has an SUV we can use."

I looked at Erasmus and Matt. "Erasmus, why don't you take *Emma*? Matt and I can take Ricardo and Anna in the SUV, and we'll meet you in Odessa. Okay?"

Ricardo and Anna hurried out of the Quaker Meetinghouse with Angelina. The older woman Helen came with them and said, "Here are the keys to my SUV. If you can get as far as Odessa, I have some friends who can take them to Colorado. Hurry."

In the black SUV, Matt, Ricardo, Anna, Angelina, and I took the backroads out of San Antonio to Odessa.

"Don't worry! I know every back road between here and Las Vegas, and even better, I have my police scanner," said Matt. "I always use it in my truck, and it'll pick up the faintest whisper of police. We'll be in Odessa before nightfall. It'll be okay."

I told Matt, "This is too unfair! People simply want to raise their families and be happy. Am I so naïve?"

"Naïve, no. The way you think is realistic. It would be much cheaper and safer to have a sane immigration policy. My radar says there are cops ahead, so I'll take a side road."

This was scary. I tried to talk to Ricardo and Anna in my little Spanish.

Ricardo said, "I worked at the meat plant for six months and made good money. Now they are making a mess of this."

The land was bleak, barren, and hot. We got a call from Erasmus.

"I was right. I've been stopped by the cops four times since we left. Good thing I have Socrates to protect me. I'll see you in Odessa shortly."

We arrived at the Stonehenge monument in Odessa, and Erasmus was waiting for us along with another car to take Anna and Ricardo to Colorado.

"Jake, Anna wanted me to give you this." Matt took out a small medallion no bigger than a quarter. "It's the Lady of Fatima. She said it would protect you."

I added the medallion to the necklace from my grandmother and felt I had all this protection surrounding me.

Erasmus looked tired and he said, "Matt, I'm glad you're here. I have been taking some medication, and it's making me a bit weary."

Seemingly out of nowhere, a police car with flashing blue lights appeared and two cops got out. The younger of the two had his gun drawn and screamed, "Hands in the air! We've got you surrounded."

The older cop said to the younger one, "Jack, you sound like a bad movie. Put your gun down. We can talk to these people."

Erasmus approached the cops with his hands up and said, "I'm not armed."

The young cop shouted, "I'm in charge! Everybody, kneel down on the ground."

The older cop said, "Jack! I'm in charge. Put your gun away!"

"They've been on the run and helping wetbacks, Sergeant!" said Jack with his gun pointed at us.

"Put the gun down!" said the sergeant.

The young cop stepped forward, tripped, and his gun went off.

Matt leaped in front of Erasmus, but it was too late.

Erasmus fell to the ground, and I ran to him. "Erasmus!"

He was bleeding all over his favorite green shirt. He opened his eyes for a minute and looked at me. "I'll be okay. Take care of Ricardo and Anna." Then he passed out.

Matt ran over and screamed at the cop, "You idiot! You had no reason to fire!"

The sergeant reached over to the young cop. "Jack, give me the gun!"

Matt ripped off his shirt to stop the bleeding and put Erasmus's feet up. "Call an ambulance."

I screamed, "Wake up, Erasmus! You can't die!"

More police cars came, and finally, the ambulance. Matt whispered to me, "Jake, go with Erasmus! I'll meet you later! I need to make sure Anna and Ricardo are safe."

I told the EMT who approached us, "Let's go! Stop wasting time!"

The EMT hooked up an IV and put compression bandages on Erasmus's chest. He said, "I know he'll make it. Come with us, and we'll get your grandpa to the hospital."

The EMT rushed him directly towards the operating room when we arrived, and I stayed with him as long as I could and held his hand. "Erasmus, we can't stop here. We got a long road ahead of us."

"Miss, we'll help your grandpa. Is there any other family here?" asked the receptionist.

"No, just me and some friends. Please save him!"

I was alone in the waiting room. I knew people loved and cared for me, but the one closest to my heart was on the other side of the door between life and death. With all my soul, I knew he would be okay. I didn't know how to pray, but I held my hands together, repeating, "Please, make him better."

I dozed off, and I heard someone call me. "Jake. Are you okay?"

People came into the waiting room from the Quaker Meetinghouse and Shiloh Church.

Josiah said, "We'll stay with you and Erasmus as long as you need."

"How did you know about Erasmus?"

"The grapevine and our police monitor." Then he whispered, "All the refugees have been taken north, including Anna and Ricardo."

Socrates barked.

"How did he get in?" I asked as he leaped into my arms.

"He had been waiting by the hospital door, and I guess he knew how to find you."

The doctor came out and said, "I'm Doctor Torres. Are you his granddaughter?"

I nodded my head. "What's the good news?"

"Your grandpa lost a lot of blood, and the gunshot barely missed his heart. It's a miracle he survived. Everything is sewn up, but it will be touch-and-go for the next few days. We should transfer him to a medical center, but I'm afraid to move him. I wish I could give you better news. Do you have other family?"

Matt and Josiah came forward. "We're part of the extended family of Erasmus. Whatever you need, let us know."

I was exhausted. "Can I see Erasmus?" I asked.

"Give us a few minutes. He's still sedated from surgery."

I couldn't believe what I saw when they let me into his room. Erasmus, who I often thought of as Superman, an extraordinary person who could climb mountains and swim across lakes, looked like a pale shadow of himself, jaundiced, with his long silver hair disheveled. He had an IV and a blood transfusion going and was hooked up to all kinds of machines.

I refused to cry and held his hand tightly.

"Erasmus, I'm here."

He breathed deeply, and I thought I felt him squeeze my hand. Maybe it was only my imagination. I carefully brushed his hair, tied it into a braid, and gently massaged his back and legs with the nurse.

I said to the nurse, "Can I sleep in the chair tonight next to him?"

"No, we're going to let your grandpa sleep in the ICU, and someone will always be with him, but we'll call you if anything changes or we need you."

"Look out the window at the yellow RV with the picture of the lady dancing. That's our home, and if he needs anything, call me."

"I promise you, if he needs anything we'll call you."

The sergeant who was there when the rookie shot Erasmus came in. "Miss, I'm sorry about what happened to your grandpa. I'm Sergeant Pedro Gonzales. Do you have a driver's license or ID?"

I shook my head. "Here's Erasmus's driver's license. Is that enough? Why did the cop shoot him? Erasmus had his hands up. No one was threatening anybody, and he just wanted to talk."

The sergeant said, "Our officers are doing their best, and this officer was new. I can't say anything until the investigation is completed. He's on desk duty now."

"Desk duty? He should be fired and arrested."

That night I had my reoccurring dream where I was running against the wind and getting blown backward. Then a cowboy in a white hat on a horse came running by and picked me up off the ground. "I got you, Jake!" said the rider. But this time, the rider wasn't Erasmus. It was Sojourner and she said, "Hold on!"

Over the next twenty-four hours, people from Shiloh and the Quaker Meetinghouse came to the hospital, brought food, prayed, and waited for news.

I was terrified of losing Erasmus. "Matt, this is damn unfair. Why did the cop do something this damn stupid?"

"I keep asking myself the same question. Let's see Erasmus one more time tonight."

"Erasmus, can you hear us?" He squeezed my hand, but his eyes were closed. "Everyone is here, Matt, Socrates, and people from the churches."

Doctor Torres came in and said, "Erasmus needs to recover. He had several blood transfusions, and you said he also has prostate cancer and other diseases caused by Agent Orange?"

"Yes, and hepatitis C," I said. "Normally, he's strong and healthy, and none of that slowed him down until the rookie cop tripped and shot him. Doctor, he's going to be fine. Right?"

She nodded her head. "We think he's through the worst of it, but he needs rest and quiet."

The idea of Erasmus dying was terrifying. I'd seen death before with my grandpa. I held Socrates close to me and felt safe.

In the morning, sunrise came in purple and orange hues, and the oil rigs dotting the horizon looked like steel dinosaurs. With Socrates, I stretched out a mat, faced the sunrise, and did my yoga. When I folded my hands, it was in prayer. Even though I wasn't sure if I believed in gods or angels, I prayed to every god or religion I could think of -- Buddhist, Hindu, Christian…any higher power or magic was sorely needed. Right now, I'd take any help I could get.

Afterward, I walked to the hospital with Socrates. There was a bed of black-eyed daisies by the side of the road, and I picked a small bunch for Erasmus.

I hated the antiseptic smell of hospitals. Despite the care and professionalism of the nurses, staff, and doctors, I couldn't shake off my despair.

"Where's Erasmus?" I asked the nurse when I saw his empty bed in the ICU.

"Don't worry. He's in the medical-surgical ward. He's out of danger."

I was shocked when I walked in. He was awake, his green eyes sparkled, and he only had one IV. "Well, if it isn't my favorite hobo," said Erasmus.

I fell into his arms. "Erasmus!"

"Careful, Jake. The shoulder is sore."

I was at a loss for words. I needed to be held and to be reassured he wasn't going away. I had seen my whole world turn upside down and spin out of control during the last four days.

I came back to visit in the afternoon. "Ras, the nurse said you could eat, so I made us your favorite hobo burritos with beans, rice, tofu, and tomatoes."

"Thank you. I'm sure it's delicious, but I can only eat a bit. I only remember a little of what happened. I tried talking to the cop, and then everything went black. I assume Ricardo, Anna, and Angelina are safe?"

While eating, I filled him in on all the adventures. "Remember they had gotten away before you were shot? I can't believe all the trouble you get into! Man, Erasmus, you're becoming a time-and-a-half job!"

"Please, don't make me laugh. It hurts too much. Where's Matt?"

"He'll be here in a minute. He's been fabulous and is ready to get his truck engine in Flagstaff whenever you're ready. Everyone we picked up has gone north on the Underground Railroad, and Ricardo and Anna are in Colorado in a safe house. Nothing to worry about. Most importantly, you're okay."

We got Erasmus out of bed, and the orderly helped him with a shower. I put his guitar, drawing pad, and pencils by his bedside.

"Thanks for all your help," said Erasmus. "I can't believe how sore I am and how much I've been sleeping! I've been taking homeopathic medicines, plus antibiotics. Ah, my doctor Anna Torres is here."

"Hi Jake, we spoke earlier about Erasmus," said Doctor Torres. "Mr. Hobbs, you have a lucky star guiding you. The bullet missed your heart, and we had to give you a few pints of blood for transfusion, and now you have to take it slow. You shouldn't travel. Is there a place you can stay around here for a few weeks?"

"Thank you for all your help, Doctor," Erasmus said. "I have a lot of angels surrounding me! I've had too many close calls in my life, more than most people would be entitled to. However, between the bullet, the surgery, the extra blood, and the hospital stay, I'm ready to hit the road. I have friends in Sedona, and whenever I need mending, I go there."

"Mr. Hobbs," said Doctor Torres. "You shouldn't travel for at least a week and then only when we've cleared you. We got the bullet, but we need to run some more tests, and with your other medical problems, it's not a good idea to be on the road. You need to be near medical help."

"Doctor, this has been one insane week. I value and do take all your advice seriously. I am deeply grateful."

Socrates patiently waited until the doctor left, then leaped into Erasmus's arms. "This is the best medicine. My Socrates, I've missed you! If they had let you into the ICU, I would have had you there."

I said to Erasmus, "You've got to stay. The doctor doesn't think you're ready."

"I'm going to be fine. How have you been doing? I've been worried about you."

"The first days after the shooting, I was terrified. I couldn't sleep. The gunshot sound stayed with me. I was afraid you'd die."

"I thought it was lights out for me. I have a profound allergy to guns!"

"They took the cop's gun away, and he's on desk duty until the investigation ends. Let's get you walking. We've got to get you back into shape."

I walked up the hallway slowly with Erasmus and Socrates. There was a patient area outside the hospital with a garden that I brought him to. "It's so sweet to smell the air. I don't like being inside. I'll be ready to go by tomorrow. Between you, Matt, and me, we can get to Arizona in the next forty-eight hours. There's a friend and a medicine man I need to see."

I looked at him. "Which part of 'no' aren't you getting? Doctor Torres said wait. There's no rush. We should wait until you get the green light from her."

"I feel my star is guiding me there sooner than the doctor would like."

"I don't agree," I said with my arms crossed.

"Jake, we have you and Matt driving, and I can drive a little. We're only about six hours from Albuquerque and then on to meet Hattie."

"Hattie?"

"I have a friend named Hatalli, a traditional Navajo medicine man, who was also a medic in Vietnam. After returning from Vietnam, he continued the tradition of healing he learned from his father. I know he'll help me."

"I'm afraid, Erasmus. We've had a lot of close calls over the past few months, and I don't want to push our luck." I looked out the window at the dusty and barren hillside of Odessa. The hospital and the surgeons had saved his life, but I couldn't stop him from leaving once he'd made up his mind.

"Matt will drive, and you need to lie back. I know taking it easy isn't your style. As far as I can tell, we have a lot more journeys ahead of us, but please consider staying."

Erasmus always convinced me, even if I didn't think something was possible. It was easier to leave than I thought. I imagined we would have to tie sheets out the window, but the front door was the easiest way to go. He had to sign a form *Against Medical Advice,* settle with the business office, and by 9 a.m., we were in *Emma Goldman* heading to Sedona.

It felt strange having Erasmus lying in the bunk bed while we were up front. Matt said, "Jake, take the first turn driving."

I checked the mirrors, pulled out of the hospital parking lot, and the signs for Odessa faded in my rearview mirror. Sunlight washed over *Emma*, and I felt the road ahead was a new beginning.

CHAPTER NINE

Surrender: The Hero's Journey Ain't Always Heroic

I had been afraid I'd lost Erasmus. I wanted to put the nightmare behind me as soon as possible. I was driving slowly and easily, avoiding the bumps and keeping between the lines. "Erasmus, you okay back there? Not too fast?"

"Straight ahead! Remember, the hero's journey isn't always heroic or in a straight line."

"How so, Erasmus?"

"The hero's journey is about facing our demons and finding our way home."

Now I understood this even more vividly with the challenges along the way after the shooting and Erasmus nearly dying.

Erasmus said, "Don't worry about me, Jake. Hero's journey or not, nothing can slow me down beside a bullet, a bit of cancer, and Agent Orange!"

"Really?" said Matt. "You've been the luckiest cat with nine lives, but even with all your good karma, I wouldn't push my luck. We still have a few hours to Albuquerque, and I have a friend who owns the Road King Motel. Jake, there's a terrific history museum in Albuquerque called the Indian Pueblo Center with many stories about the Pueblo people of the area."

"Tell me more."

"Maybe we'll go there tomorrow morning. I've often been in and out of Albuquerque, and this is the place I always come back to," said Matt.

"You're like Erasmus. He's also a museum and art junkie. I had never been to a museum 'til he took me to the one in Cleveland."

"I love going to museums. Otherwise, it would get more than a bit boring simply driving. I've been back and forth across the USA, and whenever I can, I try to find a new museum or art center."

We reached the outskirts of Albuquerque and found the Road King Motel, which looked like a big log cabin. The rooms were comfortable, with Pueblo rugs hung on the wall and comfy beds.

I changed Erasmus's bandage. "How's it feeling? It looks clean, and the sutures have healed."

"A little tender, but soon I'll be racing you up the mountain!"

"I'm looking forward to the day when we can race up mountains again."

The shooting had taken a lot out of him, and he was moving a little slow. Nevertheless, he had always been the comeback kid over the past few months. No matter the adversity, I believed he would always come back stronger and better. Though reason might say otherwise, my optimism couldn't be tarnished. In the evening, we strolled around the old town, listened to folk music, and Erasmus, Matt, and I had the most ordinary enchanted evening. With all the dramas and tumult of the past few weeks, this ordinariness with my favorite people was a huge blessing.

Matt said, "My friend came into town, so I'll stay in his room and see you in the morning."

In the middle of the night, I dreamed I was chasing Erasmus. He rode away from me up a long canyon on a white horse with Socrates. "Wait! I'm coming too!"

I awoke with a start and looked over at the other bed and saw it was empty. "Erasmus!"

I heard his voice. "Come outside. The moon is lovely."

He was swaddled in a sheet and playing his guitar softly. The stars were dancing above us, and the moon reflected on the ghostly shadows of the mountains.

"It's like the god Apollo painted this moment of perfection for Selene." I soon fell asleep with his music dancing in my dreams.

In the morning, Matt came in with breakfast, a tray of scrambled tofu, veggies, black beans, juice, and coffee.

"Jake, how come you never cook like this for me?" asked Erasmus with a wink.

I threw a pillow at him, but Matt caught it mid-flight. "Sorry, but we can't be too frisky until Erasmus is fully back in the saddle."

I slipped outside, wrapped in a blanket, and watched the sunrise. Morning colors of lilac and orange, dashes of sunlight, and the wisp of clouds danced in all the inconceivable colors of enchantment. I stood up and sang a song without words, like Sojourner, but this was my song, my prayer for the morning. My song rose across the valley and lingered like the lone cloud overhead.

Almost as if on cue, a good-looking, clean-shaven guy with long blond hair in a ponytail and a straw cowboy hat strolled out, and my sixteen-year-old hormones were bubbling fast.

"Everyone, this is Everett." Matt put his arm around him and kissed him on the cheek.

A breeze could have knocked me over. My entire fantasy of hooking up with Matt disappeared.

Everett said, "Howdy, folks! Matt and I met a few months ago at a truck stop in Mississippi, and when we met – we instantly knew we were meant for each other." Their smiles lit up the room, even though my smile had sunk to the floor with all my fading fantasies. Now, I understood why he didn't answer directly when I asked about his girlfriend.

I put on my big girl boots. "Great to meet you, Everett." Erasmus once reminded me that a gracious loser always takes the higher ground.

"Erasmus, Matt and I were planning on driving to Flagstaff to pick up my new rig. Would you like us to split up and have one of us go with you?"

Erasmus said, "I'm sure we'll be okay. Jake is getting really good at driving *Emma*. I'm sad about you leaving, Matt, but I know you two will have a lot of stories to tell when we see you next."

"Erasmus and Jake, I know our paths will cross again," said Matt as he hugged us. "I'm sure of it, and when we get to Yosemite, we'll connect. You have my cell phone number and you can call us if you need any help. It's been a pleasure seeing you both again."

"Everett and Matt, I'm glad you found each other. We'll see you before too long," I said before we watched them drive away.

Driving down the valleys with the twisting turns from Flagstaff to Sedona, the mountain forests appeared, and the stunning red mesas came into view. They were like sentinels, ancient gods who had transformed into stone, and I could feel their majestic presence.

Erasmus said, "Despite the bullet and the drama in Odessa, I feel good about the road ahead."

"Sit back and let me take over for a while." Socrates sat on Erasmus's lap as I drove from Albuquerque to Sedona. I felt like a big girl and even when a truck pulled out of a side street, it didn't faze me. I had a great co-pilot, Ras.

The skies were crisp blue, the wind fair, and I had an optimism that our worst days were behind us.

It was already noon when we pulled into the Crescent Moon Picnic Area. I said, "Let's go for a swim."

"Jake, you go ahead. I'll make some lunch." He looked tired. "Enjoy the swim."

Socrates joined me for a splash. All the hot dust from San Antonio, Odessa, and Albuquerque fell away. I was lying on my back, my arms stretched out, drifting in the cool water. I felt like I was floating in the clouds with all my cares sailing away.

Later, we parked *Emma* by the side of the stream next to a twisted twirl of junipers. "We have to find out where we can park overnight. See Cathedral Rock? There's a story that those two figures over there in the middle are like a husband and a wife, back-to-back against each other, and arguing for eternity."

"It seems like a pretty bleak view of relationships."

"I agree, but it's the legend. Don't you love how majestic this is? Whenever I'm here, I marvel at the millions of years it took to make this."

We sat on the rocky outcropping overlooking Cathedral Rock. I was mesmerized watching the landscape, the clouds rolling by, and the play of orange, purple, and red sunlight through the clouds. "Erasmus, I could sit here forever and be thoroughly enchanted by this."

"It's sublime, and tomorrow maybe you can hike up there."

"Erasmus, this has been one extraordinary journey these past few months."

"Extraordinary? That's an understatement. The past three months have been a maelstrom of good fortune, happiness, and incredible surprises. Sedona is famous as a vortex, a place of incredible energy and transformation."

I thought to myself, *Yes, more than anything I want a transformation to make all of Erasmus's illnesses disappear.*

The mesas were stunning in the sunset. The colors of the sandstone constantly changed, from ruddy to ruby bright in the evening sun, thanks to the extraordinary magic of color and light in Sedona.

Erasmus said, "It takes my breath away every time and fills me with humility. This transformation took millions of years of wind, rain, erosion, and sunlight. This land was all part of a vast ocean." He reached over for a piece of sandstone and brushed back the dirt. "If we scrape away the outer layer, we can see the remains of the clams, snails, fish, and trilobites. We're only a tiny part of this story, and one day we'll be part of these fossils. It's a good reminder of the impermanence of life and my mortality."

"All of our adventures, like the girls in the car accident we helped and getting shot, must have given you a taste of your mortality."

"Absolutely! My mortality was served up big time. Though the hardest thing of all was allowing people to help me."

"Really?"

"I've always valued my independence and freedom. I hate to rely on others and letting others take care of me when I'm sick or in the hospital is difficult. Perhaps, I'm afraid," he added quietly. "It almost makes me feel old."

I let out a deep sigh. "Ain't a damn thing old about you, Mr. Erasmus P. Hobbs."

We sat on the bench overlooking the vast canyons where the sun was setting. Despite the near disasters and all the catastrophes, I was at peace. I took out my wooden flute and played "Green Sleeves." *Emma Goldman* was exquisite in the red sunset light, and I saw how she had come to life. Erasmus said, "She is a beauty and embodies the spirit of the great revolutionary Emma Goldman."

While he was sketching the valley and the vistas, I went inside and made a dinner of seitan sloppy joes and a sesame kale salad.

Erasmus made a small fire. It cracked and popped with the dry juniper wood beneath the stars that were brightly strewn across the skies, and a shooting star blazed across the horizon.

"Look, a falling star!"

"Yes, and a meteor shower following! One Native American story says good fortune will follow when you see a shooting star."

I wished on the falling star with all my might. It was a straightforward wish. An impossible and simple wish that the road for Erasmus and I would never end.

Erasmus took a bite of his dinner and said, "Jake, this is delicious! You are an extraordinary chef!"

"I learned from the best."

"By the way, I have a surprise for you."

"What is it?"

"Jake, it wouldn't be a surprise if I told you."

"A hint?"

"Zoom!"

"That's a bit enigmatic?"

We stretched out our sleeping bags and ground mats, with Socrates snuggled between us. Starlight danced across the sky, a cool breeze blew, and I knew everything would be all right. It had to be.

"Sueños con angelitos," he said as he tucked me into sleep

I awoke shortly before sunrise and was surprised Erasmus's bedroll was gone.

I made coffee and sipped it while watching the sunrise. I did yoga on the rocky outcropping overlooking Cathedral Rock and wondered what the surprise was today. Every day with Erasmus was a surprise, but what was this special one?

Erasmus came back from his walk. "Good morning, sunshine. I took a walk up along the mesa trail to watch the sunrise. I didn't want to wake you up. Today is the day for the surprise. Are you ready?"

"I'm always surprised at everything that happens to us, so why should today be different?"

"This will be a mystery, but in order to do this we'll have to do a trust exercise."

"Trust?" That word always lingered on my tongue and in my brain. I grew up fearing and mistrusting people. I had never been able to trust those who were supposed to protect me. My mother, Sonny, rarely had a sunny day in her entire life, and her life was a trail of mistrust and betrayal.

"Because this is a trust exercise, I'll blindfold you."

"Wow, like a real trust exercise?"

"A genuine trust exercise." He put a blindfold over my eyes and helped me climb into the passenger seat.

I smelled the morning air, crisp and clean, and heard the sounds of blue jays and phoebes. We drove further away from town, and the wind blowing through the canyon got stronger.

"Do I get any clues?"

"All your clues are around us."

"Ras, sometimes you're annoyingly enigmatic," I said with a laugh.

We stopped, and Erasmus got out and opened my door. "Take my hand, Jake. The surprise is almost here." Blindfolded, he led me along, and I heard him talking to somebody. I heard a door open, and I sat in a chair and was strapped in.

"Jake, are you ready? Take off your blindfold."

I took off the blindfold and realized I was in a helicopter that was lifting off.

"This is my friend Adam, and he's going to take us for a ride."

"I can't believe this. No way! This is the first time my feet have ever left the earth except to dance, jump off a cliff, and go swimming with you. Erasmus, you sly dog, you sneaky, wonderful you!"

"Jake, happy almost seventeenth birthday from Adam and me."

We soared through the canyons of Cathedral Rock and swirled above the valleys surrounding Sedona. The colors quickly changed as the helicopter shifted and turned from right to left. "Erasmus, look at these shades of reds! I didn't even know there were this many!"

Then Adam headed toward the Grand Canyon. "Hold on tight!"

My stomach was doing flip-flops and I was sure my eyes would almost pop out of my head. I was lost for words. Erasmus had a huge grin and looked like a kid on the biggest roller coaster. He shouted out, "Yahoo! Thank you, Adam!"

Adam called out, "Everyone okay? We're going for the next big turn." We roared along the riverbanks and zoomed up to the highest peaks, and at the last turn, we got the most extraordinary view of the entire canyon and then flew up to Point Imperial, the highest point in the canyon. "This is over eight thousand feet tall! Taller than any mountains near here. Look down, and people are rafting on the Colorado."

I was spellbound and couldn't believe what I saw, from the valleys below to the tallest peaks.

Then we came down on top of Airport Mesa. I couldn't move. I didn't know what to say. My whole body was buzzing.

Adam said, "Wasn't it a blast?"

"Beyond words, Adam. Totally beyond words or anything I've ever seen. Thank you!"

"Erasmus told me what a fabulous person you are, so I had to meet you, and it's always fun being someone's first helicopter ride."

My head was spinning, and though my stomach was a bit queasy, I was exhilarated! I had gone to the heavens in Adam's helicopter, soaring above Sedona and the Grand Canyon. Erasmus, Socrates, and I had been like angels flying to heaven.

Now, down on earth, I took off my sandals. I needed to walk barefoot on the ground. "This was the best, most outrageous, amazing trip!"

Erasmus said, "Yes, it was, but even more extraordinary was the smile on your face."

We danced on the plateau's edge overlooking the mesas, and Erasmus stretched his arms wide. Like in the movie *Zorba the Greek* we saw last week, he clapped and danced. We danced the dance of life, and Socrates, our wise playful sage, also danced. I thought I would never come down.

Downtown in Sedona, we pulled into the natural food store, a place to meet people and shop. All kinds of people were there, hippies and New Age folks, and the place smelled of incense and patchouli.

When we returned to the parking lot, I couldn't believe what I saw. "Erasmus, do you see what I see to my left? Am I having one of those weird New Age Sedona moments?"

We both did a double take. How was this possible?

"Yup, we both are having one of those New Age vortex moments."

"Roshi!" I called out. I was dumbfounded.

"My dear Jake!" He stood up to his full six-foot-five height. He wore a long purple silk shirt and folded his hands in gassho as he said, "I missed you!"

I bowed and hugged him, though I was completely confused about why he was there.

My confusion grew when I saw Sojourner coming out of the store with a basket of fruit.

"Sojah!" I called out.

She looked regal with her long grey dreadlocks entwined with rainbows of ribbons, wearing gold hoop earrings and a long flowing saffron and purple dress. The bright sun made her face seem even more radiant than usual. She saw us and broke into a wide smile. "My children! Jake! Erasmus!"

Socrates was sitting on the bench and barked.

"Of course, Socrates, my dear friend," she said as she picked him up and held him.

I was overwhelmed. "Roshi, Sojah, it's incredible to see you. Without being rude – why are you here?"

"We got a call from Erasmus at the hospital in Texas," Roshi explained. "We would have come sooner but needed to wrap a few things up. Also, this is serendipitous, our friends are making a new Buddhist shrine here and we haven't been on a road trip in a long time. Plus, we missed you both."

I looked at Roshi and Sojourner. "Yeah, but why are you really here?" I said with my arms crossed.

Sojourner took my hand. "Jake, what Roshi said was true. However, we also knew Erasmus was getting sicker, and then with the shooting, it made a bad situation worse."

I bit my lip. I was afraid. "No, Erasmus is getting better. Ever since we left Odessa, he's been getting stronger. Right, Erasmus? Tell them you're getting better."

"Let's sit down in the shade under the trees and continue this," said Erasmus. "I'm the one who hasn't been completely candid with you. The last three months have been extraordinary. When I first met you in West Virginia, I thought I'd just give you a ride home, but it was kismet."

I was a big girl now and held back the tears. "Sojah and Roshi – you haven't been honest with me and you knew he was getting sicker. Erasmus, why didn't you level with me?"

"Jake, we are leveling with you – we're trying to figure this out too," said Sojah.

"I'm not a kid anymore! I'm going to be seventeen soon! Erasmus, you were in the army at seventeen and in the middle of a war. Sojah, you ran away from home at sixteen and traveled down to Mexico alone with no money. You could have told me."

"Jake, we couldn't find a way to do it. Simply because we're adults, we don't always know how to do something or what is best," said Erasmus. "I'm sorry."

"Erasmus, I'm pissed you didn't tell me Roshi and Sojourner were coming! I know you're sick, but sometimes I thought the illness wasn't real because you looked so healthy and strong. Damn it! You escaped a burning car dangling off a cliff, survived a bullet, and…"

"And what?"

"And you survived three months with me, a snarly, irritable sixteen-year-old girl."

Erasmus looked at me and smiled. "Is there more, Jake?

"Damn right, there's more. One part of me is hoping to the high heavens a miracle will happen, and we can go to California, see the sequoia trees, climb the mountains in Yosemite, and dance under the northern lights in Alaska. I want more time with you! Three months ain't enough. I don't want to lose you. I'm scared." Tears rolled down my cheek. "It isn't fair!"

I looked at Erasmus's blue-green eyes tinged with yellow. "Jake, I'm sorry. I'm as confused as you are. Even with your gnarly sixteen-year-old personality, I've genuinely enjoyed every minute of our journey together and I plan to enjoy every minute we still have."

"So, what's the answer?" I asked.

"Honestly, Jake?"

I nodded my head. "Honestly! No bullshit!"

"I asked Sojah and Roshi to come to Sedona because…" he took a deep breath.

"No! You can't die! I won't allow it! We'll figure it out! We can beat this."

Sojourner said while she reached her arms out to hold me, "We're family. We're in this together. I love you, Jake. Come here."

She sat down on a chair, held me, and let me cry.

Erasmus said, "Jake, I'm going outside Sedona to the Navajo sanctuary White Rock tomorrow. My friend Hattie the medicine man and Roshi will go with me."

"To heal you? Something to make you better?"

"No, I won't get better." Roshi put his hand on Erasmus's shoulder. "I'd love to believe I have one more extraordinary dance around the sun. Though I wanted to travel with you to the West Coast and further, I'm afraid Sedona's my last stop. My only sadness is not being able to see you grow up, finish school, go to college, and have a family. I have had the most extraordinary life! I've traveled the globe, had a family, met thousands of people, sung my songs, and danced the dance of my life. I can't be any more grateful."

I was lost. I felt like I had a huge balloon of expectations suddenly sucked out.

Sojourner looked at me. "Let's go to the Buddhist stupa. It's not far from here. Roshi and I came to see you and help with finishing building it."

"Yeah, I'm talked out! I need to scream and dance."

"Me too," said Sojah. "This stupa is a Buddhist prayer site and a perfect place for us. I'm out of words too, but we're family, Socrates, you, Erasmus, and me. We're in this together." She looked at me directly. "Jake, we're in this together."

"Sojah is right. Let's walk," said Roshi.

We climbed up the hill towards the temple. The Buddhist stupa was golden and bright in the evening sun. Surrounding it were smaller statues of the Buddha. Erasmus and Sojourner were walking behind holding hands.

"See the eagle over there on the mountain?" said Roshi.

"No."

"Just beyond the ridge to the left of the setting sun."

Then he picked me up like I was a little kid, lifted me up high over his head, and faced me in the right direction.

"How amazing! All I need to do is be six-foot-five, and it will improve my perspective."

He chuckled. "I think your perspective is perfect."

When we got to the stupa, he said, "I'm going to do kinhin and pray. Would you like to join me?"

I knew the kinhin line from Dignity, the slow walking meditation. "I can do the kinhin, but I haven't learned all of the Zen prayers."

He put on his robes and took out his prayer beads. "Jake, you embody many of the noblest prayers – compassion, kindness, and love. Not to worry. Let's walk!"

Erasmus and Sojourner walked to the promontory point while Roshi and I walked around the stupa in kinhin and recited prayers. I closed my eyes and visualized Erasmus as healthy. Each step was intentionally slow. The colors in the evening light were majestic and extraordinary, with more shades of reds and violet than I'd thought could even exist. There was no past, no future, only this moment. The simple direction of *no past, no future, only this moment* helped me with my *monkey mind,* as Erasmus called it – when my mind wandered. Slowing down and breathing opened more space in my brain. Colors shimmered in the sunset. I had been afraid of being alone, but for the first time, I could accept this, and I had Roshi, Sojourner, and Socrates as family.

Sojourner made a little fire from juniper branches. The flames popped, and we carefully nestled stones to protect the kindling. Dinner was a scrumptious salad of tempeh, veggies, and rice. We played music, and Erasmus sang one of his favorite songs, "Gracias a La Vida."

A woman nearby began to sing in Spanish, and as she came closer, she sang all the verses to the song beautifully. A crowd gathered and listened. She was an older woman with her granddaughter. The girl said, "My grandmother said, when she was a girl in Chile, Violeta Para sang this song for her, and you reminded her of first meeting Violeta."

"Who was Violeta?" I asked. I knew the song, but not the singer.

"She was a folk singer who inspired a generation of people."

It was a joy to play music and listen to the stories of the grandmother, Lucia. When the evening ended, Roshi said, "Sojah and I are staying with friends who built this Buddhist sanctuary. We'll be back early in the morning. Jake, I'm sorry we weren't forthright with you. We didn't know what to do. I'm sorry."

"What's the saying of Erasmus? Every saint has a past, and every sinner has a future. So, with that in mind and your eloquent apology, I see a bright future for you."

Sojourner said, "Another Jakism!"

Roshi said, "Jake, you are priceless."

When Erasmus and I went to *Emma*, I said, "Erasmus, before you get undressed could I hold you? But no funny business!"

"Right, no funny business." We lay on the bed in the back and looked at the stars through the skylight. "Sueños con angelitos."

"Goodnight, my dear sweet Erasmus." I wanted to hold him tightly enough that he would never leave.

When I awoke in the morning, I was alone. Coffee was brewing, and a pot of oatmeal was on the stove

Hattie, the Navajo medicine man, came in his white pickup truck. He wore a worn black cowboy hat with silver jewelry and turquoise around the hatband, a silver belt buckle with blue stones, and long grey braids, and his face was the deep brown of a man who had worked in the fields all his life. When he smiled I saw how pearly white his teeth were. "How ya do, Miss Jake? Erasmus told me all about you."

"How do you do, Mr. Hattie? Did he tell you only the good things about me, or did he include the things not so perfect?"

"Only the most charming aspects of your personality," he said with a smile.

"Can I make you some tea or coffee?"

"Coffee black is perfect."

Erasmus had gone out early with Sojourner and had left a note. Socrates and I sat with Hattie.

"How are you doing, Jake?"

"Fine, I guess, except…"

"Except?"

"Erasmus, needing help."

"I know this is hard to accept and understand."

"Accept? Accept that my best friend is dying?"

"Yes, but like many people, we Navajo believe the spirit lives on. I've known Erasmus since we were in the army years ago. I've had the privilege to see him grow and become the man he is now."

"Is he different now?"

"He would always do anything to help a friend. Once, my father was very sick here in Arizona, and he figured out a way to get me out of Vietnam and onto a military transport back to the USA. Even though I didn't know him well, he was a friend from the get-go. And now, I can see why he wanted to return to Sedona."

"He lived here?"

"On and off for some years, but he always had the gypsy wanderlust. We're glad he came back."

We sipped our coffee and then walked up to the bluff overlooking Sedona with Socrates. Hatti told me how he looked at death. "In our world, the Chindi is the spirit that lives on, and a great spirit like Erasmus will continue to inspire and guide you."

One part of me still didn't want to give up the hope Erasmus could defy the odds and get better.

When we returned to *Emma*, Erasmus, Roshi, and Sojourner were there.

Erasmus said, "Jake, can I talk to you for a minute?"

We walked over to the shady juniper grove overlooking the mesas. "Is this going to be a difficult conversation?" I asked as Socrates cuddled in my lap.

"Jake, I'd like to stay but I have to go with Hattie today. We will be heading up to his camp White Rock, not too far from here."

I was confused. "Roshi, Sojah, and I are going too, right?"

"I asked Roshi to come with me, but Sojah will stay with you."

My world stopped. "You're leaving me? When are you coming back?"

Sojourner and Roshi approached and sat next to us. "We thought we should be part of this conversation if you don't mind," Sojourner said.

"Don't treat me like a kid. Be honest with me."

Erasmus said, "We're not keeping you out of this. I don't want you to be part of my leaving."

"Sorry to be naïve, but leave? Like, as in really leaving? Like dying?"

"Jake, there is no easy way to do this. I don't want you to be there and watch me go through it."

"I disagree. We're like peanut butter and jelly, Batman, and Robin, the unstoppable duo. Rain or shine. Good or bad. We're a team. Right?"

"Jake, you can always find a way to make a difficult conversation funny. You're right. We're as tight as peanut butter and jelly, but I'm going to White Rock in another hour. I'll take every single drop of joy we've had over these past few months, all the laughter and adventures, and hold them close. Sojah and Socrates will stay with you. Is it okay?"

Nothing was okay, but I had to accept the inevitable, even though acceptance was not one of my strengths.

When it was time, I took off my purple amethyst necklace and gave it to Erasmus. "This was from Alice. It will protect you."

We hugged, and then he had to go. "Jake. I'm sorry."

"It's okay, Erasmus. One of the lessons I learned from you is I can take care of myself, but I'll miss you every day. No, I'll miss you every moment you're gone."

Roshi climbed in the back of the truck, and Cathedral Rock loomed in the background.

"Erasmus, you are always close to my heart."

"I love you, Jake." He handed me an envelope. "A letter for you. Thank you for everything, and all your kindnesses and thoughtfulness, and how you could always make me laugh."

The months of being with Erasmus were over as quickly as they'd started as I watched him disappear down the road.

I was in a state of shock. Life without Erasmus? "Sojah, I don't know what to say, but I need to go for a long cool swim."

The walk up to Wet Beaver Creek was like stepping into a dream. I loved leaping off the outcropping called the 'tongue of the beaver.' A couple of months ago, I was terrified of swimming, and now I took a flying leap off the rocks without hesitation and then lay back in the sheltered area by Oak Creek. I floated on my back and splashed the evening hours away.

"Sojah, what's next?"

There's nothing we can do now. Jake, if you want, we would love for you to live with us on the mountain. You can finish your GED, and if you'd like, there's a college nearby. Jake," she said as she looked at me with sublime tenderness. "You always have a home with us."

She held me in her arms tightly and all the tension and worry eased.

Sojourner said, "There are herbalists who worked with us at Dignity Village who have set up their shop here in Sedona, and I think it'll be a lot of fun to visit and work with them."

"I said goodbye to Erasmus, but I don't feel it in my bones. I want to be with him when he dies. It may be a week, a month, or longer. I can't explain who Erasmus is to me. Grandpa? Teacher? Sage?"

Sojah said, "He is all of that, but he is also a *soul toucher*, a rare, extraordinary person who can touch and heal your soul. Even though he would deny this and always said he was just an ordinary man with a lot of failings."

"Yes, I agree. He and you are definitely *soul touchers*."

As the moon rose, I played the guitar, and Sojourner played the flute. When it was time for sleep, I needed Erasmus to be here, to tell me "Sueños con angelitos."

I took out the letter from Erasmus, written in his meticulous handwriting. I caressed the paper and could almost smell his sandalwood aftershave.

My dearest beautiful Jake,

You are one of my soulmates. Jake, I wish there was so much more I could do for you, and there is so much more time I want to spend with you. As Jim Croce said, "There never seems to be enough time."

Sojourner and Roshi want you to live with them. Soon you'll be seventeen, and if you choose to be on your own, it is up to you, but I think you'll l be happier with them at Dignity. After all, we're family.

I left you Emma Goldman, *my gypsy mistress. If she'd had wings,* Emma Goldman *would've sailed around the world with us.*

I also left you money for college. I wish I could've left you more, but it's enough to get through four years of a state school. I asked my friends at Reed College if they would consider you for a scholarship.

I left my share of the family farm to my son Henry David and his family, and I know they are well provided for.

Of course, Socrates, will stay with you, a better companion one couldn't ask for!

I regret I can't be with you in your extraordinary journey ahead, though I will always be with you in spirit.

Thank you for this Summer of Love*!*
Erasmus P. Hobbs

My hands trembled and tears came down, but I dried them before they could blur the ink. I loved Erasmus from the first moment I met him, despite my gnarliness, his illnesses, and the ups and downs of our relationship. His love healed so many of my childhood wounds and enabled me to find my way out of the wilderness of my pain.

The moon was full and I couldn't sleep. Through the skylight, it looked like the moon was divided, and I woke up with a start. I stood out in the cool air, alone, with Sojourner asleep. I needed to be with Erasmus, sick or not. I needed to hear his laughter one more time. I took the keys to Sojourner's truck, and as quietly as I could, I headed to White Rock. The springs in the truck squealed. I knew it was wrong, but I had to see him.

I knew where White Rock was, on Route 89 north of Sedona. I had left a note. *Sojah, I will be back. I need to see Erasmus one more time. Love, Jake.*

I saw the various constellations. I thought of what Hattie had said when he was talking about each one of the stars as friendly spirits that guide and heal us.

It was dumb luck that got me to Canyon Road. I pulled over to the side of the road and looked at a map. A cop car pulled up behind me. The cop got out and tapped on my window. I was sunk. I didn't have a license or registration, and it was a stolen car.

"Miss, are you lost?"

"Officer, you might say that. I'm looking for Schnebly Point and White Rock."

"Hattie's place?"

"Yes, do you know it?"

"Sure enough. Talk about a strange coincidence. He's my uncle, and that is a sacred Navajo encampment. My name is Officer Shillah. Follow me up the mountain. We're not too far."

I followed the police car and when we came to the Canyon Road turn-off, he said, "Keep going up this road about 200 yards, and it will be on your left."

"Officer Shillah, thank you. I would never have found it." Sure enough, it was precisely where he said. I pulled off the road where other cars were parked.

Then I realized what I was doing. I was intruding when I shouldn't. Erasmus had said goodbye, and I should have respected his wish, but I was a moth drawn to the light. A shadowy figure approached the car.

"I'm sorry, Mister. I'm not sure I should be here. I'm Jake, and I'm looking for Erasmus."

"Oh, yes, Jake, he told me about you. He's here, but he's with Hattie in a ceremony. I'm not sure if he'll be free. Come with me, and I'll take you by the fire. My name is Jack. I'm Hattie's apprentice."

"Jack, if I made a mistake, I can leave. I'm confused. I'm sorry."

"I'll help you." He led me to the fire and brought me a cup of tea. "Wait, and I'll sit with you."

Waiting was not part of my vocabulary, but I felt at peace while drinking the tea. I could sense Erasmus was close by. The night sky was completely filled with stars and the wispy Milky Way illuminated the towering ghostly mesas. I felt incredibly small and insignificant in this magnificence.

The fire warmed my bones and the tea was delicious. I was feeling sleepy when I heard his voice and felt a hand on my shoulder.

Erasmus said, "What took you so long to find me?"

"How did I know you I would come?"

"You are the most tenacious person I know besides myself."

I couldn't clearly see his face, but I smelled his sandalwood aftershave and snuggled close under the blanket with him, watching the starlight, and soon I dozed off. I had the same dream I'd had before. I was in a windstorm trying to get ahead, but the wind kept pushing me back. I heard Erasmus call out, "Hold on! I'm coming!" He was astride a white horse with Socrates. "Take my hand! We're almost there."

I woke up with a start. Sojourner was holding me, and it was dawn. "Where am I?"

"You don't remember?"

"I saw Erasmus last night. How is he? Can I see him again?"

"What time did you see him?"

"About midnight, and we sat by the fire. We chatted for a few hours 'til I fell asleep."

The last star shined in the dawn light against the vast sweep of the mesas before us and the air smelled fresh.

Sojourner was with Hattie, and he said, "Jake, Erasmus died at about midnight."

"No, you're mistaken. As real as you are, he was right next to me. We were here late at night. I couldn't have dreamed this."

Hattie said, "I've seen people visit with their loved ones as they go. Perhaps, he visited you? I'm so sorry. I know how much you loved him."

Sojourner sat with me, wrapped her blue quilt around us, and Socrates lay in my lap. "Jake, we all loved our extraordinary Erasmus."

Roshi walked over and sat down. "I brought us tea and biscuits,"

I sat on one side of Roshi and Sojourner was on the other, and he held us close. We watched the sunrise wordlessly and ate our breakfast. I had shed too many tears and now felt empty.

Hattie said, "Roshi and I were with Erasmus. He didn't suffer, and he was at peace. He is a great spirit and friend. We have helped to prepare him for the next life."

Later, I saw that Erasmus was swaddled in white cotton cloth in a shelter made of twigs. "Tomorrow, according to his wishes, he'll be cremated and his ashes spread to the winds," said Hattie. "Is that okay with you, Jake?" he asked as he put his hand on my shoulder.

I nodded and needed to be held by Sojourner.

Roshi said, "I need to pray. Would you like to join me?"

Sojourner, Roshi, and I sat zazen and we chanted the Heart Sutras. As we chanted, the tears started again. I was sad Erasmus was gone, but I was also joyful that his pain was over. I thought of all the incredible fun and silly moments we had together: leaping off twenty-foot cliffs into cold water, singing with Mr. Sam at the diner, dancing in the streets of New Orleans, meeting Rumi in Cleveland, and the ordinary day-to-day fun. Even when we had long workdays it always had an element of fun and play.

Roshi prepared a small altar with candles and incense and wore traditional robes. I followed Roshi's lead as he chanted and blessed Erasmus. He bowed deeply in gassho. "My dearest old friend. May your next journey be even more outrageous and joyful than this one."

New prayer flags hung from the trees at White Rock, the crows flew overhead, and the multicolored flags fluttered in the wind.

That afternoon and evening, I was mystified by how all these people we had met over the past months now arrived to bid their last farewell to Erasmus P. Hobbs. Alice and Rumi drove from Cleveland; Marty, Liz, and Mandy came from New Orleans; Phil the Tinker drove up in a psychedelic VW bus that said, *Phil the Tinker NDAA;* and dozens of his other friends appeared for the gathering.

I was overwhelmed when I saw Henry David, Erasmus's son, who was the spitting image of Erasmus in his twenties, with the same Vermont accent and smile as his dad. When Henry David held my hands, it was like I was holding Erasmus's hands.

"Hello, you must be Jake," he said. "Dad often wrote us about his adventures with you, and though he struggled with his health, he said this was one of the best times of his life. Thank you, Jake. I was a little jealous of all the fun you were having, but I had my farm and family in Vermont. Dad and I spent a lot of time over the past years healing our relationship. He was the first to admit that he hadn't been a good father at the beginning, often gone when I was growing up, but he changed when I was a teenager. Then he worked at being the best dad that he could. I've met many of his friends today, and I know he was an exceptional man. I'm so proud of him. This is his grandson, EP Hobbs."

EP Hobbs was four months old in a blue Guatemalan baby sling. His blue-green eyes sparkled brightly as he giggled.

Suddenly, the sound of a motorcycle broke this peaceful reverie. Sojourner pulled up on a huge Harley motorcycle, her long dreads tied back, and she said, "Jake, I need to let off some steam. Jump on the back! There's a helmet for you."

"Do you know how to ride this thing?"

"Why don't you find out? Jump on! I need some open road."

As exhilarating as the helicopter ride was, this was as equally astonishing and terrifying. I had no idea Sojourner knew how to ride a motorcycle. "Hold on!" she called out.

We soared up the road from White Rock and the Schnebly Hill. I held on tight, and after a few minutes, I realized she not only knew how to ride but rode like a fearless demon.

"I need to see how this bike can handle a little speed." She gunned the bike and soon we were flying. She let out a banshee scream. "Yahoo! Erasmus Plato Hobbs, we love you!"

He would have loved to have been here and holding on tight. Sojah quickly shifted down once we got on the main road north, and there were few cars. The red canyons and mesas gave way to evergreen forests, and the snow-topped mountains rose in front. Sojah and I flew as the world raced by, and everything was fine until I heard a police siren. We pulled over to the side of the road, with the police cars flashing blue lights.

"Don't worry, Sojah. I think I know who this cop is."

"Really?"

"Officer Shillah, do you remember me from the other night? You helped me to find Hattie's place."

"Yes, you're Jake. I hope you found it okay?"

"It was perfect. Thank you for being so helpful. My best friend was dying. Because you helped me, I saw him before he passed on."

"I'm sorry to hear about your friend, but why were you going over 80 mph on the motorcycle?"

Sojah said, "Officer, it was my fault. I should have known better. I was blowing off steam, and this bike was faster than I realized."

He smiled. "Keep the speedometer under seventy and you'll be fine."

"Thank you, Officer Shillah. We're having a farewell for Erasmus at White Rock tomorrow. Will you join us?"

"I'll try. And remember to go a bit slower. These roads are tricky."

Our return was every bit as exhilarating but at a slower pace. I was squeezing Sojah so tightly I was afraid her ribs would break. I had no idea what tomorrow would bring, but this moment now was perfect. When we got back to White Rock and the encampment at sunset, a fire was ablaze, and dozens of people were there.

I got off the bike with unsteady legs. "Sojah that was the most fun, even though I was scared to death!"

We hugged. "Thanks, Jake! I needed that. It must have been at least a decade since I've ridden. Now, let me find the person I stole the bike from and return it."

Henry David came over with his son EP sleeping in a blue Guatemalan woven baby sling and a jug band was playing *Ripple* by the Grateful Dead. He said, "Jake, the music's starting. Let's dance."

"Ain't it kind of disrespectful?" I asked.

"Come on, Jake. You know my dad. You never need an excuse to dance."

EP, Henry, and I danced, and as I closed my eyes, I imagined it was my last dance with Erasmus. I looked into Henry David's blue green eyes. "For a dairy farmer, you dance pretty gracefully."

"For a hobo, you dance kind of fancy!"

"Yup, your dad taught me every step."

Then Sojourner said to me, "Jake, I don't think I've had the pleasure of dancing with you."

"Yes, my dear Sojah. Come, let us dance to the edge of time."

We danced by the bonfire with the flames leaping up and illuminating *Emma Goldman* with her luxurious metallic glow, and the figure of Emma Goldman dancing above the words, "If I can't dance, I don't want to be part of your revolution."

The world had turned, and my revolution had begun.

Epilogue:
The End is the Beginning

It's been twenty years since I saw Erasmus P. Hobbs, and though I don't perseverate on his memory I do cherish every moment I spent with him, even the times which were difficult, but time and memory have a way of coloring the past. I finished writing my memoir of my *Summer of Love* here in Venice, Italy.

When I asked him what his favorite place was, he told me, "In Venice, as you sit on the steps just down from Plaza San Marco, overlooking the Grand Canal at sunset, is the most exquisite place. At sunset, at the door of one of the ancient churches there is the enchanted music of Vivaldi. Though you may hear the music a thousand times, it's never the same unless it's here. Right here on the Grand Canal."

The road since Sedona and my last moments with him had been extraordinary. I finished my GED and went to college, something few people in Black Mountain did. I met an exceptional man and had a family, and I always hold the memory of my *Summer of Love*.

Sometimes I think I can still smell Erasmus's sandalwood fragrance and the cedar fragrance of *Emma Goldman*. I can still feel the rush when I first jumped off a cliff and dived into a freezing pond. There is a time in life that is so extraordinary that you remember almost every second of it. This was the time I had with Erasmus, Socrates, and the people we met along the way in our journey of love. *Emma* is now in retirement in our barn, not far from Sojourner and Roshi's home near Dignity Village.

Today, in Venice I found three people at random by the church at sunset, just like Erasmus would do. His genius was his love of people, and his love was his genius. I opened a bottle of prosecco. As the first lines of the Vivaldi concerto were beginning, I sat on the steps of the church and raised a glass of bubbly to my beautiful hobo:

"Here's to you Erasmus P. Hobbs – our beautiful hobo and to all of you wandering hobos, Gitano's, vagabonds, and gypsies of the soul. We celebrate your glorious journey of love and discovery."

Sunset colors of oranges and gold danced above the setting sun over the chapels of the Grand Canal. Erasmus, thank you for my *Summer of Love* that has endured throughout my life.